Cyber Attack

Book Two

The Boston Brahmin Series

A novel by

Bobby Akart

Thank you for purchasing
Cyber Attack by Bobby Akart

For free advance reading copies, updates on new releases,
special offers, and bonus content,
Go Here To Sign Up:

eepurl.com/bYqq3L

or visit us online at

BobbyAkart.com

Other Works by Bestselling Author Bobby Akart

The Boston Brahmin Series

The Loyal Nine

Cyber Attack

Martial Law

False Flag

The Mechanics (Fall 2016)

The Prepping for Tomorrow Series

Cyber Warfare

EMP: Electromagnetic Pulse

Economic Collapse

DEDICATIONS

To the love of my life, you saved me from madness and continue to
do so daily.

To the Princesses of the Palace, my little marauders in training,
you have no idea how much happiness you bring
to your mommy and me.

To the Founding Fathers, whose vision and bravery built America.

ACKNOWLEDGEMENTS

Writing a book that is both informative and entertaining requires a
tremendous team effort. Writing is the easy part. For their efforts in
making The Boston Brahmin series a reality, I would like to thank
Hristo Argirov Kovatliev for his incredible cover art, Pauline Nolet
for her editorial prowess, Sabrina Jean, my second set of eyes, with
FastTrack Editing, Stef Mcdaid for making this manuscript
decipherable on so many formats, and the Team—whose advice,
friendship and attention to detail is priceless.

Thank you!

Choose Freedom!

ABOUT THE AUTHOR

Bobby Akart

An Amazon Top 100 Author and author of six #1 bestsellers, in both fiction and non-fiction genres:

THE LOYAL NINE – #1 bestseller in Political Thriller Fiction and Financial Thriller Fiction

CYBER WARFARE – #1 bestseller in eight categories including Politics, Social Sciences; Business, Money; Engineering, Transportation; Science, Technology; International Politics

EMP: ELECTROMAGNETIC PULSE – #1 bestseller in seven categories including International Politics, Arms Control; Physics; Politics, Social Sciences; Engineering, Transportation

ECONOMIC COLLAPSE – #1 bestseller in seven categories including Politics, Social Sciences; Economics; World Affairs; International Politics; Business, Money

SEEDS OF LIBERTY – #1 bestseller in three categories including Politics, Social Sciences; Modern History; Sociology

EVIL, MEET OPPORTUNITY – #1 bestseller in two categories including Action, Adventure; Contemporary Fiction

Bobby Akart has provided his readers a diverse range of topics that are both informative and entertaining. His attention to detail and impeccable research has allowed him to write bestselling books in several fiction and nonfiction genres.

Born and raised in Tennessee, Bobby received his bachelor's degree with a dual major in economics and political science. He not only understands how the economy works, but the profound effect politics has on the economy as well. After completing his undergraduate degree at Tennessee in three years, he entered the dual-degree, JD-MBA program, obtaining a juris doctor at the age of twenty-three.

His education perfectly suited him for his legal career in banking, trusts, and investment banking. As his legal career flourished, business opportunities arose, including the operation of restaurants and the development of real estate. But after meeting and marrying the love of his life, they left the corporate world and developed online businesses.

A life-changing event led them to Muddy Pond, Tennessee, where he and his wife lead a self-sustainable, preparedness lifestyle. Bobby and his wife are unabashed preppers and share their expert knowledge of prepping via their website www.FreedomPreppers.com.

Bobby lives in the backwoods of the Cumberland Plateau with his wife and fellow author, Danni Elle, and their two English bulldogs, aka the Princesses of the Palace.

About The Loyal Nine and the Boston Brahmin Series

And this is good old Boston,
The home of the bean and the cod,
Where the Lowells talk only to Cabots,
And the Cabots talk only to God.

Works of fiction are frequently based upon historical fact. In the case of Book One of The Boston Brahmin Series, *The Loyal Nine*, and the entire upcoming Boston Brahmin Series, history repeats itself. *The Loyal Nine* takes its name from nine patriotic Bostonians who chose freedom over the tyrannical rule of Great Britain. As the British exerted more control over the colonists, especially in the form of taxes, anger and resentment rose to a crescendo, resulting in the War for Independence.

Author Bobby Akart has observed similar acts of rage and discontent in America today. Sadly, they perceive an America which is in decline socially and economically. There are many perspectives and theories all across the political spectrum on how to save her. Methods may differ, but does it matter if the ultimate goal is achieved?

The Boston Brahmin series will take the reader on a journey based in historical fact—both in its character development and the events that take place during the timeline of the series. This is a series about the societal and economic collapse of America. This type of collapse event is gradual and not sudden. The events portrayed in The Boston Brahmin series will rise to a crescendo, forcing the characters to make a decision—choose tyranny or freedom. They will be challenged physically and emotionally. As always, nothing is exactly what it seems.

Writing a series of this magnitude takes a considerable amount of time and research. It also asks the reader to become invested in the journey of the characters. Creating a book series about societal and economic collapse is a marathon, not a sprint. Read with us. Learn with us. Get involved in the backstory and details of the novels by frequently visiting our fan-dedicated website www.TheBostonBrahmin.com. We encourage you to interact with us on social media. We truly enjoy conversing with our fans—all of whom we consider friends.

If you have not had the opportunity to read *Seeds of Liberty*, a #1 best seller in the Politics, Social Sciences category and the Modern History category. *Seeds of Liberty* is a nonfiction companion guide to The Boston Brahmin series, which provides both a sociological analysis and a complete historical perspective of America's penchant for rebellion.

We hope you enjoy this epic, history-rich thriller series. Torn from the headlines, The Boston Brahmin series presents a nation plunged into chaos by enemies "foreign and domestic." Only The Loyal Nine, a patriotic group of descendants of our Founding Fathers, can navigate the collapse and restore the American republic.

As the country slowly descends into economic and societal despair, America is one bad news story away from collapse. In *Cyber Attack*, Book Two of The Boston Brahmin Series, the reader is taken through a very realistic scenario that would bring America to its knees.

Dramatis Personae

THE LOYAL NINE:

Sarge – born Henry Winthrop Sargent IV. Son of former Massachusetts Governor, Godson of John Adams Morgan and a descendant of Daniel Sargent, Sr., wealthy merchant and owner of Sargent's Wharf during the Revolutionary War. He's a tenured Professor at the Harvard-Kennedy School of Government in Cambridge. Sarge resides at 100 Beacon Street in the Back Bay area of Boston.

Steven Sargent – younger brother of Sarge. He is a graduate of United States Naval Academy and former platoon officer of SEAL Team 10. He is currently a contract operative for Aegis Security—code name NOMAD. He resides on his yacht — the Miss Behavin'.

Julia Hawthorne – descendant of the Peabody and Hawthorne families. First female political editor of The Boston Herald. She is the recipient of the National Association of Broadcasting Marconi Radio Award for her creation of an internet radio channel for the newspaper. She is in a relationship with Sarge and lives with him at 100 Beacon.

The Quinn family – Donald is the self-proclaimed Director of Procurement. He is a former accountant and financial advisor who works directly with John Adams Morgan. Married to *Susan Quinn* with daughters *Rebecca* (age 7) and *Penny* (age 11). Donald and Susan coordinate all preparedness activities of The Loyal Nine. They reside in Brae Burn Country Club in Boston.

J.J. – born John Joseph Warren. He is a direct descendant of Doctor Joseph Warren, one of the original Sons of Liberty. The Warren family founded Harvard Medical and were field surgeons at the Battle of Bunker Hill. J.J. was an Army Battalion Surgeon at Joint Base Balad in Iraq. He finished his career at the Veteran's Administration Hospital in Jamaica Plain, where he also resides. He is affectionately known as the Armageddon Medicine Man.

Katie O'Shea – graduate of the United States Naval Academy who trained as a Naval Intelligence officer. After an introduction to John Adams Morgan, she quickly rose up the ranks of the intelligence community. She now is part of the President's Intelligence Advisory Board. She resides in Washington, D.C.

Brad – born Francis Crowninshield Bradlee, descendant of the Crownindshield family, a historic seafaring and military family dating back to the early 1600's. He is the battalion commander of the 25th Marine Regiment of 1st Battalion based at Fort Devens, Massachusetts. There nickname is *Cold Steel Warriors*. He is an active member of Oathkeepers and the Three Percenters.

Abbie – Abigail Morgan, daughter of John Adams Morgan. United States Senator for Massachusetts since 2008. Independent, with libertarian leanings. Resides in Washington, D.C.

THE BOSTON BRAHMIN:

John Adams Morgan – lineal descendant of President John Adams and Henry Sturgis Morgan, founder of J.P. Morgan. Morgan attended Harvard, obtaining a master's degree in business and a law degree. Founded the Morgan-Holmes law firm with the grandson of Supreme Court Justice Oliver Wendell Holmes, Jr. Among other concerns, he owns Morgan Global, an international banking and financial conglomerate. Extremely wealthy, Morgan is the recognized head of The Boston Brahmin.

Walter Cabot – direct descendant of John Cabot, shipbuilders during the time of the Revolutionary War. Wealthy philanthropist and CEO of Cabot Industries. He is part of Morgan's inner circle.

Lawrence Lowell – descendant of John Lowell, a Federal Judge in the first United States Continental Congress. Extremely wealthy and part of Morgan's inner circle.

ZERO DAY GAMERS:

Andrew Lau – MIT professor of Korean descent. Brilliant mind that created the Zero Day Gamers as a way to utilize his talents for personal financial gain.

Anna Fakhri – MIT graduate assistant to Professor Lau of Arabic descent. She prides herself on her "internet detective work". She speaks multiple Arabic languages.

Leonid "Leo" Malvalaha – MIT graduate assistant to Professor Lau of Russian descent. He is very adept at creating complex viruses, worms, and Trojans used in cyber attack activities. He speaks fluent Russian.

Herm Walthaus – newest member of the Zero Day Gamers. MIT graduate student. Introverted, but extremely analytical. Stays abreast of latest tools and techniques available to hackers.

AEGIS TEAM:

Nomad – Steven Sargent.

Slash – Drew Jackson. Former SEAL Team member who worked briefly for private contractors like Blackwater. Born and raised in Tennessee where his family farm is located. He has excellent survival skills.

Bugs – Paul Hittle. Former Army Special Forces Medic who left the Green Berets for security contractor work. He owns a ranch in East Texas.

Sharpie – Raymond Bower. Former Delta Force who now operates a lucrative private equity fund venture with former classmates from Harvard. He resides in New York City.

SUPPORTING CHARACTERS:

Malcolm Lowe – John Morgan's trusted assistant. Former undersecretary of state during Morgan's tenure as Secretary of State. He *handles* sensitive matters for Mr. Morgan.

J-Rock – Jarvis Rockwell, leader of the unified black gangs of Dorchester, Roxbury and Mattapan in south Boston. He rose to power after the death of his unborn child during a race riot at Copley Square in April 2016.

Joe Sciacca – Boston Herald's chief editor.

PREVIOUSLY IN THE BOSTON BRAHMIN SERIES

The Boston Brahmin series begins in December of 2015 and the timeframe of The Loyal Nine continues through April 2016. Steven Sargent, in his capacity as Nomad, an Aegis deep cover operative, undertakes several black ops missions in Ukraine, Switzerland, and Germany. The purposes behind the operations become increasingly suspect to Steven and his brother Sarge. It is apparent that Steven's true employer, John Morgan, is orchestrating a series of events as part of a grander scheme.

Sarge continues to teach at the Harvard-Kennedy School of Government. He begins to make nationwide appearances after publishing a New York Times best seller, *Choose Freedom or Capitulation: America's Sovereignty Crisis*. During this time, he rekindles his relationship with Julia Hawthorne who is also celebrating national notoriety for her accomplishments at The Boston Herald newspaper. The two take a trip to Las Vegas for a convention and become unwilling participants in a cyber attack upon the Las Vegas power grid. Throughout The Loyal Nine, Sarge and Julia observe the economic and societal collapse of America.

The chasm between the haves and have-nots widens resulting in hostilities between labor unions and their employers. There are unintended consequences of these actions and numerous deaths are the result.

Racial tensions are on the rise across the country and Boston becomes ground zero for social unrest when a beloved retired bus driver is beaten to death during the St. Patrick's Day festivities. In protest, a group of marchers descend upon Copley Square at the end of the Boston Marathon resulting in a clash with police.

The Quinn family, Donald, Susan and their young daughters, are caught up in an angry mob scene at a local mall relating to the Black Lives Matter protests. Donald decides to accelerate The Loyal Nine's preparedness activities as he gets the sense America is on the brink of collapse.

The reader gets an inside look at the morning security briefings in the White House Situation Room. Katie O'Shea becomes a respected rising star within the intelligence community while solidifying her role as a conduit for information to John Morgan.

John Morgan continues to act as a world power broker. He manipulates geopolitical events for the financial gain of his wealthy associates, The Boston Brahmin. He carefully orchestrates the rise to national prominence of his daughter, Senator Abigail Morgan.

As a direct descendant of the Founding Fathers, Morgan is sickened to watch America descend into collapse. Morgan believes the country can return to its former greatness. He recognizes drastic measures may be required. He envisions a reset of sorts, but what that entails is yet to be determined.

Throughout The Loyal Nine, the Zero Day Gamers, make a name for themselves in the *hacktivist* community as their skills and capabilities escalate from cyber vandalism to cyber ransom to cyber terror. Professor Lau and his talented graduate assistants create ingenious methods of cyber intrusion. At times, they question the morality of their activities. But the ransoms they extract from their victims are too lucrative to turn away.

The end game, the mission statement of the Zero Day Gamers, is succinct:

One man's gain is another man's loss; who gains and who loses is determined by who pays.

But who else loses in their deadly game? Cyber Attack begins …

Epigraph

There are risks and costs to action. But they are far less than the long range risks of comfortable inaction.

   ~ John F. Kennedy

*****

Experience hath shewn that even under the best forms of government, those entrusted with power have, in time, and by slow operations, perverted it into tyranny.

   ~ Thomas Jefferson

*****

Civilization is like a thin layer of ice upon a deep ocean of chaos and darkness.

*****

Timeo Danaos et dona ferentis ~ Beware of Greeks bearing gifts.

   ~ Vergil's words for the voice of Laocoon in the Aeneid

*****

By failing to prepare, you are preparing to fail.

   ~ Benjamin Franklin

*****

What the world needs now is a do over.

   ~ Anonymous

PART ONE

CHAPTER 1

May 8, 2016
3:07 p.m.
American Airlines Flight 129
33,000 Feet
Near St. Louis, Missouri

"Good afternoon from the flight deck. This is Captain Randy Gray, and it is my honor to pilot our American Airlines Boeing 757 into Washington Dulles this afternoon. We have reached our cruising altitude of thirty-three thousand feet, after averting the initial turbulence caused by the area of weather north of the Dallas–Fort Worth metro area. With a little help from a tailwind, we should arrive on time at Washington Dulles International by two o'clock local time," said Gray. "I will be turning off the Fasten Seat Belt signs to allow you free access to our newly enhanced cabin. Our flight attendants will begin cabin service shortly. As always, we thank you for flying American Airlines."

Gray began his career as a pilot in 1989 with Command Airways, a small regional carrier based in upstate New York. Initially checked out on the ATR 42, a Czech-made plane, Gray continued his training and became a highly respected pilot within the American Airlines ranks. The flight to Washington Dulles was routine. He shared the cockpit with First Officer William Applegate and his longtime friend Stacy Bird, a Frontier Air captain riding in the jump seat to D.C. after a hunting trip in West Texas.

"Bill, Stacy and I would like to say hello to a friend in first class. Would you mind taking over for a bit?" asked Gray.

Applegate had flown right seat with Gray in the past and had earned Gray's confidence.

"Absolutely, fellows, go ahead. She's flyin' herself anyway," said Applegate.

Gray and Bird unbuckled their harnesses and took a quick glance at the controls to confirm everything was in order. He and Bird slipped into the galley through the secured cockpit door, which automatically locked behind them.

"Hi, guys," said Karen Mosely, the chief flight attendant. "May I get you boys anything?"

"I don't think so, Karen, but thanks," said Gray. "We're gonna holler at 3B for a minute before we descend into Dulles."

Captains Gray and Bird strolled down the aisle behind her to greet a former Air Force buddy—when the aircraft took a sudden lurch upward. Gray grabbed the headrests of the seats on both sides of the aisle and ducked to look out the windows for a cause—clear blue skies. The plane quickly corrected, steadying for a moment before nosing downward into a steep descent. Gasps and screams erupted throughout the cabin.

"Is your FO okay?" asked Bird.

Gray knew what he meant by this question. Since the mysterious disappearance of Malaysia Flight 370 and the deliberate crash of Germanwings Flight 9525, every pilot looked at the members of their crew with a different set of eyes. He locked eyes with Bird, both of them sharing the same thought. If they'd hit turbulence, why didn't Applegate activate the Fasten Seat Belt signs?

"Back to the cockpit," he said, edging brusquely by Captain Bird.

Gray reached the intercom console next to the cockpit access door and pressed the pound key, praying for Applegate to respond.

CHAPTER 2

May 8, 2016
3:07 p.m.
The Hack House
Binney Street
East Cambridge, Massachusetts

Andrew Lau stared intently at the iMac monitor array as Leonid Malvalaha deftly navigated the mouse. Malvalaha and Lau's other longtime graduate assistant, Anna Fakhri, had continued in their new endeavor, despite the potential risk of criminal prosecution.

Through the process of pen testing, Lau identified zero-day vulnerabilities in a computer network and took advantage of the security holes before the network's IT department could find a solution. Once the vulnerability window was identified, the zero-day attack inserted malware into the system. The *Game*, as Lau called it, required the attacked entity to pay a ransom in exchange for a patch to their security. Prior to today, their hacks didn't directly risk lives, though their February hack on behalf of the Las Vegas service employees union resulted in many unforeseen deaths. They were more selective in their project after Las Vegas, until now.

"Malvalaha, run us through the hack," said Lau, patting his trusted associate on the shoulder as he walked by.

Lau's core group consisted of Malvalaha, Fakhri and newcomer Herm Walthaus, who had proven himself by creating a cascading blackout of the Las Vegas power grid—no small feat. In a way, this was a team of misfits—although talented ones. They came from diverse backgrounds but shared a common goal of advancing their personal wealth.

"We're monitoring American Airlines Flight 129, which departed

Dallas around forty-five minutes ago," stated Malvalaha.

His desk resembled the cockpit of a sophisticated aircraft, with six flat-panel monitors at his disposal. He pointed to the screen that displayed FlightAware, an online tool providing up-to-the-second statistics on any airline flight.

"Flight 129 is currently over St. Louis and has adjusted its flight path directly to Washington Dulles airport. The aircraft is a Boeing 757-200, flying at approximately four hundred eighty knots, or five hundred and fifty miles per hour. Altitude thirty-three thousand feet."

"Tell us what your research has shown," said Lau.

Fakhri addressed her former professor, now hacking partner. "Since 9/11, there have been conspiracy theories surrounding the commandeering of the four aircraft by the terrorists," said Fakhri. "One such theory is the aircraft was part of a false-flag attack initiated by the government. As the theory goes, based upon 2001 technology, NORAD—the North American Aerospace Defense Command—took control of the planes and purposefully crashed them into the World Trade Center and the Pentagon. The most prevalent reason cited for the false-flag operation is that the government wanted to justify initiating a war in the Middle East."

"For our purposes, we're not interested in the false-flag theories," said Malvalaha. "We focused on the concept of the remote takeover of a commercial aircraft. The technology exists, and it has, in fact, been used by the military in the past. Today, we will hack the aircraft via the flight management system, *and* make ourselves known."

"My father is a pilot for the 757-200 airframe," said Walthaus. "We always had sophisticated flight simulators in our home growing up, and naturally they provided more entertainment for me than a PlayStation. I've never physically flown an aircraft, but I am an expert on the flight sim."

"I thought the FAA disproved the theories surrounding remote access of the onboard computers," said Lau.

"True to an extent," said Fakhri. "A security consultant from Germany claimed to have hacked an aircraft using an Android telephone application. Later, one of his peers accessed the aircraft's network by connecting through the in-flight entertainment system. He then used a modified version of Vortex software to compromise the cockpit's system."

"When pressed for a response, the FAA was selective in its choice of words," said Malvalaha. "They equivocated using the phrases *described technique* and *using the technology the consultant has claimed.*"

Lau laughed after this statement.

"The government has a lot of experience with misdirection," said Lau. "Our most sophisticated operations were panned as impossible by the experts and their friends in the media—even after we successfully accomplished them!"

"When researching this online, we discovered that American Airlines and Boeing launched a Bug Bounty program, offering a million free air-miles to the good guys—the white-hat hackers," said Walthaus. "These *ethical and conscientious* hackers shared their findings online. We took their findings as a starting point and found the vulnerability window we were looking for."

"Continue," said Lau.

If Lau could publish his work, he would surely win the Carnegie Foundation award as Professor of the Year. Then again, he might be teaching second-grade math to his fellow inmates.

"We're going to use the government's safeguard technology against them in two steps," said Malvalaha.

Lau turned his Red Sox cap backward—an unconscious signal that it was time to go to work.

"First, we access the Boeing Uninterruptible Autopilot system," said Fakhri. "The patent for the system was granted to Boeing in 2006, as a method of taking control of a commercial aircraft away from the pilot or flight crew in the event of a hijacking. The uninterruptible autopilot can be initiated by the pilots via onboard sensors or remotely through government satellite links."

"As far as the public knows, no Boeing aircraft has been retrofitted to include this technology, although rumors abound to the contrary," said Walthaus. "After the disappearance of Malaysia Flight

370, the Prime Minister of Malaysia claimed Boeing or *certain government agencies* utilized the uninterruptible autopilot to down the aircraft. I'm sure he alluded to the CIA."

"An online search supported his theory," said Fakhri. "We researched the rules issued by the FAA on the Federal Register website and found a Special Condition granted to Boeing for the Model 777 aircraft, allowing the installation of the uninterruptible autopilot software."

"But we're tracking a 757," said Lau.

"Yes, we are," said Walthaus. "The FAA, in its action, authorized Boeing to conduct tests of the new system in six of its 757 aircraft, plus the system was initially designed for the 757. We researched all of the top contractors who work under Boeing's Defense division. Typically, new technology ends up in the hands of our Defense Department."

"We found the company hired to install the system—Alion Science and Technology," said Fakhri. "Their technology solutions sector manager, Robert Hurt, gave a presentation at a Raytheon trade show last year, which was published online. After some digging, we have the details on the six 757 aircraft participating in the program."

"American Airlines Flight 129 is one of them," said Malvalaha.

CHAPTER 3

May 8, 2016
3:12 p.m.
American Airlines Flight 129
33,000 Feet
Near Evansville, Indiana

Gray exhaled deeply when the green light on the keypad illuminated. He and Bird quickly entered the cockpit and slammed the door shut.

"What the hell is going on, Bill!" exclaimed Gray as he climbed into his seat and strapped in. Bird positioned himself in the jump seat. Gray quickly examined the onboard computer monitor and activated the Fasten Seat Belt sign.

"Talk to me, Billy!"

"The controls are unresponsive," muttered Applegate. "We are in a rapid descent, and the controls will not respond to any of my commands."

"You have to call a Mayday, Randy," said Bird.

Gray looked at the altitude control indicator. They were in a descent, but not an insurmountable one—yet. The altimeter read twenty-four thousand feet.

"Billy, are you with me?" asked Gray.

Applegate barely muttered a response.

"Billy, why don't you trade seats with Captain Bird," said Gray. "You need a break, and Stacy is an experienced captain. Come on now, let Stacy swap with you."

Applegate slowly removed his seat harness and traded seats with Bird, who immediately leaned across the center console.

"Should I escort him off the flight deck?" asked Bird.

7

"He's just shook up," said Gray. "Call in the Mayday, and let me figure this out."

Bird's attempt to access the onboard computer proved fruitless. The keyboard was unresponsive.

"We're one hundred miles east of St. Louis," said Gray. "Try SDF. Wait, not Louisville. We'll need Indianapolis Center."

"Mayday, Mayday, Mayday, Indianapolis Center. American Airlines one-two-niner heavy declaring an emergency," said Bird. "I say again. Mayday, Mayday, Mayday, Indianapolis ZID. American Airlines one-two-niner heavy declaring an emergency."

"American one-two-niner, this is Indianapolis Center. We copy your Mayday," said a representative of the Indianapolis Air Route Traffic Control Center. The primary responsibility of Indianapolis Center was to monitor and separate flights within the seventy-three thousand square miles it covered in the Midwest. Today, a new task presented itself. "What is the nature of your emergency?"

"Indianapolis Center, onboard controls are unresponsive. We are under power and in a steady descent now passing twenty-two thousand feet," said Bird. "All other flight deck functions appear normal."

"Roger, American one-two-niner. All stations. All stations. Indianapolis Center. Mayday situation in progress. Stop transmitting. Repeat. Mayday situation in progress. Stop all transmissions."

Gray sat back in the pilot's seat and looked around the Orbiter flight deck, searching for clues—and answers. Nothing made sense. The entire console appeared normal. The monitors functioned properly, displaying their current flight parameters; however, the keyboard for the onboard computer continued to be unresponsive.

"We're leveling off," said Bird, pointing at the altitude control indicator. "Son of a bitch, we're holding steady at twenty K. I've never seen anything like this."

Neither had Gray.

"American one-two-niner, this is Indianapolis Center. Boeing technical team is en route, and Homeland Security has been notified."

"Roger, Indianapolis Center," said Bird. "Be advised, altitude has leveled off at twenty thousand feet. Steady on original course."

"American one-two-niner. Indianapolis Center. Roger."

"Homeland Security?" asked Bird.

Gray understood the gravity of their situation. If he couldn't demonstrate positive control of the aircraft, it would not be allowed to reach Washington.

CHAPTER 4

May 8, 2016
3:13 p.m.
The Hack House
Binney Street
East Cambridge, Massachusetts

"Now that we've entered the plane's Wi-Fi system, it's necessary to hack through the firewall of the aircraft communications addressing and reporting system, or ACARS," said Malvalaha. "This will give us access to the plane's onboard computer system and the uploaded flight management system data."

Lau watched intently as his protégé navigated through the plane's servers.

"You're in!" exclaimed Walthaus. "My turn, Leo."

Malvalaha relinquished his chair to Walthaus, whose only experience with an airplane was playing on his father's computer as a teen.

"The aircraft is flying on autopilot," said Fakhri. "That's good. Right about now, the pilots are relaxed and completely unaware of our presence."

"First, I will initiate the uninterruptible autopilot system, which will prevent the flight crew from interfering with us," said Walthaus. "These controls are considered *fly-by-wire,* which have replaced the conventional manual controls of the aircraft with an electronic interface. The yokes that control the aircraft may provide certain inputs into a flight-control system, but with the uninterruptible autopilot system initiated, the crew can flail around all they want, and their actions will not be recognized.

"First, we'll adjust the altitude to twenty-six thousand feet—just to let them know we're flying their plane," he continued. "Watch here."

Walthaus pointed to FlightAware, and Lau turned his attention to the screen. When Walthaus refreshed the screen, the airspeed had declined, along with the aircraft's altitude.

"Whoa!" exclaimed Walthaus. "Sorry about that! It's hard to adjust the controls using a mouse and its cursor. I just took the plane into a dive and probably scared the shit out of everybody on board. Let me level this off at twenty thousand feet."

"Is that too low?" asked Lau.

"No, eighteen thousand feet is considered the upper end of an air traffic's transitional level, where the most activity takes place," said Walthaus. "We'll maintain this altitude and course for a few minutes, to give everyone on board an opportunity to catch their breath. Then we'll climb back to thirty-three thousand feet."

Ordinarily, the Zero Day Gamers had a profit motive. The hijack by hacking of the American Airlines flight was a test. Today, they would determine whether the hack could be achieved, in addition to gauging the government's response.

"At this point, the pilots have probably reported a Mayday to the nearest air traffic control tower—either St. Louis or Louisville," said Malvalaha. "Their flight training would dictate a simple procedure of turning off the autopilot and resuming control of the aircraft manually. Unfortunately for them, the Boeing Uninterruptible Autopilot system has built-in safeguards that prevent the pilots from overriding our controls."

"What prevents NORAD or the FAA from taking over the operation of the plane via its satellite controls?" asked Lau.

"We've installed a version of the TeslaCrypt Ransomware onto the plane's servers," said Malvalaha. "This malware blocks access to the aircraft's onboard computers by everybody until released by us. In the future, we'll provide them a message with a monetary demand. Today, we're just sending a message."

CHAPTER 5

May 8, 2016
3:17 p.m.
NORAD—Air Defense Operations Center
Cheyenne Mountain Air Force Station, Colorado

"Sir, Wright Patterson has been notified of the situation," said the technical sergeant who was manning the console tracking American Airlines Flight 129. "I have Lieutenant Colonel Darren Reynolds on the line, sir."

Colonel Arnold pressed the remote transmit button for his headset. "Colonel Reynolds, this is Colonel James Arnold. Please stay on the line as we assess the situation."

"Colonel Arnold, we have scrambled two F-16s. Time is running out. Once ADOC was notified, we ceased communications with the Indianapolis Air Traffic Control Center and turned comms over to you."

"Thank you, Colonel," said Arnold. "Sergeant, contact the aircraft."

"American Airlines one-two-niner, United States Air Force Air Defense Operations Center. Over," said the airman.

After a moment, the response came through the overhead speakers.

"Air Defense, this is Captain Randy Gray."

"Captain Gray, this is Colonel Arnold. What steps have you taken to gain control of your aircraft?" asked Colonel Arnold.

"The most logical step is to turn off the plane's autopilot," said Gray. "But the autopilot is unresponsive. In fact, all of our controls are unresponsive. We've had no flight control for nearly seventeen minutes now."

"Stand by, Captain Gray," said Colonel Arnold.

He pointed to the sergeant to mute the conversation, waiting several seconds before addressing his team.

"If this 757 is outfitted with Boeing's new autopilot system, why haven't we simply taken control of the aircraft?"

"Malware has been inserted into the aircraft's onboard server network, preventing any type of outside access," said another airman. "Boeing technical support is working on a solution, but so far they have been unsuccessful."

"Colonel Reynolds, what is the ETA on your F-16s?" asked Colonel Arnold.

Arnold took a deep breath during the pause and studied the global positioning of Flight 129. The plane would be over a desolate area of Eastern Kentucky in roughly ten minutes. He had to escalate this to USNorthCom. He was not going to sentence 237 passengers and crew to their death without further orders.

CHAPTER 6

May 8, 2016
3:23 p.m.
F-16 "Fighting Falcons"
180ᵗʰ Fighter Wing
24,000 Feet
Near Lexington, Kentucky

"Roger, Giant Killer, awaiting orders," said Smash Seven, the lead F-16 pilot dispatched to intercept Flight 129. "We will maintain two four thousand at the four o'clock and eight o'clock positions."

"Copy, Smash Seven," said Smash Eleven, maintaining his position above the left rear of the 757 aircraft. "Smash Seven, switch to alternate frequency Charlie. Repeat, switch to alternate frequency Charlie."

"Go ahead, Smash Eleven."

"Are we going to shoot down a commercial airliner?" asked Smash Eleven.

"Certainly not what I had in mind when I woke up this morning," said Smash Seven. "It must be hijacked."

"Look, they're climbing. Return to primary frequency."

"Switching," said Smash Eleven.

"Giant Killer, Smash Seven. Aircraft appears to be in ascent. Repeat, aircraft is ascending. Now climbing to two four thousand," said Smash Seven. "Now two eight thousand. Please advise."

"Roger that, Smash Seven," said Giant Killer. "Maintain present heading and adjust altitude to three six thousand."

The F-16s rose in altitude to maintain a height advantage over the 757.

"Aircraft has leveled off at three three thousand. Heading has not changed," said Smash Seven. "We have bull's-eye on one-two-nine at three six thousand now. We are a half mile in trail."

CHAPTER 7

May 8, 2016
3:23 p.m.
American Airlines Flight 129
20,000 Feet
Near Lexington, Kentucky

"Those are F-16s," said Bird. "They've remained just behind us since they checked us out a few minutes ago."

Gray was aware the military would not hesitate to shoot them down if the plane was hijacked. Although their altitude had leveled, no one knew whether the plane would fly directly into the Atlantic or nose-dive into Washington. The government would not take that chance. He suddenly felt the urge to call his wife.

"I'm going to call Betty," said Gray.

At lower altitude, he might reach a cell tower. A second after pressing send on his phone, the plane began to climb. He initiated communications once again with the Indianapolis ZID.

"Indianapolis Center. American Airlines Flight one-two-niner. Aircraft has begun uncontrolled ascent," said Gray.

Bird called out the altimeter readings. "Twenty-three thousand. Twenty-six thousand. Thirty thousand."

"American Airlines one-two-niner, roger that. Are you able to gain control of your aircraft?"

"Negative." Gray was sweating profusely.

They were running out of time.

"Where are the F-16s, Stacy?"

"I don't have a visual. My guess is they're a thousand feet above and behind us," replied Bird.

"Captain Gray," interrupted the voice of the Air Force colonel, "I'm not going to sugarcoat this. You have about two minutes to gain control of your aircraft before you enter populated areas and D.C. airspace. Homeland Security has established certain protocols in this type of situation."

Gray and Bird exchanged glances. *How could this be happening? I really want to talk to my wife.*

"Colonel, I assure you that we have nothing to do with this," pleaded Gray. "There has to be a solution. This airplane is acting normally, except for the controls. It must be a malfunction. You can't shoot us down!"

"Randy, look!" exclaimed Bird, tapping the monitors for the onboard computer.

Gray immediately grabbed the controls, remembering that the autopilot was activated. He flipped the switch, and the plane responded to his touch. Flight 129 was his again!

"All stations, this is American Airlines one-two-niner. We have positive control of the flight. I say again, we have positive control of the flight!" said Gray.

As he and Captain Bird exchanged relieved looks, the monitor display changed:

Thank you for flying with Zero Day Gamers Airways.

CHAPTER 8

May 13, 2016
5:51 p.m.
Senate Chamber
North Wing of the United States Capitol
Washington, D.C.

Senator Abigail Morgan stopped to catch her breath and take a sip of water from an Aquafina bottle provided by Sen. Rand Paul. The Senate had been called *the world's greatest deliberative body* since the mid-nineteenth century, but this marathon filibuster orchestrated by Abbie and her libertarian comrades in the Senate was more rumination than deliberation. As she gathered her thoughts, she soaked in the grandeur of the Senate chamber. For over one hundred and fifty years, great American orators made their case to the American people and their fellow senators in this hall. Flanked by the red Levanto pilasters and facing a large marble rostrum, the senator who *had the floor* was granted the opportunity to speak unimpeded. Abbie had the floor and the National Defense Authorization Act of 2017 was the topic du jour.

"Our objection to Section 1021 of the NDAA goes beyond the ability of the military to detain American citizens without the right to a civilian trial," said Abbie. "We believe the House amendment, if adopted, specifically states that the NDAA will not deny the writ of habeas corpus or any other constitutional rights afforded any citizen of the United States."

Abbie, along with Senators Paul, Cruz and Lee, had commandeered the Senate floor to lambaste the NDAA provisions on domestic surveillance, the militarization of police departments

18

and, most importantly, the attempts of the act to gut the Second Amendment. It was not a filibuster, per se, by Abbie and her fellow senators. The *Gang of Four*, as these Senate libertarians had become known, were trying to draw attention to the provisions slipped into the act at the eleventh hour by Senate leadership with full support of the Minority and the President. The overreaching by the National Security Agency into domestic surveillance had been debated for years. This act took the assault on Americans' civil liberties to new heights. Abbie continued.

"However, the proposed Senate amendments are being sold to the American people as a way to deal with insurrection within the United States," said Abbie. "We all recognize that social unrest is on an unprecedented rise across the nation. Americans are distraught and rightly so. But the solution is not to pass draconian laws which take away our citizens' civil liberties. Americans will not stand for being placed upon a domestic terror watch list simply because they stated an opinion on social media or perhaps purchased too many rounds of ammunition for their legally owned firearms."

Cable news networks were enjoying the spectacle provided by Abbie and especially Senator Paul, who was the front runner for the Republican nomination for President. Most accused Senator Paul of claiming the spotlight to draw attention to himself and raise funds for his presidential candidacy. Abbie was accused of similar political grandstanding—seizing the opportunity to show her vice presidential bona fides. At best, their *filibuster* was self-aggrandizing. At worst, some critics said, it was an act of pure cynicism.

These criticisms were not without merit, but their objections reflected the abilities of those who'd mastered parliamentary arcana for a living. Senator Paul learned political maneuverings from his father—longtime Texas Congressman Ron Paul. Abbie learned from the master manipulator, her father—John Adams Morgan.

"The defense of the country requires that we have adequate intelligence to detect and to counter threats to domestic security," said Abbie. "But this requirement must not take priority over maintaining the civil liberties of our citizens. Our Constitution and the Bill of Rights should not be suspended even during a time of war, much less during a difficult period of social unrest. Intelligence agencies that legitimately seek to preserve the security of our nation must be subject to transparency and oversight. Thus, we oppose our government's use of secret classifications to create a so-called domestic terror watch list—*an enemies list*—based upon one's free speech, political beliefs or purchases of firearm-related merchandise."

Shortly after her election in 2010, Abbie learned senators had very powerful levers at their fingertips. At any moment, like this one, a senator could grind the chamber to a halt without any real accountability other than an admonishment from their leadership. Were this a real filibuster, the Gang of Four could have stopped the legislation dead in its tracks, but that would have a devastating impact on the nation's security. Everyone knew that, including the Gang of Four. By occupying the Senate floor and speaking for hours on end with great political fanfare and the world watching via the cable news networks, attention could be drawn to these objectionable provisions with the hope that a public outcry might develop. It was an inherently attention-seeking tactic that had unsurprisingly effective results.

"I am an unapologetic supporter of the Second Amendment," continued Abbie. "I accept the premise that the only legitimate use of force is in defense against aggression of one's individual rights—life, liberty and justly owned property. While this right resides permanently with the individual, our First Amendment right of association allows us to be aided by any other individual or group without fear of being labeled an enemy combatant of our government."

Abbie looked around the Senate floor and realized that she was virtually alone except for her comrades and a few tired, disinterested Senate staffers. But the cameras were always on and her words held profound meaning. This was not just about political posturing, although it was an ancillary benefit. Abbie spoke from the heart and was principled in her beliefs. For that reason, the words flowed easily.

"We affirm the individual right recognized by the Second Amendment to keep and bear arms and oppose the persecution of

American citizens for exercising this right," said Abbie. "The American people should be free to establish their own conditions regarding the ownership and use of firearms without fear of confiscation as this Act allows. We will continue to vehemently oppose all laws at any level of government restricting the ownership, manufacture and transfer of firearms or ammunition for any lawful purpose."

From her right, Abbie saw Senator Cruz approach. Abbie admired Cruz for his shrewd initiative and spirited resourcefulness. He had the gumption to stand up for his principles and oppose even the most popular of Republican proposals. Over the last couple of years, Cruz grew more alienated within the GOP conference than ever, earning him the well-deserved designation firebrand.

"Well done, Abbie. Take a breather and let this long-winded Texan have a go at it," said Senator Cruz, whispering to Abbie as he placed his hand over the microphone. "Just be aware, our sellout of a Senate Majority Leader is headed your way."

Abbie knew the pontificating was coming to an end and the presence of the Senate Majority Leader on the Senate floor was evidence of the gavel from the bully pulpit being dropped on their Libertarian party of four.

"May I speak with you, Senator?" asked Senate Majority Leader Mitch McConnell from Kentucky. He gently led Abbie away from the prying eyes and ears of others. Like a protective sheepdog, Abbie's chief of staff remained close by.

"Of course, sir," said Abbie.

"Senator," started McConnell, "I'm aware Senator Paul has a vested interest in ennobling Rand Paul just as high as his goal of thwarting the ability of our government to use lawful surveillance measures to protect the homeland. I am quite surprised, however, that you would join in this mockery of doing the people's business."

"Sir, I am very committed to the defeat of these objectionable provisions and late added amendments by the Senate Armed Services Committee," said Abbie. "I objected when they were proposed in committee and I am continuing to object now. They are overreaching."

"I admire your commitment to your cause," said McConnell. "When I gave you high-valued assignments on the Emerging Threats and Capabilities subcommittee and on the Senate Intelligence Committee, I knew that you would bring a unique perspective. However, I need not remind you of the criticism I received from my caucus for placing a political independent such as yourself in these prized assignments."

"Sir, I mean you no disrespect by advancing my arguments on the floor today," said Abbie. "I feel strongly about these issues."

"Well, no matter," said McConnell. "I have reached an agreement with Senator Paul to bring this charade to an end. He will be allowed to bring a few amendments to the Senate floor for consideration together with a limited amount of time for more *eloquent speeches*. But then we will vote. The members of both houses are interested in winding this up in order to hit the campaign trail for summer recess. I am sure you have some campaigning to do as well, Senator."

"Yes, sir, of course," said Abbie. She could sense something was about to blindside her.

"Senator, I have spoken with your father," said McConnell. He turned to Abbie's chief of staff. "Young lady, I imagine you have a phone message for the senator."

Abbie was handed a transcribed message from her father. She looked at her chief of staff, who nodded her head affirmatively. The note read—*take the deal, see you Sunday*. Senator McConnell was smiling at her. Abbie did not like her vote being sold.

"Senator, after the vote authorizing the NDAA, the President will be signing an Executive Order," said McConnell. "In the interest of making the new Act budget-neutral, the President will be divesting certain lands determined to be a cost burden upon the taxpayers. The Department of the Interior has already made the arrangements. One such parcel is located in Massachusetts."

"I am sorry, sir," said Abbie, beginning to get the picture. "Which parcel are you referring to?"

"Senator, your father will explain the details to you," said McConnell. "This will be a magnificent feather in your political cap. Use it wisely."

"But, sir—" said Abbie.

"We're done here," said McConnell. Abbie was dismissed as she watched the Senate Majority Leader approach Senator Mike Lee from Utah. Abbie wondered what other feathers were being doled out to caps of the Gang of Four today.

CHAPTER 9

May 15, 2016
John Morgan Residence
39 Sears Road
Brookline, Massachusetts

Morgan milled around and cordially engaged in conversation with his guests. The executive committee of the Boston Brahmin met monthly, usually at his 73 Tremont office. After last month's excitement as viewed from the Top of the Hub restaurant, Morgan thought a more relaxed atmosphere was appropriate. It was doubtful a race riot would break out on his pristine four-acre front lawn.

"The rise in interest rates is unprecedented," said Lawrence Lowell, a wealthy philanthropist and direct descendant of John Lowell, a federal judge in the first United States Continental Congress. "I'm told the Federal Reserve will raise rates to five percent on Thursday."

"It is untenable," said Morgan. "As you know, we turned off the lending spigot to our European interests several months ago. As these rates rise, they will not be able to afford the payments. I am not in the business of collections, are you?"

Lowell's stout frame shook as he laughed. "No, our borrowers do not appreciate our collection efforts, do they?" Lowell asked rhetorically. "My concern is for the American economy. The nation's debt is unsustainable. Logically, as rates rise, the deficit will grow exponentially. This takes money out of the hands of businesses and squanders it down the drain of interest payments to Japan, China and others. A government that borrows a lot will have to pay the piper— or hope for some form of a reset."

"A day of reckoning is coming, Lawrence," said Morgan. "Rest assured we will be well positioned when the time comes." Morgan slapped his old friend on the back as Walter Cabot approached them. Cabot, heir to the Cabot shipping fortune, was a direct descendant of Captain John Cabot, a Revolutionary War hero.

"I sense a conspiracy is brewing over here." Cabot laughed as he shook hands with his fellow Boston Brahmin. "You two are either solving the world's problems or creating a few—for someone else, of course."

"Walter, our astute friend Lawrence and I were simply envisioning a world without water," said Morgan. "What would all those Cabot ships do if they were high and dry?"

"Blasphemy, gentlemen," replied Cabot. "We would simply turn them into high-dollar condos with great ocean-front potential!" The powerful men shared a laugh and a clink of the glass. Morgan knew their resources would always enable them to prosper—in good times and bad.

"John, we love what you've done with the place," said Cabot as he turned to survey the grand entry. Morgan's home was a fifteen-thousand-square-foot, 1929 Georgian Revival manor located in the heart of prestigious Brookline. The nine-bedroom, fourteen-bath mansion was adorned with gold-leaf ceilings and intricate architectural millwork. After recent renovations, Morgan added a billiards room, a state-of-the-art home theater and even an elaborate tree house in the event Abigail rewarded him with grandchildren.

Morgan thought often of Abigail and her lack of serious relationships in the past—except for Henry Sargent years ago. Morgan clearly discouraged the relationship with Sarge because of the plan he had for both of their lives. As his only child, Abigail had many shoes to fill. As the Sargent boys' godfather, Morgan had a special bond with Henry and Steven, but he also needed them for important roles that Morgan knew were inevitable. With every passing week, Morgan knew the time was near for the Sargent brothers to prove their mettle. He had seen it coming for many decades.

"Thank you, Walter," said Morgan. "I must say the tree house in the woods is my favorite addition. Hopefully, I will be a grandfather someday. Abigail's career takes precedence at this time."

"I've seen the polls," said Lowell. "Her path to victory looks strong. I've also seen her rise to national prominence. She seems to be spending a lot of time with Senator Paul." Morgan perceived Lowell was making a point about her association with the GOP frontrunner.

"If you are referring to their marathon session on the Senate floor, I am aware," said Morgan. "She and Senator Paul have shared this opinion of so-called governmental intrusion into people's lives since they both ran for the Senate six years ago. Senator Paul may have been politically motivated by Friday's grandstanding, but I believe Abigail was principled in her rhetoric. In any event, her actions have benefitted us tremendously, as you will soon learn."

One of Morgan's butlers approached them without intruding. Morgan, acknowledging his presence, spoke first. "Yes, Robert."

"As you requested, sir. Abigail is here."

"Excuse me, gentlemen," said Morgan as he went to find Abbie. She deserved an explanation about the mysterious change of events in the Senate chamber Friday. As Morgan passed through the ornate columns guarded by large Chinese fan palm trees, he paused to admire his daughter. Abigail never failed him. She shared a passion for the law and followed his educational path through Harvard. She gradually gained an inclination for politics. His wealth and power allowed her to avoid the normal path of local politics to the national stage. She enjoyed the benefit of his prominence and powerful friends, enabling her to become a powerful junior senator with even greater ambitions. There were times decisions would be made on her behalf. Friday's wrangling with the Senate Majority Leader was one of those times. He did not like to shut her out, but as a sitting senator, plausible deniability was necessary.

"May I borrow my lovely daughter?" asked Morgan to a handful of well-wishers surrounding Abigail. "This will only take a moment." Morgan leaned down to kiss her cheek, which was slightly out of character for him. Her cold response told him she was still unhappy. He led her into the billiards room and shut the door behind them.

"Abigail, I need to explain," said Morgan, but she interrupted him.

"Father, you know I don't like to sell my vote," said Abbie. "We agreed I would always look after your interest, *and theirs*." Abbie gestured through the door, obviously making reference to the Boston Brahmin.

"Yes, dear, we did agree," said Morgan. "You have always performed admirably."

"I am not one of your employees who expects a pat on the back," said Abbie. "Those provisions of the NDAA are onerous and need to be removed." She walked away from him and mindlessly rolled the cue ball down the red felt of the full-size, modern billiards table. He hoped his explanation would make this right.

"Before I provide you the details of my arrangement with Senator McConnell, please know that I will never put you in a position to compromise your principles, even if they conflict with my own needs," said Morgan. "I will not be at cross-purposes with my daughter. I would simply find another way." Morgan discerned his daughter was still raw with emotion.

"The objectionable provisions of the NDAA will be struck from the final draft prior to passage," said Morgan.

Abigail looked up at him, probing his eyes for subterfuge. She knew him well.

He continued. "Politics is about give and take, as you have learned. We take far more than we give. I have worked with Senators McConnell and Reid their entire careers. I helped Harry rise to his leadership position. The two are interchangeable. The fight between political parties is less about ideology than it is about who controls the purse strings. Republicans and Democrats rotate in and out of political power, but they conduct the same political business while there—control the flow of money to their benefactors. Abigail, we are the benefactors to both sides of the aisle." He could see her relax. Morgan had taught her over time that his methods might appear objectionable at first, but the results typically improved a given situation.

"What kind of deal did you make? What land was McConnell talking about?"

"Abigail, we have established a charitable trust and will be acquiring Prescott Peninsula," replied Morgan.

"What part of it—the old town of Prescott? For what purpose?" asked Abigail. She leaned on a barstool next to a mounted eight-point buck.

"No, dear, all of it, including the Quabbin Reservoir." Morgan allowed this to sink in for a moment. The Quabbin Reservoir was the largest body of water in the State of Massachusetts. Located in the central part of the state, it was formed by the creation of dams and dikes in the 1930s, and became federal government owned and was largely undeveloped. Prescott Peninsula was completely surrounded by the reservoir and was largely unimproved except for an abandoned radio astronomy observatory where the old town of Prescott Center once stood. The entire acquisition encompassed nearly forty square miles.

"Father, the media will have a field day with this," objected Abbie. "Every Executive Order the President signs receives heavy scrutiny. If my vote is tied to this, my political career is over."

"It is for this reason Senator McConnell agreed to drop the provisions of the NDAA you find objectionable. The President has ascertained another way to achieve his goals. You—*we*, will reap the benefits."

"How will we benefit?" asked Abbie.

"Politically, you will have a very public ribbon-cutting ceremony on a new facility for abused families," said Morgan. "The facility, owned by a charitable trust with many layers of anonymity, will be portrayed as a shelter for victims of domestic violence and abuse. For that reason, the media and local residents will be asked to respect the privacy of the developers before and after its completion. It would be unsafe to the families to be exposed to their abusers."

"On paper, this is a very noble cause," said Abbie. "I could take credit for bringing this type of facility to our state." Morgan saw she was warming to the concept.

"Yes, Abigail," said Morgan. "You will not be required to compromise your vote and you will gain political capital in the process."

"But this will still be picked apart by the media," said Abbie.

"We have orchestrated these events to fall on this particular weekend. The media will be preoccupied for days to come."

"How?" asked Abbie, only to be interrupted by a knock at the door.

"Come in, please," said Morgan.

Malcolm Lowe, his longtime assistant and former Undersecretary of State, entered the room. He was carrying a phone.

"Sir, an urgent call for you," said Lowe, handing the phone to Morgan. "Hello, Abbie."

"Yes," said Morgan into the receiver.

CHAPTER 10

May 15, 2016
The White House Situation Room
Washington, D.C.

Katie O'Shea knew something of vital national importance was brewing. Weekend briefings in the White House Situation Room were not completely out of the norm. The world, after all, didn't take weekends off. What made this particular briefing extraordinary was the presence of Valerie Jarrett, the seniormost advisor to the President. Officially, her title was Assistant to the President for Public Engagement and Intergovernmental Affairs. Unofficially, she was much more.

Born in Iran, Jarrett wielded unprecedented power in the White House. She was rumored to be the closest confidant of the President, surpassing even the voice of his wife. Her presence in today's emergency briefing told Katie the White House was circling the wagons and had a serious incident on its hands that required the narrative to be closely monitored.

In addition, Secretary of the Treasury Jack Lew was present. To her knowledge, matters of State and National Defense did not ordinarily involve Treasury. Katie was still new in her position as a member of the President's Intelligence Advisory Board, but she had earned the other members' respect with her excellent analysis of the Las Vegas cyberattack on the downtown casinos. At first, both David McDill, White House Chief of Staff, and Susan Giles, the National Security Advisor, were skeptical of Katie's role on the board. They were aware of John Morgan's influence in placing Katie in her position. NSA Giles instantly warmed to Katie's blunt manner and candid analysis of intelligence matters while being mindful of the political impact of reports. Most importantly to Katie, however, was pleasing her real boss—John Morgan.

"Let's get started," said Lew, breaking the whispered conversations in the room. "We have been contacted via official channels by my counterparts in Spain, Greece and Italy today. The decision by Greece was somewhat expected. They began issuing a form of IOU, which was used as payment to government employees and retirees. In addition, six new drachma banknotes were designed and printed. When their banks reopen, the new drachma will become the country's official currency." Secretary Lew sat back in his chair, which prompted Chief of Staff McDill to interject.

"The President will be returning from a fund-raiser in San Francisco this evening," said McDill. "He will be in contact with Chancellor Merkel and French President Hollande in the next several hours to assess their reactions."

"The International Monetary Fund is working with national authorities in Europe on contingency plans," said Secretary Lew. "The Greek banks are big players in some of its neighbors' financial systems. In Bulgaria, for example, subsidiaries of the National Bank of Greece own a quarter of the country's banking assets. The situation is similar in Romania, Albania and Serbia."

Katie followed the collapse of the Eurozone for several years. Before Abbie's senatorial reelection campaign ramped up, the two would enjoy movie nights at Katie's apartment. Abbie likened the Eurozone collapse to watching a bad B-movie that you just can't turn off. Everyone knew Greece would exit the Eurozone—*Grexit* as the process was termed. What was surprising about today's news was the complicity of Spain and Italy. While both nations had their financial difficulties, their withdrawal from the Eurozone would catch everyone by surprise. Secretary Lew continued.

"Several scenarios have been advanced regarding the departure of Greece from the Eurozone," said Secretary Lew. "It was our opinion that the biggest threat to the continuance of the euro is not that Greece might leave, but that it might exit and then thrive with a clean financial slate. The Italians would question whether it made sense for them to continue its financial pain when it could simply bring back the lira. I don't want to get into the weeds here, but Italy is running a government surplus that is constantly strained by the low growth and deflation caused by the euro. The Grexit is simply an excuse for Italy to advance their already laid plans."

Katie's mind raced as she thought about the national-security issues surrounding this train wreck. This would cause substantial unrest throughout Europe and could potentially spill over into the United States. Terrorists never sleep and typically took advantage of distractions to conduct their attacks. NSA Giles was studying her. *Has the NSA developed a mind-reading app—which is implanted in Susan Giles brain? Wouldn't surprise me.*

"What happens next?" asked the President's Chief of Staff.

"The government did not put up a default notice, but it did advise several key officials in the Greek trade unions and a run on the banks began," said Secretary Lew. "As word spread and the lines at the banks grew, the decision was made over the weekend to close the banks indefinitely. The IMF has requested national banking supervisors to ensure all subsidiaries of Greek banks throughout the Eurozone have enough assets to allow exchanges of emergency financing at their own central banks in case financing from the Greek parent institutions is suddenly cut off."

"We expect President Pavlopoulos to address the Greek people and ask for calm," said NSA Giles. "As President, he is a figurehead, but he is respected. Prime Minister Tsipras is the driving force behind the default—together with his allies, Prime Minister Rajoy in Spain and Italian Prime Minister Renzi."

"We expect Portugal to join their Southern Europe neighbors by the end of today," added Secretary Lew.

"Europe is America's largest trading partner," said McDill. "The most common currency for transactions between the United States and European businesses is the dollar. But the euro is a close second, which will leave American businesses that deal with Europe exposed to devastating losses."

"The value of the euro had already dropped below the one-to-one ratio with the dollar," added Secretary Lew. "Many of our businesses began writing their contracts with European companies in dollars, but a few of the larger institutions hedged and used forward contracts—betting on the additional loss of value."

Katie absorbed as much of this information as possible because she would have to relay these details to Morgan. However, she was hesitant to take notes. Valerie Jarrett continued to study the faces seated around the table in the Situation Room. *What is she looking for? Does the White House suspect a leak?*

"How does all of this affect our national security?" asked McDill.

"There are a lot of possible scenarios, none of them are very good," said NSA Rice.

"Give us the best-case scenario, Jack," said McDill.

"We expect the breakup to destroy twenty-five percent to sixty percent of the gross domestic product in the stronger countries who choose to remain with the euro—namely France and Germany," said Lew. "Banks throughout Europe and to some extent elsewhere will suffer catastrophic losses and need to be nationalized. There will be massive wealth destruction in the private sector. European export markets will practically disappear because devaluation will make those products expensive and uncompetitive. On a societal level, unemployment, uncertainty and shortages of basic necessities will result in large-scale unrest across Europe."

"I asked for the best-case scenario."

"That is the best-case scenario, Dave," replied Lew. "The worst-case scenario is a total collapse. Such a collapse would lead to a multiyear depression in Europe and several years of recession here. The collapse of the euro would have a more damaging impact on the American economy than the events of '07 and '08."

"What do you mean?" asked McDill.

"A rush of financial assets out of the Eurozone would wreak havoc with currencies and the price of oil, for starters," replied Secretary Lew. "Even worse, interbank lending will be destroyed worldwide. Should there be a run on banks worldwide as a result of the Eurozone collapse, credit markets will freeze, making it near impossible to borrow money."

"We pulled ourselves out of the '08 debacle through Federal Reserve activity," said McDill. "Can't you coordinate with the Fed and the IMF to formulate stopgap measures?"

"Ordinarily, the answer is yes," replied Secretary Lew. "The crisis in 2008 originated in the United States and was manageable by the Fed. There is no single global entity that wields as much power internationally as the Federal Reserve. The Fed has its hands full with the rapid rise in inflation in the United States. A reduction in rates for the purposes of bailing out Europe would make our inflation look like Zimbabwe of ten years ago."

In 1998, the President of Zimbabwe, Robert Mugabe, instituted a series of government programs to elevate his country's poor population. The programs included land grabs from multinational corporations who allegedly took the properties from the poor during the early years of colonialization. Because the lands were primarily used for farming and food production, the economy of Zimbabwe was devastated. Exports came to a halt, tax revenues dried up, and the government's operating expenses skyrocketed. The Reserve Bank of Zimbabwe produced more currency in higher denominations. Hyperinflation destroyed the value of the currency. Inflation rose to an unprecedented six hundred percent in 2004. By 2008, hyperinflation rose to two million percent. Katie knew Zimbabwe was not an isolated occurrence, although it was considered the worst example. In the last one hundred years, major countries, including Germany, Mexico, Argentina, Iraq and Romania, had experienced hyperinflationary periods.

Secretary Lew paused and a tense silence filled the room. Jarrett broke the silence, speaking for the first time.

"The President is very concerned about the impact all of this will have on the American people," said Jarrett. "Whatever one might think of the euro, the possibility of its total collapse, or even rampant speculation about its collapse, is going to devastate economic growth in Europe and will negatively impact our own economy. If this news creates market volatility with no feasible solutions, then U.S. consumers will be hesitant to spend money in the face of the economic uncertainty."

"Each of you has a unique role and contribution to the President's Intelligence Advisory Board," added NSA Rice. "I want a full assessment of these events from your perspective to be presented in tomorrow morning's briefing. Ordinarily, I believe there is little that time and money can't solve. We are short on both, people."

CHAPTER 11

May 15, 2016
John Morgan Residence
39 Sears Road
Brookline, Massachusetts

"Sir, this is Katie O'Shea. I have just left the Situation Room at the White House." Morgan gestured for Lowe to leave the billiards room and close the door behind him. He looked at Abigail before responding.

"Yes, Miss O'Shea," said Morgan. "What do you have for me?"

"I was called to an emergency meeting in the Situation Room conducted by Secretary Lew," said Katie. "The Eurozone will collapse tomorrow. Greece, Spain and Italy are all intentionally defaulting on their payments to the IMF. Portugal is expected to follow suit. Banks across Europe will be closed indefinitely as the Germans and French sort things out."

"Anything else?" asked Morgan. He looked at Abigail to assess her mood.

"Yes, sir," said Katie. "Valerie Jarrett was also present throughout the meeting. Her primary concern was market volatility and the lack of a feasible solution."

"Interesting. Who will be running point on behalf of the administration with the media?"

"Secretary Lew," responded Katie.

"Thank you, Miss O'Shea. Keep me informed." Morgan ended the call. He turned his attention to Abigail.

"Is everything okay?" she asked.

"Tomorrow the house of cards formerly known as the Eurozone

will come to an end," said Morgan. "Greece, Spain and Italy are willfully defaulting on their obligations to the International Monetary Fund. All banks across Europe will be closed until further notice. This will have global repercussions on the markets." Morgan saw Abigail look at him with skepticism.

"Did you know this was going to happen?"

"I did."

"For how long?" she asked.

"I've known for several weeks, Abigail," replied Morgan, who was growing weary of his daughter's tone. *There is work to be done.*

"So you knew the compromise on the NDAA reached Friday night would be buried by the financial catastrophe in Europe?"

"Yes, I did—for several weeks now," replied Morgan. Both of them stood silently for a long moment.

"I understand, Father. Thank you." Perhaps his daughter was beginning to understand the burdens he carried. She came to hug him—a rare, brief moment of affection between them.

"You're welcome, Abigail," said Morgan. Morgan opened the doors and spoke to Lowe, who was dutifully waiting outside.

"Malcolm, discreetly advise the others to meet me in the study to discuss a serious matter." He walked across the hallway towards his study. He turned to Abigail, who followed him.

"It is best that you are not present in this meeting, Abigail," said Morgan. He noticed the look of hurt on her face. "You do understand the reasons?"

"Of course, Father, plausible deniability."

***

Morgan walked to the bar and poured himself a Macallan. Not bad, but certainly not his beloved Scotch whisky—Glengoyne, which was in short supply. As he took a moment to gather his thoughts, he admired the renovations to his study. Intricate walnut carvings adorned the walls, filling the room with the colors of chocolate brown and smoky swirls of honey. This was a man's room, and the gold-leaf ceiling capped off its opulence. Morgan studied his original painting of John Adams—his most prized possession and one of only three known to be in existence. Silently, he toasted his glass to his ancestor.

Paul Winthrop, a descendant of Massachusetts' first governor, and Samuel Bradlee, a direct descendant of Nathaniel Bradlee, one of the organizers of the Boston Tea Party, entered the room first.

"Is everything all right, John?" asked Winthrop.

"Is this about Secretary Kerry?" asked Bradlee as he approached the bar.

"What about Kerry?" asked Morgan, pouring his friend a Scotch.

"Damn fool broke his leg falling off his bicycle." Winthrop laughed.

"This is very true, John," added Bradlee. "He bounced off a curb and crashed, breaking his leg. His helmet and knee pads couldn't save him." Despite the seriousness of the circumstances, Morgan couldn't resist a little humor of his own.

"Let me guess, all the king's horses and all the king's men couldn't put the flip-flopper back together again." Morgan laughed.

"Cheers to that!" announced Henry Endicott as he entered the study. Endicott, whose grandfather was one of the first Secretaries of War, despised John Kerry for what he deemed traitorous statements in front of Congress during the Vietnam War.

Morgan greeted Cabot and Lowell as they entered the room and closed the door behind them.

"Gentlemen, refresh your drinks and get comfortable. There is much to discuss."

CHAPTER 12

May 15, 2016
John Morgan Residence
39 Sears Road
Brookline, Massachusetts

"I have received information regarding the Eurozone," started Morgan. The idle chat amongst the executive committee of the Boston Brahmin died down as he spoke. Morgan was the titular head of the committee and was granted the utmost respect as a result. Over the years, no member had questioned his authority or judgment. During that time, he had increased their wealth and power exponentially.

"As expected, the countries of Spain, Italy, Greece and now Portugal will officially declare themselves in default on their debts to the Troika—the Eurozone Central Bank, the IMF, and the Eurozone countries that helped bail them out."

"John, I assume this has not made the news," asked Winthrop.

"That's correct, although a formal announcement is expected within hours," replied Morgan. "This should be a lesson learned by all governments in the world. High structural deficits and unsustainable debt-to-GDP levels will ultimately lead to a sovereign debt crisis. If this leads to a crisis in confidence in the markets, both Europe and the United States could face a 1929 scenario." Morgan watched as expressions of concern came over the faces of his fellow Brahmin.

"Do not be concerned, gentlemen. As always, I have our finances in order." Morgan had met with each of the men over the last several weeks to prepare them for the inevitable collapse of the Eurozone.

They were all heartily invested in physical gold and precious metals. Soon, he would disclose his plan for profiting from the inevitable economic collapse.

"To quote our friends in the White House," started Morgan, "*One must never let a good crisis go to waste.* The primary repercussion of this failed experiment will be the tightening of credit. Business in Europe will be looking for willing lenders outside the European banking system. I have spoken with K. V. Kamath, president of the BRICS bank. They have no interest in lending to European concerns. They are singularly focused on advancing the economies of their member states. That leaves only one group other than us capable of filling the lending void."

"The Bilderbergs," offered Cabot.

"Yes, Walter, but more specifically, the leading financial members of the Steering Committee representing the largest European banking houses—Credit Suisse, BNP Paribas and Deutsche Bank. I have identified four individuals who have opposed our activities in Europe's finances in the past. Some are persuadable, others are not."

"John, will you be in contact with these four?" asked Lowell.

"Most definitely, Lawrence," said Morgan. "We have several weeks before we host the conference at The Liberty Hotel. I will have all possible contingencies addressed prior to then. Our resources, under the umbrella of Morgan Global, will become the lender of first and last resort for Europe. It is time to come out of the *shadows*, gentlemen—pardon the pun."

Morgan toasted his fellow Brahmin, who laughed. *Shadow banking*, as the term was first used, referred to nontraditional, nonbank methods of lending. The term received a derogatory connotation after the 2008 banking crisis. The use of hedge funds and credit derivatives to finance the growth of America's real estate market was not illegal. There would not have been a problem if people had simply paid their loans as they were contractually obligated to do. Morgan considered the insinuation of malfeasance unfair. He preferred to refer to his methods as the *facilitation of credit*.

"The collapse of the euro will have a profound effect on the markets and our own currency," said Bradlee. "I have no confidence in this administration's ability to handle the fallout."

Morgan had considered this as well. This was also an opportunity to gain favor with the President and reap financial gain.

"I have thought of this, my friends," said Morgan. "This administration's appetite for quantitative easing—the printing of money to buy up our own debt—has to cease. At this point, the Fed now owns nearly one hundred percent of all ten-year Treasury Bonds. When this tool was initiated in 2009, the administration's goal was to divest its bond holdings and normalize its balance sheet once the economy fully recovered. The recovery never happened. Now, inflation is forcing rates higher, which in turn are creating a staggering debt. Gentlemen, our nation is not that far behind the Eurozone. As one of our protégés likes to say—*all empires collapse eventually*." Morgan allowed reality to settle in for a moment. All of these men were descendants of the Founding Fathers. They were freedom-loving, patriotic Americans who would spend their fortunes to protect America from failure. They knew tough decisions had to be made.

Morgan continued. "Gentlemen, our Founding Fathers worked just as tirelessly building our fledgling nation as they did in their fight for our independence from Great Britain. As fighters for the freedoms we enjoy, their causes for seeking independence followed a common theme—ensuring the freedoms and the rights of its citizens. Why should our fight for the protection of American freedoms be any different today?

"We are a nation in decline, politically, economically and socially. I, along with many of you, believe drastic measures are necessary to put America back on sound footing. I don't think our country's best days are behind her. But I do believe a *reset* is in order. Some of you have discussed this concept with me in the past. I do not know what a reset entails, but I do know it will be painful for some. As our forefathers knew, revolutions are nasty business, but necessary at times."

CHAPTER 13

May 16, 2016
The *Boston Herald* Editorial Board
Conference Room
Boston, Massachusetts

Julia Hawthorne reluctantly accepted the praise being heaped upon her by Joe Sciacca, the chief editor of the *Boston Herald*. Julia just received another nomination for a prestigious award. Earlier in the year, Julia was awarded the Marconi Radio Award for the paper's newly launched Boston Herald Radio—a first for an Internet radio station.

Now, the Society of American Business Editors and Writers granted Julia the Distinguished Achievement Award. Established in 1993, the SABEW singled out individuals who made a significant impact on the field of business journalism. It was another honor bestowed upon Julia that was sure to vault her to the top of every journalism headhunter in the county. For now, she was happy in her job, and her relationship with Sarge.

After their dinner together in December, she and Sarge became inseparable. Trips to the West Coast and getaways to Martha's Vineyard gave them the opportunity to step away from their lives and focus on each other. Julia wanted to marry Sarge and she was certain he felt the same way. The time didn't seem right yet.

"Julia, would you like to say a few words before we get started?" asked Sciacca.

Julia composed herself. Today was a busy day at the paper. The news of the day could fill a morning and evening edition.

"Thanks, Joe," replied Julia. "It would be cliché to say this was a team effort, but I'll say it anyway. Everyone in this room contributes to the publication of our paper. For one hundred and seventy years, journalists have taken great pride in producing the news and excellent editorial content for our fellow Bostonians. Our work on Herald Radio got us noticed again and I believe the SABEW award is just the beginning for this group. I say we step it up and show those guys at *The Globe* they better watch their backs."

The other members of the editorial board provided Julia a brief moment of applause, but the serious looks on their faces indicated the accolades were short lived.

"Thank you, Julia, and despite your humble nature, the praise is well deserved," said Sciacca. "Now, where the hell do we start?" Sciacca paused and then he answered his own query.

"I've been in the newspaper business my entire adult life. This is my thirty-third year at the *Herald*, covering everything from the crime beat, to Massachusetts politics and now as editor-in-chief. I will be honest with you. I've never been more concerned about the stability of the world from an economic or societal standpoint than right now. As journalists, it is our duty to convey the news to our readers without bias or hyperbole. The reader shouldn't have to discern between reporting and editorializing. I am proud of this group for your ability to keep the two separate. Most news organizations fail at this task—often intentionally. We are now presented with a number of news stories across the globe, all of which could be front-page headlines. This is now the norm, rather than the exception. Our challenge is to bring the news to our readership, and listenership, in a way that doesn't diminish the importance of the story."

Julia became a little emotional listening to this iconic journalist pour his heart out. These were troubling times and her associates in the room were responsible for informing the public of every crisis. The media's reputation had been tarnished and she hoped to do her part to restore integrity to the journalistic process.

"Okay, enough already. Let's start with the European situation," said Sciacca. "Sandra, what's the latest?"

Sandra Gottlieb was the highly respected business editor of the

Herald and was providing excellent reporting on the continuous increase in interest rates by the Federal Reserve. She had warned the other editors of the *Herald* about a potential exit by Greece from the Eurozone.

I bet she didn't expect this.

"In a word—chaos," said Gottlieb. "We've discussed the potential default by Greece for some time, but as I pointed out in December, the attack by Ukrainian Special Forces on the Russian convoy at Mariupol seemed to accelerate the demise of the Eurozone. The relationship between European governments and Moscow was tenuous at best. After the attack, which smacked of CIA involvement, by the way, the delicate balance has fractured. The countries with the least to lose by the Eurozone collapse are Spain, Portugal, Italy and Greece. They have planned for the default and orchestrated the pullout over the weekend."

"How have these four countries prepared?" asked Sciacca.

"First, they have all adopted their pre-Eurozone currencies," replied Gottlieb. "Second, as a condition of their banks reopening, the governments have uniformly instituted capital controls. The anticipated reaction of depositors is to make a run on the banks. Closing them for several days was a good decision. This will allow the heads of state to issue appeals for calm."

"Julia, from a political perspective, how do you anticipate the various governments responding?" asked Sciacca.

Julia wasn't prepared to jump into the Eurozone collapse situation, but she and Sarge had discussed this subject over dinner the night before.

"Governments and their politicians have a common goal—remain in power," said Julia. "I'd expect them to strike a nationalistic tone and separate their particular country from the others in the Eurozone. I foresee large political demonstrations orchestrated by the predominantly left-leaning governments of these four southern European nations. They will portray the wealthier nations of France and Germany as the bad guys. If they are successful, the people will rally around the decision and the new currencies."

"Julia is spot on," added Gottlieb. "I have seen the proposed currency notes issued by the central banks of the four nations. They are very patriotic, featuring symbols and leaders of their historic past."

"What will be the effect on the United States economy?" asked Sciacca.

"Obligations to *official* creditors like the IMF, the European Central Bank and the other European governments account for the vast majority of the three trillion dollars of indebtedness," replied Gottlieb. "These global financiers will bear the brunt of the foreign losses resulting from the default. The foreign bank exposure, including those of the United States, totals around eighty billion dollars, which is widely dispersed around the world. The direct effects on these banks should be manageable. However, this action will plunge the former Eurozone into recession. Europe is America's largest trading partner and its demise will probably have an immediate impact on our floundering economy."

Instinctively, Julia looked at her watch as the opening of the stock market approached. "Markets don't like volatility," said Julia. "How bad can it get?"

"The markets in France are our best indicator," replied Gottlieb. "Like most cash and derivative markets, mitigation strategies are in place to prevent mass hysteria from collapsing an entire stock market. History has shown that crashes are driven by panic as much as by underlying economic factors. They are truly social phenomena where certain external economic events combine with crowd behavior, creating panic selling."

It was human nature to follow crowd behavior. Julia had observed this at sporting events. During a football game, a fan might suddenly turn around and look at the sky. Suddenly, fifty thousand individuals began to act as a single unit, almost a single brain, focused intently on what was happening off the field. Sociologists claimed crowd behavior was partly responsible for the market crash of 1929.

"What happened in France?" asked Sciacca.

"The French equivalent of our Dow Jones Industrial Average of thirty benchmark stocks is known as the CAC40," replied Gottlieb. "Their mitigation strategy is fairly complex, but transactions are suspended for one hour when certain levels are met and the markets close completely when twenty-five percent of the value of the CAC40 has been reached."

"What happened after the markets in France opened?" asked Sciacca.

"After a series of suspensions of trading and corresponding resumptions, the markets closed. The CAC40 bottomed out at twenty-five percent of value within three hours," replied Gottlieb.

The room became deathly silent as the magnitude of the crash in French equities soaked in. More than one person in the room checked their watches.

"Do our markets have similar mitigation strategies?" asked Sciacca.

"We do," replied Gottlieb. "There are three thresholds, each of which represents different levels of decline in terms of points in the Dow. These are computed at the beginning of each calendar quarter to establish a point value based upon the market's present value. They are known as circuit breakers."

"I remember this," said Sciacca. "During the market crash of '08, trading was halted after drops in ten percent increments."

"That's correct, Joe," said Gottlieb. "The SEC and the New York Stock Exchange have since amended Rule 80, which deals with the benchmark index to seven percent, thirteen percent and twenty percent. At twenty percent, trading will be halted."

"What are we talking about here?" asked Sciacca.

"If trading is halted, indicating a twenty percent loss, the market capitalization of the United States will have decreased by nearly seven trillion dollars," replied Gottlieb. "That's half of the entire Gross Domestic Product of the Eurozone. Our investors have the most to lose by this."

Julia checked her watch again. It was 9:30. This was going to be a newsworthy day.

CHAPTER 14

May 17, 2016
73 Tremont
Boston, Massachusetts

"You know, I just realized something," said Donald as he rode up the elevator with Steven and Sarge, while ignoring the two bulky security personnel standing to their rear.

"What's that, DQ?" asked Steven.

"In all the years we've known each other, we have never been here together," replied Donald.

Steven nodded and Sarge thought for a moment.

"You're right, Donald, and other than recent events, I have no clue as to why we're here today," added Sarge.

Yesterday's news of the Eurozone collapse was dominating the major networks, not just cable news. When it was announced the European banks would be closed indefinitely, panic turned to anger throughout Europe. Rioters opened the doors of banks on their own, and cell phone videos began to show the destruction. By day's end, nearly one hundred bank locations across Europe were destroyed by outraged citizens. As financial markets opened on day two, stocks crashed as investors sought the safe-haven investments of precious metals.

The elevator doors opened and Sarge led his companions to the reception desk. Despite attempting to exchange pleasantries with the ladies manning their posts, Sarge noticed a constant darting of the eyes in Steven's direction. Animal magnetism, mesmerism and hypnosis were all at work when Steven encountered beautiful women.

"Gentlemen, Mr. Morgan requests you wait for him in the studio," said a stunning blonde who could just as easily peel off your toenails as curl your toes. The boys dutifully followed her into the media room of Morgan's offices, which comprised the entire top floor of the 73 Tremont building. Originally built in 1829 as the Tremont Hotel, the neoclassical building was known for its innovations of the time such as indoor plumbing, locking guest rooms and free toiletries. Some of the Tremont Hotel's early guests included Davy Crockett and Charles Dickens, who would marvel at the modern alterations incorporated into Morgan's studio. Decorative shelving and built-in television monitors gave the room a distinctive library feel. The titles included the works of Dickens, Hawthorne and Faulkner. You could choose a classic book or a classic movie, all in one place.

"Thank you, Danielle," said Morgan as he entered the room with the ever-present Lowe. "Gentlemen, thank you for being prompt. We have a number of issues to address." Morgan was getting right down to business.

Sarge nudged Steven to pay attention to Morgan and not the young lady's departure.

"Malcolm, bring up the video on Prescott Peninsula," said Morgan.

Lowe interacted with a tablet computer and two screens came to life. One showed a continuous video of the entire Quabbin Reservoir by helicopter and the monitor showed an overall map of the area. Morgan approached the screen. "As you know, the Quabbin Reservoir is the largest inland body of water in the state. This area is known as the Prescott Peninsula. A charitable trust has been formed to take ownership of the area outlined here." Morgan pointed along a boundary surrounding the entire area, which included the former town of Prescott and the entire peninsula on which it sits.

"Mr. Quinn, Malcolm will provide you a packet of materials on the acquisition together with the legal documents. For public purposes, the charitable trust is owned anonymously and has been established for families fleeing domestic abuse. For our purposes, I want you gentlemen to plan a private community to be used in the event a catastrophic occurrence requires the city to be abandoned."

"You want a bug-out location," said Donald.

Sarge and Steven couldn't conceal their looks of curiosity. Morgan always had a plan, which was based upon an event foreseeable only to him. His methods never came into question.

"That's correct, Donald," said Morgan.

"What's that dome-shaped building?" asked Steven.

"This is the former Five College Radio Observatory built in 1969 by the University of Massachusetts, Amherst, Hampshire, Mount Holyhoke and Smith colleges," replied Lowe. "Its purpose was the training of astronomy students and to conduct research. At the time, it contained state-of-the-art technology."

"Next screen, please, Malcolm," instructed Morgan. The next screen was produced, showing the exact same aerial vantage point, but the domed building was no longer there. "In 2011, the observatory was decommissioned, requiring the government removal of the building and astronomy equipment. However, there is something else about this facility that cannot be seen by these aerial photographs. Run the next sequence, Malcolm."

"Looks like a giant golf ball," said Steven. A series of images flashed across the screen, revealing the before and after images of the facility. The final image revealed a small lake and a large grassy area devoid of trees.

"Most ground-based observatories consist of an optical telescope like the one shown in these images, surrounded by a dome-like structure—Steven's giant golf ball," said Lowe. "As you can see in these images, the structure and the telescopic apparatus were removed. What you cannot see is what is underground."

"At the time of the design and construction of the observatory, the Cuban Missile Crisis was still very much on people's minds," said Morgan. "Senator Ted Kennedy insisted the facility include an underground, nuclear-proof shelter. In addition, following the successful testing of an electromagnetic pulse weapon, the good senator required the shelter be protected from an EMP as well.

Despite a series of nuclear disarmament treaties being executed in '69, the Quabbin Observatory was designed as a state-of-the-art nuclear fallout shelter."

"In 1962, the government was testing a number of EMP weapons," said Donald. "One of the tests known as Starfish Prime exploded an EMP thirty miles above the Earth about thirteen hundred miles west of Honolulu. Electronics from Hawaii to New Zealand were damaged by the electromagnetic pulse."

"Is the shelter still present?" asked Sarge.

"It is," replied Morgan. "When the facility was decommissioned and dismantled, the contractor hired for the demolition worked for one of my associates. He removed the visible portions of the facility but left the subterranean compound intact."

"What is still underground?" asked Sarge.

"Malcolm, if you please," said Morgan. A series of images crossed the screen, which included blueprint drawings and images of the interior, including bunk rooms and storage lockers. "There is roughly five thousand square feet in the bunker, allowing for thirty occupants and several years of provisions."

"Wow, this is incredible," said Donald. "This is a prepper's paradise."

"I'm glad you feel this way, Mr. Quinn, because you will be busy over the next few months," said Morgan. "First, you will orchestrate a charade for the media. I want this entire project to have the appearance of a home for wayward families. My daughter will be conducting a high-profile political event there on June 7th, primary day. Afterwards, you will proceed quickly to ready the facility. My thoughts for the construction and use are detailed in the packet of materials Malcolm has provided you."

"When is the facility to be ready?" asked Donald.

"End of August," Morgan replied flatly.

Sarge sat back in his chair and once again glanced in the direction of Steven. *Something's afoot.*

"Mr. Quinn, of utmost importance is secrecy. Use all of the tools available to insure your activities go undetected. Am I clear?"

"Yes, sir," said Donald.

"Now, let's discuss our hosting of the Bilderberg conference next month," said Morgan, addressing Steven and Sarge. "I want the two of you to coordinate security and logistics for The Liberty Hotel and our guests. There will be a few guests who will require special attention. Further, there will be a couple of guests who will be unable to attend." Morgan allowed the words to soak in. *Looks like Steven will be going out of town for a few days.*

"Steven, expect a call from your employer within twenty-four hours. Henry, I need you to coordinate the hotel logistics with Aegis in his absence. I will rely heavily upon you both during the conference and be aware that plans can change on a moment's notice. We will meet here weekly until the conference. Do any of you have questions?"

"No, sir," replied Sarge on behalf of the group.

"There is one more thing," said Morgan. "Abigail is doing very well in the polls, and barring unforeseen circumstances, she should be reelected in November. Henry, have you discussed the campaign with my daughter?" *He's snooping.*

"Only briefly last month, sir," replied Sarge. "We had an impromptu fund-raiser on her behalf at 100 Beacon the day of the Boston Marathon. She also indicated the campaign was on track."

"There are occasions when my political viewpoints conflict with Abigail's," said Morgan. "I do not publicly state my political positions, but this doesn't mean I am devoid of opinion. I have established a nonprofit organization for the purposes of a political think tank. I want you to assemble a team, produce the necessary policy statements, coordinate a research arm and develop the necessary means of disseminating information."

Sarge was caught off guard by this request. Mr. Morgan never alluded to a project of this type and it was completely out of character for him. Further, Sarge could talk about politics and its impact on world affairs. But becoming involved in the process was never on his career-advancement radar.

"Sir, naturally I am flattered you chose me for this project, but aren't there more politically inclined people at your disposal?" asked Sarge.

Morgan's reaction was annoyance.

Fatal Error. Don't question the boss.

"Henry, I give every decision a thorough analysis before I implement it," said Morgan. "I've read your book and your flawless analysis of America's standing in the world comports with mine. Because of my position, I am unable to advance my views publicly. You, on the other hand, have become a recognized expert on the importance of America's sovereignty. There is no better spokesman for the preservation of this concept. Further, this will advance your stature as a defender of the Constitution."

Sarge exchanged glances with Steven and Donald. *He has a plan for me. This is just the beginning.* "Thank you for the confidence you have placed in me," said Sarge. "I look forward to the challenge and appreciate the opportunity to raise awareness of the importance of protecting America from global intercession."

"Gentlemen, we are entering troubling times for America," said Morgan. "The key to the survival of our nation will depend upon the outcome of certain events in the next few months. I believe in preparation for all contingencies and I expect perfection in the implementation of my directives. Are we clear?"

"Yes, sir," was the response, in unison.

CHAPTER 15

May 20, 2016
Harvard Kennedy School
Cambridge, Massachusetts

Sarge was in his eleventh year as a professor for the prestigious Harvard Kennedy School. As a teen, he enjoyed reading and research. Every topic caught his attention, but his family's political roots put him on this career path. His father, now deceased, was the former governor of Massachusetts and the Sargent lineage was filled with Revolutionary War heroes.

Unlike many of his friends in college, Sarge was not idealistic. He was not interested in political activism—neither party seemed to get it right. His dedication to studies and hunger for knowledge led him to the top of his class throughout his years in college, culminating with a doctorate in political economy and government from Harvard. He was honored when he received the offer to teach at his alma mater.

As a junior, untenured professor, Sarge focused on building a record through research papers and articles written for relevant journals. Journals were nothing more than the primary product of professorial research. He wrote between four to six articles a year with the help of his research assistants. Sarge supplemented his journal submissions with travel. Being single, he was not constrained by family commitments. He traveled throughout the world, giving lectures and workshop presentations. Although it took time to develop a concise, entertaining presentation, he eventually became adept at public speaking. He became known internationally and rapidly built a respected reputation abroad and amongst his peers at Harvard.

When a professor was offered tenure, it was an up or down decision. If you accepted the offer, you had a job for life. If you received the offer and turned it down, you needed to look for another job because you would soon be fired. Upper-crust universities didn't like rejection from their faculty. Harvard's tenure process was rigorous and invasive. Twenty or more unsolicited letters were sent to senior members of your community. There were background checks, interviews of associates and in-depth reviews of your lectures. Sarge's bona fides were never in question. His lineage dating back to the Revolutionary War helped. Being John Morgan's godson sealed his future as a tenured professor at Harvard.

Once tenured, Sarge was able to pursue his craft without fear of dismissal. Many professors used this Teflon status as an opportunity to advance their political agendas without fear of reprisal. Sarge simply enjoyed the job security and the ability to teach what he was passionate about—global governance.

After receiving his offer of tenure, Sarge had the time, and staff, to write a full-length book on the topic of global governance. Sarge's best-selling book, *Choose Freedom or Capitulation: America's Sovereignty Crisis*, became a regular topic on the presidential campaign trail. In the book, as well as lectures, Sarge warned against the overreach of globalists. He frequently opined that the Founding Fathers anticipated a power grab by a strong federal government, so autonomy of state governments became a central premise of the Constitution.

As the world advanced technologically, nation states, corporations and international organizations were required to coexist without a set of defined rules. This resulted in a blurring of national boundaries and ideologies. Proponents of global governance had a hidden agenda leaning toward a single totalitarian government. This would lead to the destruction of America, in Sarge's view, and his goal, as a patriot, was to lead people to respect America's sovereignty and oppose the globalist agenda.

Sarge's methods were subtle and his classroom lectures reflected his tact. These young minds had been influenced by so many—family, the mainstream media, Jon Stewart, Stephen Colbert. Sarge provided them an alternative view, without being blatantly obvious. Some minds were changed; others were reinforced. But all of his students respected his point of view.

"Okay, everyone, here we are," said Sarge. "It's the end of another riveting semester taught by your all-knowing professor."

Happy to hear the news, the class allowed themselves some cheeky applause. As always, Sarge enjoyed the response as the realization of another semester was checked off the list for these future public administrators, think-tank contributors, politicians and world leaders.

"Lest we forget, dear students, finals will be on Tuesday," said Sarge to the usual groans and protestations. "Yeah, I know. Boom, boom—out go the lights." Sarge loved the response and grinned as he brought up the screen. This would be his last lecture—for a while.

WHO IS RUNNING THINGS?

Naturally, the comedians throughout the classroom had their opinions. Muffled voices volunteered answers ranging from a shadow government to wealthy elitists to ancient aliens. Sarge suspected all of the above had a role in the world's affairs.

"Miss Crepeau, we started with you this semester and we will allow you the first opinion on this topic," said Sarge.

"Professor, follow the money," said Michelle Crepeau, a veteran of Sarge's lectures. "Wealth provides a tool to improve your bargaining position in any negotiation, at any level. Money represents power and control."

"This is quite the pessimistic view of the world's wealthy," said Sarge. "Aren't there wealthy individuals who are philanthropic—therefore doing noble deeds with their excesses?"

"That is true," replied Miss Crepeau. "But everyone has an agenda and the ultra-wealthy are in a better position to shape opinions."

Sarge saw a number of heads nod throughout the room. Over the past year, Miss Crepeau, articulate and attractive, had gained a tremendous amount of respect in the Kennedy School of Government. Sarge looked forward to following her career path.

"Miss Crepeau makes an interesting point, and if you were paying attention, she added some nuance to her response," said Sarge. "Did you notice she used the qualifier *ultra-wealthy*? Miss Crepeau, why did you add this to your statement?"

"Professor, there are many millionaires in the world," said Miss Crepeau. "I don't believe they have the ability to shape opinion on a national scale, much less international agendas. The ultra-wealthy have the ability to buy the equivalent of most nations' gross domestic product. They have the resources to pay off our national debt. Someone with that much money either uses it to gain more, or to wield power and exert control over others."

"The world's ultra-wealthy use their resources in many ways," said Sarge. "They participate in a vast network of secret societies, think tanks and charitable organizations to advance their agendas. They have the ability to control public perception through their ownership of the media and their dominance over a nation's education system. They are able to influence the affairs of nations via their funding of political campaigns." Sarge paused to catch his breath and to command their attention for the main point.

"Finally, this control ultimately provides them the ability to impact the operations of the leaders in global governance—the United Nations, the World Bank, the International Monetary Fund and the World Trade Organization. When you consider the big picture, global governance is a people business and the power of money controls the agenda." *Let's identify the evil ultra-wealthy and see if any familiar names pop up.*

"Who are the ultra-wealthy?" asked Sarge. He pointed to Mr. Lin, who was originally identified as shy by Sarge but broke out of his shell on the second question of day one.

"The tech giants lead the way, sir," responded Lin. "The names Bill Gates, Larry Ellison, Jeff Bezos of Amazon, and the nouveau riche Mark Zuckerberg of Facebook."

"Do you believe these individuals are part of the world's power brokers?" asked Sarge.

"Not really. I believe they are too high profile to get involved in behind-the-scenes policy-making," replied Lin.

"Not shadowy enough for you, Mr. Lin?" asked Sarge. "I'm guessing only the cloak-and-dagger ultra-wealthy stick their noses in global affairs. Does anyone else believe this?" Sarge saw a few hands pop up, but he chose Nikolas Dukakis, son of the former governor and presidential candidate Michael Dukakis.

"I don't know about the cloak-and-dagger aspect, sir," said Dukakis. "Wealthy individuals have plenty of minions to distribute their resources. They may use their banking or investment houses. They may enlist their subordinates in their multinational corporations to advance their goals." *The answer to this question should be enlightening.*

"Mr. Dukakis, you heard Lin's list," said Sarge. "Do you have a list illustrative of your theory?"

"I do. I'd include, based on the most recent Forbes richest people list, the Walton family of Walmart fame, the casino mogul Sheldon Adelson, and the Koch brothers."

"All republicans," said Sarge.

"Naturally," responded Dukakis. The room filled with laughter. *The apple doesn't fall far from the tree.*

"Without arguing which of the ultra-wealthy individuals in the world use their resources for good, *or evil*, as Mr. Dukakis seems to imply, I believe we can all agree their influence on world organizations is far greater than ours," said Sarge. *Let's see who has been paying attention.*

"Mr. Ocampo," began Sarge, "earlier this semester we discussed the Bretton Woods Conference in 1944. We identified the participation of the United States as an important step in the advancement of global governance. Who were the driving forces behind the conference and what did they hope to accomplish?"

"John Maynard Keynes and Harry Dexter White were considered the founding fathers of the World Bank and the International

Monetary fund," said Marcos Ocampo, the grandson of a former high-ranking United Nations official. "The stated purpose of the World Bank and the IMF was the reduction of world poverty."

"Hard to argue with such a lofty goal," said Sarge sarcastically.

"True, and consistent with the beliefs of Keynes and White," continued Mr. Ocampo. "Keynes was a believer in government intervention in the economy to maintain a proper balance between the needs of consumers and goods produced. Mr. White was accused of disclosing military secrets to the Soviet Union during World War II. I believe their world view translated into the working apparatus of the IMF and the World Bank."

"So you believe politics plays a role in the two most important financial institutions on the world stage?" asked Sarge.

"Undoubtedly," replied Ocampo. "In addition, both institutions are dominated by a small number of powerful countries who choose the leadership through a largely political process."

"It seems Ocampo and Dukakis have a difference of opinion on who is running things, in part based upon politics," said Sarge. "Perhaps the statement my rich and powerful guy is better than your rich and powerful guy is apropos—right, gentlemen?"

"He has more on his bench than I do," replied Dukakis.

Sarge laughed. *You'd be surprised.*

"What about the United Nations?" asked Sarge. "Although established in Europe as part of the post-World War reconstruction effort, it was quickly moved to New York City on land owned by the Rockefeller family. David Rockefeller wrote in his memoirs the Rockefeller family stands guilty of conspiring with others around the world to build a more integrated global political and economic structure—*one world, if you will.*"

Sarge walked through the classroom and looked intently at his students. *Who among you will lead?*

He changed the slide.

WHO IS RUNNING THINGS?
NOVUS ORDO SECLORUM

"The reverse side of the Great Seal of the United States features the Eye of Providence and this Latin phrase—*novus ordo seclorum*," said Sarge. "This is translated literally as *new order of the ages*. Some historians believe the phrase signifies the beginning of the new American era as of the date of the Declaration of Independence in 1776. Others, through a mistranslation, read the phrase as *new world order*. When David Rockefeller proposed a one-world, integrated global structure, led by the UN, IMF and the World Bank, do you think he envisioned a new American era envisioned by our Founding Fathers or a *new world order* that controls the institutions dominating global governance today?

"One thing I believe we will all agree upon," said Sarge. "The rich and powerful are big believers in the ends justify the means. The power brokers in the world have an agenda and will not hesitate to use their wealth to accomplish their purposes."

Ahh, conspiracy. It's good to be a tenured professor for life. They can't fire me.

CHAPTER 16

May 24, 2016
The Aegis Team
ICE High Speed Train
Between Zurich, Switzerland and Frankfurt, Germany

Steven was surprised Control would send the team into Switzerland so soon after their very public gunfight in Lausanne last February. Following the shooting, his team cautiously abandoned their Range Rover across from the Hotel Lausanne and found their high-speed ride waiting for them at the Ouchy Marina. Afterwards, the guys were quiet, as is often the case when a mission required the loss of life. Then again, it might have been their concern the mission would be disavowed by blowing his team out of the water with the Semtex provided in their backpacks.

A few days after the Lausanne debacle, he spoke with Drew Jackson, code name Slash, about the incident. Slash was pretty vocal about the mission's intent, but like every good soldier, he accomplished his mission and came home alive—rules number one and two. His instincts were impeccable, and after the kills, he was the first to voice concern about the targets being spies rather than terrorists as represented by Control. Steven and Slash talked it through and agreed to put it behind them.

Slash had been a part of the Aegis Team as long as Steven. It was Slash who suggested Steven adopt the code name Nomad. Steven's first inclination was the accepted definition, which included a person who doesn't stay in the same place for long, such as a wanderer or traveler. While it was true Steven hadn't been married and spent most of his time between Sarge's place and the *Miss Behavin'* docked at

Marblehead, he told Slash the tag name Nomad just didn't seem to fit.

Slash had a different definition, which fit Steven perfectly. Slash explained NOMAD was an acronym—*None Of My Actions Detected*. During his years with SEAL Team Ten, Steven was described as catlike, silent and *moves like a ghost*. Despite his muscular frame, he was adept at moving through any structure without detection by his prey. He was a flawless assassin.

It was just before five local time when Steven settled into the plush leather seating of the first-class compartment. The Deutsche Bahn Intercity Express, or ICE, was a high-speed train connecting major cities across Germany with other major European destinations. The trip to Frankfurt would take about four hours, giving him time to spend some rare personal time with his team.

Slash was the first to find him. The men shook hands and sat down. Typically, these two longtime friends would chest bump in a hearty bro-mance sort of way, but it would be out of place for Europe.

"Hey, buddy," said Steven. "Switzerland is our new home away from home."

"It appears so, although the terrain isn't that different from our place in Tennessee," said Slash. "I see lots of fishin' and huntin' opportunities out there." Slash grew up on his parents' farm atop the Cumberland Plateau of Tennessee about halfway between Nashville and Knoxville. His parents were retired and spent their days farming while raising ducks, rabbits and some livestock. While other kids spent their free time on PlayStation, Slash grew up in the woods, learning survival skills. During his time with the SEAL Teams, he earned a reputation as an expert in close-quarters combat, especially using a variety of knives—hence the nickname Slash.

"Beats the fuck out of the desert, doesn't it?" asked Steven. After his service ended, Slash tried a few different security outfits like Blackwater, protecting the Saudi royal family or standing guard outside some safe house in Oman. "I'm not saying the desert won't call us back someday, but I'll take the Swiss cheese and German chocolate over shawarma and falafel every friggin' day!"

"Hell yeah," said Slash. "When are you comin' down for some ham and beans, along with some butter-soaked cornbread? My folks really wanna meet you."

"I need to, buddy," replied Steven. "This summer will be nuts for me. Hey, when does deer hunting season open?"

"Late September for crossbow and around Thanksgiving otherwise," replied Slash. Before the guys could set a date, their partners Paul Hittle and Raymond Bower approached their seats.

Hittle, code name Bugs, was a former medic with Army Special Forces who left the Green Berets for a well-paying job with DynCorp. DynCorp was a private military contractor headquartered in McLean, Virginia, which provided most of the security detail for former Afghan President Hamid Karzai. Aegis signed him to a lucrative contract, which included ownership of a remote farm in East Texas.

Bower did not fit the black ops mold. Dubbed Sharpie, he was a Harvard grad that hit it big with a private equity firm on Wall Street. He loved Europe and was always on Steven's team when operations brought them to this part of the world. Steven admired Bower for keeping his skills honed despite the coat-and-tie lifestyle required in New York City.

"Hello, gentlemen," said Bower. "Fancy meeting you fucks here!" The guys enjoyed a few laughs and back slaps.

Steven knew this four-hour ride through the Alps would pass quickly. Their mission would not be discussed on the train for fear of prying eyes and ears. Let the team relax. Only Steven would know the two high-value targets were handpicked by John Morgan, and their deaths would have to be staged prominently for maximum public exposure. The Aegis Team faced a tremendous risk of exposure in Frankfurt.

A message is being sent. My team won't be happy.

CHAPTER 17

May 25, 2016
Deutsche Bank Twin Towers
Debit Tower
Frankfurt, Germany

"I'm thinkin' about gettin' out." Slash's words broke the silence.

"What for? Now?" asked Steven. Steven glanced around the panel of monitors contained in their state-of-the-art surveillance truck, searching for a reason for Slash's plan.

"No, I'm talking about finishing up my contract this fall and moving back to Tennessee," replied Slash.

"Oh, okay. Why?"

"I've been thinkin' on it for a while now. My folks are getting older, my twin brother and my sister started college and could use their big brother around for guidance. I don't know. Let's just say I need to get *settled.*"

Steven listened to his friend as he continued to watch the monitors. Bugs and Sharpie were on time and were trailing their mark as planned.

"Listen, I know these last few jobs were *questionable,*" said Steven. "We talked about this and it's something I plan to address when we get stateside. But the money is incredible and I am sure I could get you something on the security side of Aegis."

"Yeah, that is an option. But, there is something else I can't seem to wrap my brain around."

"C'mon, dude, spill it," said Steven.

"I mean, look at these monitors," started Slash. "The world's goin' to shit. You see what it's like back home. Europe's no different."

Slash pointed towards the monitors, which portrayed a picture of collapse.

From their vantage point atop a parking garage, the men had a perfect view of the Deutsche Bank Twin Towers, nicknamed *Soll und Haben*—Debit and Credit. Today, hundreds of their customers lined up outside the entrances to both towers, intending to debit their accounts. The crowd became hostile when the bank refused entry and the ATMs ran out of money. The largest bank in Germany, Deutsche Bank, had recently instituted capital controls on their customers' accounts after the collapse of the Eurozone. The cash reserves of banks were at record lows and their customers' fears created a crisis. Deutsche Bank and HSBC led the way by instituting a largely debit-card economy in Europe. Initially, their stated purpose was to avoid the hefty fines levied upon them by governments for alleged duplicity in money-laundering schemes. In actuality, the central banks and governments used this as a justification for preventing an economic collapse and bank runs. The crisis of confidence this created was playing out on the monitors before them.

"This happened the other day in Boston," said Steven. "People are freakin' out and I can't blame them. My brother talks about this shit all the time."

"My folks and most of my friends back home are preppers," said Slash. "You know, some of them are more into it than others. Everyone up our way has a garden and some livestock. It's just a way of life. Over the last several years, I watched as they started stockpiling foods, canning and stuff like that. My dad has a bunker under his house, for fuck's sake."

If you only knew what my friends have.

"Are you worried about your family?" asked Steven. "Is that why you want out?"

"No, they worry about me, if you can believe that. They can take care of themselves as it relates to food, water and medical needs. I'm worried about those who might try to take what my parents have—whether its bands of thieves or the government. My experience would make a difference."

"*Bands of thieves or the government.*" Steven laughed. "Sounds like the same thing to me. Let's talk about this some more, but we need to get down to business." The communications system interrupted their conversation.

"You boys awake up there?" The voice of Sharpie came across the comms.

"Fuck yeah, it's almost showtime," replied Steven. Steven watched as the operatives closed in on Johan Fuersberg, a senior trader of collateralized debt obligations, CDOs, for Deutsche Bank. "Good ole Johan shit in the wrong mess kit. Time to pay the piper. Let's call in some air support, shall we?"

"*Air support?* So dramatic," said Slash.

Steven laughed. "Control, you copy?" asked Steven.

"*Naturlich,*" replied the Frankfurt-based Aegis Team in their native German.

"Let's liven up this party and provide some cover for my friends," said Steven, now immersed in his role as Nomad. "Watch here." Steven tapped on a monitor providing an aerial view of the Debit and Credit towers.

Aegis, via its contacts at DHL—Germany's express-delivery company, developed a drone that was initially designed to carry urgently needed packages such as medicines to remote locations. The white and sky blue octocopter, known as the *Paketkopter*, carried a payload compartment as well as several cameras, allowing surveillance of the targeted area.

Steven and Slash watched the drone wind its way through downtown Frankfurt as it approached Deutsche Bank. Keeping a careful eye on his team, Steven provided them a countdown as the *Paketkopter* approached. Bugs and Sharpie closed on the mark. Bugs would make the hit as Sharpie covered him.

"Drop the payload," said Steven. "Gentlemen, on your ready. See you at the rally point. Control, we'll need an image uploaded upon completion."

"*Verstanden.*"

Approximately two hundred feet above the crowd, the payload

doors of the drone opened and thousands of newly minted Deutsche Marks filled the air like confetti. As chaos ensued, Bugs deftly moved in on the German banker and inserted the knife in the base of his skull. An instant kill, and symbolic, as instructed. The printer inside the van came to life within seconds, revealing Fuersberg's lifeless body in a pool of blood. As the worthless money fell from the sky, none of the frenzied customers of Deutsche Bank noticed the assassination.

CHAPTER 18

May 25, 2016
Der Junge Haus
Frankfurt, Germany

"This disgusting piece of shit needs to die!" exclaimed Slash as he thumbed through the dossier provided by Aegis. "We should just go inside and take all of these sons of bitches out!"

"Calm down, buddy, you'll get your chance," said Steven. "We have some info to gather first. Orders, remember?"

Bugs drove the van across the Main at the Baseler Strasse Bridge. "Five minutes, boys."

"All right, listen up," said Steven. "This place is in a residential area, high density. Regardless of our feelings, there are kids in this house."

"Young boys!" exclaimed Slash. "Sick fuckers!"

"I'm with you, Slash, but you gotta keep your head on straight," said Steven. "We're in and out. Grab and go. I'll fire two rounds in the floor to scare the piss out of 'em. We'll get our guy and then do our jobs. Questions?" The van was silent, but the tension was deafening. Steven hoped Slash wouldn't massacre every adult in this whorehouse for pedophiles—*Der Junge Haus.*

Bugs navigated onto Rheinstrasse and then left onto Savignystrasse. Curb appearances would never reveal the horrors inside this stately European home. The wrought-iron fence contained a gate with cherubs adorning the posts.

"This is the place. Guards are in front. Silencers for them," said Steven.

Sharpie hopped out of the front seat and casually approached the two guards. They were dead in seconds. Steven and Slash exited through the rear and hopped over the short fence next to an overgrown rhododendron tree. They approached the entrance.

"Casually, Slash. Let's clear the first floor before we go bustin' into rooms," said Steven. They climbed the concrete steps and entered through the double doors. The interior was filled with red velvet furnishings and a variety of patrons, young and old, but all male. Music was playing to a festive crowd—Elton John, of course.

Steven's eyes darted around the room, assessing any threats and looking for Karl Ferdl, head of Global Transaction Banking for Deutsche Bank. More importantly for the client's purposes, he was the Chairman of the Bilderberg Steering Committee. The Aegis team was dispatched to this cesspool to abduct Herr Ferdl and extract the sought-after information. The overall purpose was to deliver a clear message—don't fuck with John Morgan.

"Upstairs," whispered Steven. The two men made their way back to the foyer and up the winding staircase. "I'll take left, you go right. If anyone raises hell, fire off a round to get everyone's attention."

Door by door, Slash and Steven made their way through Der Junge Haus. Steven found it interesting none of the doors were locked. Was that for the protection of the boys in the event the staff required access? *We should burn this place down on the way out!*

Let's see what's behind door number three. Steven carefully entered and was momentarily sickened by what he saw. *Fuck me!*

"Keep your pants on, you fat fuck!" exclaimed Steven. Steven heard Slash running down the hallway in his direction.

"*Was hat das zu bedeuten?*" asked Ferdl.

"Shut up and put on your pants!"

"I've got this," said Slash, pushing past Steven, and then he immediately bloodied Herr Ferdl's nose with the butt of his pistol. "*Hose auf!*"

The naked, young boy was curled up in the bed, attempting to hide his nude body. Steven threw a blanket over the boy and pointed a gun at Ferdl's head.

"*Mach schnell*, asshole!" said Steven.

"Nice," said Slash. "Where did you learn that?"

"*The Dirty Dozen.*" Steven pushed Ferdl through the doorway towards the stairs. A few heads poked out of the rooms, but Slash stared them down with his weapon and that scared off any witnesses.

As they led their captive down the stairs, Slash shouted instructions in German. His mother, born in Berlin prior to World War II, taught Slash her native language when he was a child. He retained a pretty large vocabulary but rarely had an opportunity to use it. Steven was glad Slash had the ability to communicate with the crowd forming below.

"*Blieb zuruck!*" exclaimed Slash. "Stand back! *Schnell!*"

They made their way out of the house with their overweight patron. Sharpie waited for them with the front gate open.

"Thanks," said Steven. "How'd you get the gate open?"

"Our friends helped," said Slash, kicking the legs of the dead guard further under the bushes. He turned his attention to Ferdl. Slash withdrew a syringe from his pocket and injected Ferdl with phenobarbital to insure his cooperation during the ride to the Aegis interrogation house. "*Guten Abend,* fuck face!"

CHAPTER 19

May 25, 2016
AEGIS warehouse
Frankfurt, Germany

The ride north to Eckenheim took only fifteen minutes by design. After the high-profile assassination of Fuersberg earlier in the day, and the very loud abduction of Ferdl, the Aegis team wanted to get what they came for and get out of Germany.

Bugs and Sharpie remained outside of the building to stand watch. Sharpie was comfortable they weren't followed because he utilized several driving techniques for escape and evasion. Their primary concern was the amount of noise their *guest* would make during questioning.

"Wake up, asshole," said Steven as he poured water over the face of the German banker. Ferdl was strapped to a large pallet and tilted against a bench. As he awoke, he struggled against the harnesses holding him tightly in place.

"*Lass mich gehen!*"

"Nope, not gonna happen," said Slash. "You aren't goin' anywhere." Slash threw another bucket of water on his face, causing Ferdl to cough and spit out the excess. Steven and Slash towered over Ferdl, whose frightened eyes searched the men for an explanation. In broken English, he spoke.

"What want sie from me?"

Steven took the lead. "You've upset my employers," said Steven. "We need information."

"*Ich verstehe nicht,*" said Ferdl.

Steven looked at Slash.

"He says he doesn't understand," said Slash. "Let's see if he understands this!" Slash brought both fists down hard on Ferdl's belly, causing him to gasp for air. Slash followed this with another bucket of water to Ferdl's face.

"Nein, nein!"

Steven gestured for Slash to hold off. He needed Ferdl to stay alive long enough to get two things. The first was a commitment. Steven retrieved a resignation letter to be signed by Ferdl.

"Translate for me, Slash," said Steven.

Slash nodded his head while staring intently at Ferdl.

"Herr Ferdl, you must resign your post as chairman of the Bilderberg Steering Committee," said Steven. "If you do not, we will be back. Understand?"

Ferdl looked to Slash, who repeated the statement.

"Warum?" asked Ferdl, earning another bucket of water in his face from Slash.

"Because he said so, *verstehen!*"

"It's gonna get wet in here," said Steven.

"I'm just gettin' started," replied Slash.

Steven continued. Over the next several minutes, Steven and Slash interrogated Ferdl about a series of financial transactions he conducted in February prior to the collapse of the Eurozone. Without the knowledge and consent of John Morgan, Ferdl siphoned off millions of dollars into investment instruments held in Bilderberg accounts at Societe Generale, a French multinational banking group based in Paris. They were a primary conduit for Bilderberg financial activities. Ferdl, using trust powers granted to him by the Boston Brahmin, invested heavily in Bilderberg-sponsored CDOs. After the collapse of the Eurozone, the account was supposedly lost. Morgan learned the funds were actually transferred into cash accounts and the money was used to increase the cash reserves of Societe Generale. Morgan wanted their money returned and demanded to know who instructed Ferdl to take the action.

"Sie werden mich töten," pleaded Ferdl.

"I will kill you right now if you don't tell me!" replied Slash.

Turning to Steven, Slash was clearly tired of waiting. "He won't talk unless we make him."

"I agree. Let's get on with it."

The two men abruptly grabbed the pallet to which Ferdl was bound and dropped it to the floor. Then they elevated it slightly so his feet were above his head. Ferdl's eyes stared wildly and he thrashed his head back and forth.

Steven grabbed a small towel and soaked it in a bucket of water. He looked up at Slash and nodded. Steven looked into Ferdl's eyes while covering his nose and mouth with the soaked towel. Slash began slowly pouring water over the towel from about twelve inches away. This continuous application of water lasted for about twenty seconds until Steven removed the towel.

Ferdl gasped for air and flailed uncontrollably.

"*Nein, nein! Bitte!*"

Steven reapplied the towel and the process continued. Waterboarding was first used during the fifteenth century. The Spanish Inquisition, instituted by Catholic Monarchs in Spain, was intended to ensure converts to the faith of Christianity from Judaism and Islam remained true to their new Christian faith. A similar technique to waterboarding was just one of the many tools used by the Monarchy. Simply burning heretics at the stake was a more favored option.

After the fifth round lasting nearly forty seconds, it appeared Herr Ferdl was ready to provide some answers. Steven turned on the voice recorder of his iPhone to insure accuracy. He uploaded the recording to Control and awaited further instructions. He and Slash walked out of earshot of Ferdl.

"I don't care what they say," said Sharpie. "That waterboarding shit works."

"Yeah. The fear of getting killed is a terrifying experience," said Steven. "They used to train the SEALs on how to survive waterboarding. They had to stop because the SEALs couldn't pass it. And that was in a controlled environment. Make no mistake, waterboarding isn't simulated drowning—*it is drowning.*"

"Let's get out of here," said Sharpie. As the men walked back to Ferdl, he appeared to have passed out.

"Let's go, Ferdl. Party's over," said Steven. Ferdl was unresponsive. Steven leaned down and felt for a pulse. "Fuck me. He's dead. Heart attack maybe."

"Good, pedophile deserves it!" said Slash. "What are we gonna do with the fat fuck?"

Steven called Control with the sitrep. The intel they received from Ferdl was accurate. Good news. They wanted his body taken back to Der Junge Haus. Bad news.

"That cesspool will be crawling with *Stadtpolizei*," said Slash. "Let's just take him to his car. Dump his dumb ass there."

"Too risky," said Steven. Steven summoned Bugs and Sharpie from outside.

"What happened to him?" asked Bugs.

"Too much bockwurst," replied Slash.

"Wasn't there a park not too far back?" asked Steven.

"Yeah, about halfway," replied Bugs.

"Let's dump him on a park bench with his pants around his ankles," said Slash. "He deserves it."

"With his pecker hangin' out?" asked Sharpie.

"Why the hell not? He won't need it anymore."

CHAPTER 20

May 26, 2016
100 Beacon
Boston, Massachusetts

Sarge rode up the elevator with a sense of relief after an extremely hectic semester. He posted grades today and was pleased with everyone's performance. He was coming into his own as an educator, both within the Harvard confines as well as on the speaking circuit. His book, *Choose Freedom or Capitulation, America's Sovereignty Crisis*, was a *New York Times* best seller for four consecutive months and Sarge was in high demand for speaking engagements. His publicist was now earning him a lucrative fee as well as high-quality travel arrangements. He scheduled a few trips with Julia in mind and he hoped she could accompany him.

He hated being apart from her. Over the last six months, since that fun evening at Stephanie's in December, they were inseparable. She moved in with Sarge—but not just in a *this is your dresser drawer* sort of way. He loved her very much and needed her even more. He wanted to make this permanent and contemplated marriage all the time. *I guess it will happen when the time is right.*

As the doors opened to the Great Hall, he was immediately struck with the smell of braised beef and George Gershwin's *An American in Paris.* Julia was pulling out all of the stops tonight, including the stunning black cocktail dress. *What did I forget?*

"Hi, honey, I'm home," announced Sarge. "Sargent, party of two?"

"Come here and kiss me, smartass," said Julia. She wrapped her arms around him while he struggled to hold the bags of produce she requested from Whole Foods. "I missed you today."

"I see that. I love you and missed you too. School's out for the summer and I'm all yours. Well, mostly."

"How 'bout some wine?" asked Julia. "I popped open a bottle of Beaujolais."

Sarge nodded as Julia poured the glass. He set the grocery bags on the island.

"Listen, I am a boy and forgetful about certain things," said Sarge.

"Like what things?" asked Julia teasingly.

Oh shit, what did I forget? "You know, *couple things* that men tend to forget but women always remember."

"Relax, Sarge, I knew you wouldn't remember what today is, but I did. I won't hold that against you as long as you hold me against you."

"Deal! What did I forget?" he asked.

"Ten years ago today, we had our first date. Do you remember now?" asked Julia.

"Of course I do, darling. John Morgan invited us to the Garden of Flags event on Boston Common and he sat us next to each other for dinner in his home that night."

Every Memorial Day weekend, the Massachusetts Military Heroes organization planted a garden of thirty-seven thousand flags in front of the Soldiers and Sailors Monument on Boston Common to commemorate the service members from Massachusetts who gave their lives to defend the United States. Morgan had a private dinner at his home that evening. Sarge and Julia were seated next to each other at the table. This event came towards the end of Sarge's relationship with Abbie and it was obvious Morgan was nudging Sarge in Julia's direction.

Sarge continued. "That seems like a long time ago. I always wondered if Morgan had an ulterior motive."

"He always has an ulterior motive, as do I, Henry," said Julia, using his given name. She bowed and handed him his glass of wine.

"I love it when you talk dirty to me, Lady Hawthorne."

Julia emptied the contents of the Whole Foods bag and looked perplexed.

"Whole Foods wasn't able to confiscate your *whole paycheck* this time?"

"No. In fact, it was eerie," replied Sarge. "The shelves were bare and the produce department was decimated. One of the employees told me their produce trucks were not running on a regular schedule."

"I'll call DeLuca's on Newbury Street and have them deliver what I need," said Julia.

"Don't bother. I drove by DeLuca's, but they closed early."

"Who is buying up all the food, Sarge?"

"I think it's a matter of why aren't they producing more food," he replied.

"We discussed this in the editorial meeting today. Listen to this. The drought conditions in California are beyond severe, especially around Sacramento. Governor Brown ordered the national guard to raid a family farming operation in the San Joaquin Valley."

"Why?" asked Sarge.

"The farmer was accused of using well water for his crops in violation of the governor's mandated water restrictions," replied Julia. "According to the governor's directive, farmers are prohibited from over-pumping the wells for irrigation purposes. Based upon an EPA study, the value of the crops produced is insignificant to the damage caused to the environment by over-pumping. Before the EPA could issue its own regulations, California acted quickly to create its own mandated restrictions."

"What happened?"

"These reports are being suppressed by the media, but the man stood his ground and refused the National Guard access to his land. He was holding a flag and stated he was a patriot. His family stood behind him, shouting at the guardsmen. According to reports, a guardsman ordered the farmer to get on the ground because he was under arrest. When the farmer began waving his flag instead, they shot him."

"You've got to be kidding."

"No. It gets worse. The National Guard, with the assistance of the Bureau of Land Management, confiscated the crops, arrested the remaining family members, and seized the land under federal forfeiture provisions."

As Julia fixed them a small salad, Sarge made his way to the windows overlooking the Charles River. This story was troubling on many levels. The government was halting food production in favor of saving the environment? Moreover, the full force of the military was used to arrest a farmer, confiscate his crops and seize his land because he used the water *under his land* to *irrigate his crops. If this isn't tyranny, what is?*

"Sarge?"

"Okay," replied Sarge. "Let's not talk about the rest of the world. I like ours right here, right now, just fine."

Julia used her best French hostess voice. "Monsieur, this will be an enchanting evening featuring a refreshing salad, braised beef and a dessert that will be, shall I say, breathtaking."

"I like anniversaries."

PART TWO

CHAPTER 21

June 2, 2016
100 Beacon
Boston, Massachusetts

"What are they building in the fire escape?" asked Steven as he exited the elevator.

Sarge was intently watching the television monitors as Steven spoke. "I have them reinforcing the access doors to our floors and putting bars on the inside of the fire escape windows," replied Sarge as he studied the various news reports. Sarge felt Steven staring at him.

"Are you expecting zombies, bro?" asked Steven.

"No, but have you noticed the way people are acting?"

"Yeah, they're going bat-shit crazy," replied Steven. "I guess it makes sense. What about the windows on the street level?"

"The Boston Historical Society wouldn't approve it," replied Sarge. "It wasn't *consistent with the period*. They're sheep."

"What's the latest?" asked Steven. Sarge wished his brother would pay more attention to the news, but then Steven's job was more *executioner* than planner.

"It's hard to find any good news," replied Sarge. "The economy's tanking. The recession numbers are far worse than the sugarcoated version Washington feeds us. Farmers can't afford to produce crops and grocers can't stock their shelves. Food distribution channels are totally disrupted due to the cost of fuel. Our economy is built on consumption. Americans have lost their consumer confidence and retail is suffering for it."

"I saw some of the same in Europe last month," said Steven. "It's more than confidence. People are angry, on edge."

"World governments have lost the ability to control their economies. After the Eurozone collapsed, the bond market sank with it. Believe it or not, the Greek default is exactly what they wanted. What they did not want is Spain and Italy to default at the same time. Now there is a void in southern Europe and Russia is ready to fill in the financial gaps. They have already bailed out Greece by reaching a natural gas distribution agreement, which further destroys Ukraine's economy."

"What does all of this mean for the United States?"

"The world's economies are interrelated," replied Sarge. "It's sort of like a codependent relationship. The world has tolerated our deficit spending while we tolerate bad actors getting away with agendas contrary to our national security. Every nation is circling the wagons around their own self-interests and the global house of cards could collapse at any time."

"When does it hit the fan?" asked Steven.

"I don't know. We're one catastrophic event away from a collapse," said Sarge.

"What do you mean?"

"Have you seen the huge increases in cyber attacks?" asked Sarge.

"Yeah. They're increasing in frequency and magnitude."

"They're testing the fences, like the velociraptors in the first *Jurassic Park* movie," said Sarge. "State-sponsored hackers are rifling through our government files. They are manipulating financial transactions. There have been rolling blackouts of the power grid. They have successfully hijacked airplanes. There is no limit. So far there has not been a coordinated attack, but it could come without warning."

"I agree," said Steven. "So what are we doing about it?"

"Other nations are preparing, but I don't know if our politicians are ready. Look at the price of gold, for example."

"It's skyrocketing," said Steven.

"Exactly. China is moving towards a gold-backed yuan. They are repatriating record amounts of gold—three hundred twenty tonnes in the last month. If the Chinese successfully adopt a traditional gold standard, the price of gold would increase exponentially. Their currency would be deemed more reliable as a reserve currency than the dollar. Honestly, at this point, there is very little we can do to deter Russia and China from their economic machinations other than a hot war."

"Great," said Steven. "I used to think these power-broker games between politicians and the super wealthy was above my pay grade, but I think I'm wrong about that."

"How so?"

"My last three missions for Aegis have been *questionable*," replied Steven. "You know I'm a good soldier, and if the boss wants something done, I won't refuse him."

"I know the feeling," interrupted Sarge.

"When I look at the results of Ukraine, Switzerland, and now Frankfurt, I begin to wonder if there is a national interest at stake or am I just a well-paid hit man. You follow this stuff more than I do. What's the boss up to?"

"I'm sure he has a plan," replied Sarge. "He's *always* had a plan. But I agree with you. Financial and geopolitical motivations are at play here, more than the protection of America from her enemies."

"This Bilderberg Conference plays into it as well," said Steven. "One of the targets in Frankfurt was the head of some committee of the Bilderbergs."

"The Steering Committee," said Sarge.

"Right. Our instructions were to force him to resign. He *resigned* all right."

"Are you talking about the Deutsche Bank guy?"

"One and the same," replied Steven.

"News reports stated he had a heart attack in a park getting a blow job from a hooker," said Sarge.

"Nope, he died after we waterboarded him."

"Fuckin' fabulous," said Sarge.

"Bro, you know I'm not supposed to spill these details to you. But the shit's gettin' weird and you understand how all of this plays together."

Sarge stared at the television screens as one talking head after another analyzed the upcoming northeast presidential primaries. He wondered if Abbie would be in town. *Let it go!*

"Hey, bro, you with me still?" asked Steven, interrupting Sarge's wandering mind.

"Yeah, yeah," replied Sarge. "Do you have any specific instructions for the Bilderberg Conference?"

"Nope," replied Steven. "They have their own security team and we will supplement their program. It's unprecedented that their annual conference would be held in a city like this. Normally, they find some secluded backwoods fortress to hide behind."

"I thought the same thing. It is part of the Bilderberg's goal of raising the veil of secrecy although I think it's just a facade."

"In any event, they are bringing their COBRA unit—elite Special Forces made up primarily of German and Austrians. I'm sure they are charming."

"Quite," said Sarge. "You know Julia is traveling this weekend to interview the candidates. You wanna go out to eat, or order in."

"Let's pop some brewskis and order pizza through GrubHub. I have last year's *Strike Back* to catch up on. Plus, we'll need the inspiration for Brad's war games at Camp Edwards this weekend." The brothers fist-bumped as they started their boys' weekend with a couple of Samuel Adams lagers.

CHAPTER 22

June 3, 2016
Camp Edwards
Joint Base Cape Cod, Massachusetts

This was the first trip for Brad to Joint Base Cape Cod since the installation of Sgt. Major Carlos Rivera as the new commander of JBCC. Rivera, a longtime member of the Massachusetts Army National Guard, also maintained a stellar career as an investigative specialist for the Drug Enforcement Administration. From first impressions, Rivera ran a tight ship, immediately gaining the respect of his counterpart from Fort Devens.

Lieutenant Colonel Francis Crowninshield Bradlee, Brad to his friends, was the consummate military man. In the early, pre-Revolutionary War days, the Crowninshields were known for their seafaring adventures. But as the War for Independence came to full fruition, the prominent family, close friends of Thomas Jefferson, became the backbone of the United States military for years to come. A member of the Crowninshield family held the positions of Secretary of the Navy and Secretary of War under several presidential administrations.

Like so many of the Founding Fathers, the Crowninshield lineage included the surnames Adams, Endicott, Hawthorne, DuPont and Bradlee. Brad's father was the editor of *The Washington Post* before his death and his mother was a highly respected, influential journalist. While the Bradlee branch of the Crowninshield family tree generally abhorred the military, Brad lived for it. He attended the Naval Academy and during his second-class year he chose Leatherneck for his summer training. He received praise from his mentors and surpassed all of the academic and physical standards required to graduate as one of a few dozen Marine Selects.

Brad's career was stellar, and after three years as a major, he earned the rank of lieutenant colonel. Under his command were 750 infantry designated service members comprising the 25th Marine Regiment of 1st Battalion. At age forty, he had fast-tracked his career to battalion commander.

Brad met Steven at the Naval Academy and the two became good friends despite their age difference of several years. He encouraged Steven to become a Marine. But he was hell-bent on becoming a SEAL via the Navy rather than through the BUDS training option offered by the Marines. Either way, Brad admired Steven for becoming one heck of a soldier and the two stayed close friends over the years. They also realized they had common interests, which they immediately pursued. When Steven called Brad about getting together with Sarge for a little rest and relaxation, Brad thought this particular weekend would be perfect. Of course, his definition of R & R was different from most.

Fort Devens was part of a three-installation military training program along with Fort Dix in New Jersey and Fort Drum in New York. Fort Dix and Fort Drum had extensive combat-training facilities while Fort Devens did not. Fort Devens considered Camp Edwards as its home field. While each base had its own unique training attributes, Camp Edwards was known as the only installation in the northeast with a training center meant to simulate a Middle Eastern town. Built in 2008, Camp Edwards was dedicated to Theater Immersion Training. The theater immersion training technique placed units into an environment comparable to the one they would encounter in combat in order to rapidly build combat-readiness. Tactical Training Bases like Camp Edwards were developed to prepare troops for missions in Afghanistan, Iraq and the Balkans.

This weekend, the teams from Devens, Dix and Drum would receive a thorough briefing on urban warfare operations on Saturday morning. The weekend schedule included specific field training in urban warfare followed by a friendly competition between teams of two. Brad wasn't participating; he was there to train his men and those who participated from the other installations. The Sargent brothers were the only civilians, but Brad knew they could hold their own.

CHAPTER 23

June 4, 2016
Camp Edwards
Joint Base Cape Cod, Massachusetts

"Let's get started, everyone. Grab a seat, as we have a long day ahead of us," said Brad. "I'm glad that all of you have gotten to know each other a little bit." Brad observed the faces of the soldiers in the room as well as his ringers—Sarge and Steven. He also caught a glimpse of eye contact and smiles between Steven and Second Lieutenant Michaela Dodge from Fort Drum. *Does the boy never rest?* Dodge may have a sweet smile, but Brad had seen her in action. She was a third-degree ball breaker who took no prisoners. *He'll see.*

Dodge was part of a four-soldier team from the 10th Mountain Division stationed at Fort Drum, New York. Each of the two soldier teams was the winner in the Best Ranger competition within their squads. Dodge and her teammate, 2LT John Rose, represented the 1st Brigade Combat Team. First Lieutenant Michael Bergman and 2LT Duane Rosenberg, son of the garrison commander, represented the 2nd Brigade Combat Team. Dodge and Rose had trained at Camp Edwards before and Brad was extremely impressed. But it was Bergman and Rosenberg who won the title of Best Rangers at the nationwide competition held at Fort Benning, Georgia, last fall.

Attending from Fort Dix were two new teams. The first team was part of the 174th Infantry Brigade. This brigade was a training unit responsible for preparing other soldiers to train the trainers. As soldiers prepare for deployment throughout the military, they were briefed and trained on maneuvers, equipment and other details pertinent to their theater of operation. These members of the 174th trained the trainers, who in turn trained the military personnel before deployment.

The other two-man team was from the United States Coast Guard Atlantic Strike Team. This was a new group to the Camp Edwards program, and Brad knew very little about their function. When their CO contacted Brad about participating, he was a little puzzled. The Coast Guard operated primarily as a maritime law enforcement branch of Homeland Security. Their primary responsibilities had been responding to environmental disasters off the United States coast. *Why does the Coast Guard need their personnel trained in urban tactics?*

Finally, Brad was very pleased with his team from Fort Devens. Master Gunny Sergeant Frank Falcone was an old-school master gunnery sergeant under Brad's command for years. He would trust this man with his life. His partner, Chief Warrant Officer Kyle Shore, had become known as an expert in one form of long-range fire support—sniping. In Afghanistan, Shore had recorded kill shots on two Taliban machine gunners at roughly 2,500 yards, just short of the longest confirmed kill of slightly over 2,700 yards.

The other two members of the Fort Devens contingent were members of the 366th Military Police Detachment. First Lieutenant Craig Russo and Captain Pedro Torrez were specifically trained in urban tactics although they had never served in combat. Part of the Army Military Police Corps, the 366th and their counterparts, the Military Intelligence Detachments based at Fort Devens, did not fall under the direct command of Brad. He suspected their deployment would be on United States soil at some point—not something he wanted to contemplate often.

"Before you is a packet of materials, which is the latest intelligence and summation provided us by the Pentagon on the subject of UO—urban operations—which has replaced the previous acronym, MOUT—Military Operations on Urban Terrain," said Brad. "I know that most of what we will cover is familiar to you, but a refresher course prior to this afternoon's LFX will be beneficial." Brad did not bother to explain the military's many lexicons for Sarge's benefit. He knew Sarge, as a civilian, was well versed in military jargon and did not need an explanation of what a live fire exercise entailed.

"The Army has not updated the field manuals on urban operations since June 2003, yet a lot of information has been gathered from our operations abroad since then," said Brad. "FM 3-06 spends a lot of time on theoretical and historical perspectives on urban operations. The most recent information at our disposal provides a more accurate picture of what our soldiers faced in Iraq and Afghanistan. Today's urban warfare puts a heavy emphasis on distinguishing between civilians and enemy combatants—such as armed militias, insurgents and even gangs. As you know, the rules of engagement and use of combat power are more restrictive than in other conditions of battle."

Brad did not verbally express his biggest fear concerning the United States military's new emphasis on urban warfare. Falcone and the Sargents recognized our soldiers were being trained for ground operations—in America.

"Urban environments are highly advantageous to the defender. Buildings in an urban setting provide high levels of cover and concealment for enemy combatants. Multistoried buildings with basements allow the defenders of urban territory the ability to maneuver in what we call the third dimension. Your unit may have a group of insurgents pinned down in front of you only to be surprised when they reappear behind you by making use of underground passageways through basements. Modern cities have elaborate sewer systems and often have underground tunnels for transit systems. Defenders may move laterally or vertically, completely out of sight of the attacker." Brad walked around his desk and wandered the room as he continued.

"For the aggressor, buildings in an urban environment provide significant obstacles to the movement of heavy equipment, which necessarily limits the ability of a superior military force to take advantage of their advanced armored vehicles. The tall buildings in urban terrain also permit defenders to shoot antitank weapons at angles able to penetrate the relatively thin top armor of infantry fighting vehicles."

Turning in the direction of CWO Shore, he added, "Long fields of fire are scarce, so the technological advantages our forces enjoy in tactical long-range fire are neutralized. In fact, those of you who have deployed to the Middle East know the majority of engagements are up close and personal. Gun battles occur at such a close range that rifle rounds retain the sufficient velocity to penetrate flak jackets."

Brad saw the nods of acknowledgement by these brave soldiers. Many of them had seen their buddies die within a few feet of where they stood, knowing it could have been them.

"As we all know, intel is critical to any military operation," said Brad. "In an urban-warfare scenario, intelligence can become outdated in a blink of an eye. For the defender, your lack of information is a tremendous advantage to them. You should always expect that the locals will enjoy a far superior knowledge of the battlefield—the urban environment."

As Brad spoke, his mind processed the application of urban tactics to American cities. Clearly, the Pentagon anticipated the application of these tactics on American soil. Were they training us to implement martial law?

"In traditional open warfare, the advantage clearly leans to the attacker who holds a technological advantage. Our overhead reconnaissance assets feed us real-time images and maps of the battlefield—as well as real-time situational awareness during the mission. GPS systems enable the attacker in open warfare the opportunity to be as well oriented on the enemy's terrain as the defenders are," said Brad.

"But it is not clear that modern technology offers this kind of leverage in urban settings. Again, the defending enemy will have a far better understanding of the city or town than will the outsider." *To what extent would Washington use advanced technology against its own citizenry in times of unrest?*

"In *The Art of War*, the famous Chinese military strategist Sun Tzu surmised the worst policy is to attack cities, and throughout our history, this advice has been followed. Today, seventy percent of the world's population resides in urban areas. The rapid increase of population coupled with the accelerated growth in the cities brought the Pentagon to this realization—urban areas are expected to be the future battlefield and combat in these areas cannot be avoided.

"Urban combat against a well-armed enemy can quickly erode the strength and capability of the attacker. In order to overcome this tactical advantage, the attackers will need to employ combined arms tactics with disciplined, coordinated movement techniques to control its own losses," said Brad. "Highly trained and skilled soldiers are required for this type of warfare."

Brad paused for a moment and took a drink of water. American forces had suffered heavy losses due to lack of training and also because of certain political realities. Our soldiers were hampered because the rules of engagement tended to place limitations on urban operations. Further, under the current downsizing agenda, the military simply did not have enough soldiers trained in these tactics to meet the mission requirements. Training in simulated villages would not prepare soldiers for combat in large metropolitan areas should the need arise. Camp Edwards was designed to train soldiers in the proper terrain, but it was only one of a handful of training centers of its kind. Every major military installation should have a mock urban training facility.

"Every urban environment is different," continued Brad. "Yet they all have similar structural characteristics. A platoon leader will need to assess the type of building to be attacked before moving forward with an urban assault. Let's review the six integral components of an urban assault." Brad thumbed through his binder to find the outline provided by the Pentagon although he could've written it himself. *Know thy enemy...*

"First, realize you can't attack every building at once," said Brad. "Your first step is to isolate your objective—the building housing the enemy combatant. Recon the surrounding buildings, being mindful you are fighting in a three-dimensional environment. The enemy may have supportive fire assets placed in the surrounding buildings. During your assessment, identify potential escape routes, including catwalks, subways, utility tunnels and cellars. Clearing a building in an urban setting requires a lot of manpower to ensure you don't simply flush the cockroaches to another location."

This drew laughs from the participants who had served in Iraq and Afghanistan. The fleeing insurgents were typically referred to as *cockroaches*.

"Second, consider the threat before you assign personnel to supporting fire. Although I never advocate underestimating the enemy's capabilities, if your intelligence indicates the enemy combatants are poorly trained, have low morale, are underequipped and have poor leadership, they may be convinced to surrender or withdraw simply by using skilled psyops or a great show of force initially. Assume the enemy is capable of viable resistance. You must be sure to concentrate direct and indirect fire together with other combat support assets onto the objective area. This has the effect of neutralizing the threat before positioning troops in preparation for an assault."

Brad was prepared to summarize their battle movements followed by a summary of the afternoon's activities. The warming trend melted the snowfall from Thursday night, leaving a muddy training field. Rather than simulating Afghanistan, EO site Calero would be more representative of Eastern Europe—or *Small Town, USA.*

The Loyal Nine had discussed many times the issues surrounding martial law or the occupation of a foreign military force within the United States. Sarge suggested the principles of urban tactical warfare should be learned to enhance their defensive capabilities. In other words, a cityscape might be easier to defend than a rural bug-out location—where open warfare benefits an attacker with superior air assets. Donald Quinn aptly related it to his career as an accountant. He said the best accountants are trained by the IRS in the early parts of their careers. This *fox in the henhouse* approach gives accountants a unique insight when they enter private practice. *Learn from the enemy,* Donald said.

"Third, once the decision is reached for a full-on assault of the building or objective, tactical movements will need to be employed," said Brad. "Again, being fully aware of the three-dimensional aspect of urban terrain, fire teams may use bounding overwatch, traveling overwatch or even a modified wedge type of column to advance. The battlefield will dictate your TTP—tactics, techniques and procedures."

Brad walked towards Shore and placed his hand on his shoulder. "Let me bring in some assistance from you for a moment. Chief Warrant Officer Kyle Shore is from my unit at Devens and knows a little about a related issue."

"Shore," said Brad, "why don't you stand and summarize the importance of a sniper on the battlefield."

"Yes, sir, Colonel," said Shore. "Put simply, our job is to take out any enemy asset that will benefit my buddies the most. In a ground operation like this one, I would observe the target area, gather raw data and intelligence, and use my long-range weapons to strike the enemy by surprise."

"When the platoon is moving through a combat area, there are some countermeasures available to limit exposure to sniper fire," said Brad. "What are those, Shore?"

"Sir. Active countermeasures are designed to detect and destroy the sniper before he can fire or neutralize him after he fires. The most common active countermeasures involve the establishment of perimeter OPs, recon and security patrols and rules of engagement that permit appropriate return fire. May I speak frankly, sir?"

"Go ahead, Shore," replied Brad. Brad watched as Sarge furiously took notes. The active-duty soldiers in the room and Steve did not. Brad wondered if the others observed Sarge's note taking. Brad knew what Sarge was thinking about Sun Tzu—*know your enemy as you know yourself.*

"The last active countermeasure—rules of engagement regarding return fire—is the most confounding, sir," said Shore. "Currently, the rules of engagement in the Middle Eastern theater are skewed in favor of protecting civilians and therefore in favor of the enemy. This puts our troops at significant risk. The best way to prevent casualties from sniper fire is to utilize both preemptive fire and overmatching fire. With preemptive fire, in a high-density urban combat arena, we can attack likely sniper positions with a variety of unit weapons to deter sniper activity. With overmatching fire, our boys can respond to a sniper's rifle round with a volley from something like an M203, sir. Simply put, our 40mm grenade trumps your .50-cal round. Game over."

"Thank you, Shore," said Brad. "The M203 grenade launcher is designed to attach to either the M16 or the M4. While its range is under one hundred sixty yards, I suggest to you that a football field is the equivalent of a mile in an urban environment. Clearly, there could be collateral damage to the civilian population. Shore, you mentioned active countermeasures. Given the present rules of engagement, what are some passive countermeasures?"

"Sir, another effective countermeasure is the use of projected smoke and, when the rules of engagement allow, the use of riot-control agents," said Shore. "Smoke is used often to protect the platoon from long-range fire. Also, if the sniper's location is known, smoke can be projected close to his location, which greatly limits his ability to acquire targets. Riot-control agents like tear gas are optimal, but typically not allowed under the present ROE."

"Thank you, Shore," said Brad. "You may be seated. Other passive countermeasures are also typical of well-disciplined tactical movements. These include covered and concealed routes, avoiding open intersections, staying away from doors and windows, and moving along the side of a street in a dispersed formation. These are all common sense, infantry basics."

Brad covered the elements of assaulting a building objective after identifying the breach point and the best ways to avoid friendly fire. He covered the fundamentals of entering and clearing a building, which will be an important part of this afternoon's activities. Finally, he gave them all an overview of the challenge parameters.

"Why don't we take some time for lunch before we get started," said Brad. "I want everybody to report to Urban Operations Site Calero at zero eleven hundred hours. Dismissed."

Everyone shuffled out of their chairs and made their way toward the mess hall. Brad approached Steven and Sarge to get their opinions on the program so far.

"What do you boys think?" asked Brad.

"Great stuff, Brad. Listen, I need to break away for a little bit," said Steven. "You guys go ahead without me. I'll grab something to eat on the fly."

"Don't zap your testosterone, buddy, we'll need it later," said Sarge.

Brad saw Steven had lunch plans of his own as 2LT Dodge milled about, waiting on her prey.

"Hey, she'll eat you alive, pal," said Brad with a grin, grabbing Steven's arm.

"Then it'll be mutual destruction. Later," said Steven and he was off.

Brad turned to Sarge. "Will he ever grow up?"

"Let's hope not. The best we can hope for is to keep the boy harnessed and release him when necessary," said Sarge. "Listen, Brad, I understand the need for this type of training. War has changed and we need to be prepared for all contingencies. But when is the last time our military fought in an urban environment with sewers, subways and tall buildings with catwalks? That type of battlefield exists primarily in one place and it isn't Tikrit."

"Very astute, Sarge," said Brad. "This is why I'm glad you two came this weekend. We need to know both sides of UO. I'm hearing rumblings from my like-minded friends throughout the service, Sarge. Our country is in for a jolt. In the not-too-distant future, there may be a time in America when the lines between a friendly and a hostile will become very blurred. We need to be ready."

"Let's go catch up," said Sarge.

CHAPTER 24

June 4, 2016
Camp Edwards
Joint Base Cape Cod, Massachusetts

The teams began to gather at the training site. Sarge found it interesting that each team had lunch alone without any attempts to make small talk with the other participating members of the exercise. This competition would be intense. There was no prize, only bragging rights for their respective squads. Sarge always studied people and was intrigued by the interactions between the soldiers. He'd read several research papers on the mentality of military personnel. The age-old question of why soldiers fight might surprise many. After World War II, many returning soldiers simply said they wanted to keep fighting so the war would end and they could go home. The secondary response provided by the World War II vets related to the group ties their unit developed during combat. Sarge believed the premise held true today. He believed the motivation of today's soldier was primarily sustained by his comrades and secondarily by his weapon.

Sarge observed the interaction between 2LT Dodge and her teammate 2LT Rose. *He's pissed.* Steven finally arrived on the scene.

"Howzit?" asked Sarge.

Steven was adjusting his gear. "Psyops mission accomplished," said Steven. "She won't be worth a shit this afternoon."

"Will you?" asked Sarge, adding, "Be worth a shit?"

"Oh yeah, just watch," replied Steven.

Brad was trying to get everyone's attention. Fortunately, the sun had melted all of the snow and the wind had stopped. Other than the

97

mud, it was a beautiful day.

"All right, teams, please gather around," said Brad. "We have set up a series of three challenges for you today. The first challenge will be a timed drill. The second challenge will be an accuracy and analysis drill. The third challenge will be a speed and agility challenge. The two highest scoring teams in these first three rounds will then move to the final challenge, which will involve the principles we discussed this morning."

"Is everybody ready?" yelled Brad.

"Sir, yes, sir!" exclaimed the participants.

"Everyone remember, we will be using live rounds throughout this exercise. Nobody gets shot on my watch, got it?" said Brad. He received another reply of *yes, sir.*

"This first challenge will test your speed and accuracy under a high pressure, live fire scenario," said Brad. "First, you will be required to run down the hill approximately one hundred yards to obtain your weapon, ammunition and your tactical spotting scope. Come back up the hill to your designated firing position identified by your preassigned colors. Once you have reached your firing position, the targets will be revealed to you. Red targets are always hostiles and white targets will always be friendlies. Any questions?"

CWO Shore spoke up first. "Sir, what is our assigned weapon today?"

"You didn't think I would make it easy for you, did you, Shore?" said Brad. "You will not be using your beloved Barrett 82A1 .50 cal. You folks from the Army will be pleased to hear that today's long-range weapon will be the M2010 ESR—enhanced sniper rifle. It has a shorter range than the Barrett and must be used due to the proximity of civvies in the area. Welcome to the rules of engagement."

Steven leaned into Sarge and gave him the rundown on the M2010. "It's a good weapon, bolt actioned. It's really just a modern-day version of the basic Remington 700," said Steven. "Let's pay attention to see if it's outfitted with a suppressor or a muzzle brake. Both of those attachments reduce recoil by about half, which will affect our second shot if we miss on the first go-around. There may also be multiple hostiles. The magazines hold five .300 Winchester Magnum cartridges. My guess is there will be at least six tangos, requiring two magazines. Be prepared to hand me the second magazine, or hand me single rounds, which I will reload manually. That will save time. I'll take the shots. You spot me in. You good?"

"Yep," said Sarge. This was the first time he and Steven had practiced like this. The training was invaluable and he hoped they could do it again. They were a team.

"On my whistle," yelled Brad. "Go!"

The teams started running through the barren oak trees down a slight incline towards wooden crates painted in their team's colors.

"Just don't fall," said Steven. "We'll make up our time going back up the hill."

Sarge followed his brother through the trees as he watched one of the members of the Coast Guard team slip and then roll head over heels until finding an oak tree to break his fall. I guess they don't have many hills and oak trees on the USCG cutters.

Reaching the bottom of the hill essentially tied with the other teams, Steven grabbed the M2010 and Sarge grabbed the ammo can and the scope. They began to run up the hill. It was more of a slog.

"Don't fall," Steven repeated as both men turned to watch one of the trainers from the 174th at Fort Dix lose his footing and drop his scope in the mud. Fort Dix was off to a rough start. "See what I mean?"

The Fort Devens team of Shore and Master Gunny Falcone adopted an interesting strategy. Shore walked up the hill at a brisk pace, keeping his footing and saving his breath. The twelve-pound M2010 was not a burden. The older Falcone made a quicker pace with the intent of getting his scope ready. Sarge suspected Shore would have a steady hand when he was ready to shoot.

The Sargents were neck and neck with Falcone when they topped the hill and approached their station. About three hundred yards downrange stood a makeshift building. Suddenly, the front of the building opened up like a trapdoor and hit the mud with a splashy thud.

"Seven hostiles, five friendlies," muttered Steven.

Sarge admired his composure. Approximately half of the red hostile targets were visible. One hostile target towards the front swayed back and forth on a pendulum. Sarge followed Steven's lead.

"What've you got?" asked Steven.

Sarge had used a spotting monocular before but never one as compact as this Vortex. He altered the eyecup for comfort and adjusted the focus.

"Range is four hundred meters. Hostile target is twenty inches wide and thirty inches tall. Silhouette of the friendly is the same. Slight headwind," said Sarge. Sarge heard someone say send it and their M2010 cracked to life. "No muzzle attachments."

"Yeah," said Steven. He adjusted the Leopold Mark 6 scope and fired.

"Hit," said Sarge. "Center mass." Several shots were being fired now. Focus. Sarge recalled the old golf adage—*play the course, not the players.* Steven fired again.

"Hit, center mass, slightly right," said Sarge.

Steven was on. He emptied the magazine. Steven was right about the number of targets and the need to either reload the magazine or hand-feed the ammo through the bolt action. When he hit the last target, Steven rose up on his knees and exhaled.

"How'd we do?" asked Steven.

"All seven tangos down. Looks like a close second to Brad's boys from Devens," said Sarge. "The Coasties are dead last."

"What about Dodge and Rose?" asked Steven.

"Mid-pack," responded Sarge. Both men stood up as the firing halted.

"Nicely done, soldiers," said Brad. "This next challenge comes directly out of urban combat zones like Baghdad. This will require accuracy and an analysis of the most efficient way to neutralize an enemy sniper. It is also a timed challenge." Brad started walking down the still-muddy road towards another group of stations. At the bottom of the hill appeared seven thirty-foot-tall sniper hides on stilts. At the top of each tower was an enemy gunman represented by a red hostile target.

"This is a two-step challenge," said Brad. "Consistent with our discussion this morning, you will be required to take out the enemy sniper first followed by the tower itself. The tower targets are four inches in diameter. Here's another twist. The team member that fired last round must rotate out in favor of the other team member."

Sarge was up for it.

"I should've known," whispered Steven. "Brad can be a tricky fucker. You've got this."

"I'm ready," said Sarge.

"Remember, steady your breathing and gently pull the trigger," said Steven. "No need to rush. We'll still be using the M2010, which is a bolt action. If we were using a semiautomatic .50 caliber like the Barrett, Shore would have a big advantage. Let's just stay up there in second next to them and we'll make up the time downstream. Cool?"

"Cool," said Sarge.

"On my signal," yelled Brad. "Go!"

Sarge and Steven hustled to their position, running past the other teams to reach their station first. Steven manipulated the Vortex and brought the red target gunman into focus.

"Okay," said Steven. "A headshot is your only option. Target is four hundred twenty meters. Target exposure is fourteen inches high, eleven inches wide. Slight left to right crosswind. Tough shot, buddy."

Sarge was silent as he adjusted his rifle's scope. He fired.

"Miss, high left," said Steven.

Sarge made the necessary adjustments as other rifle reports could be heard. He fired. The target exploded into hundreds of pieces.

"Tannerite," said Steven. Tannerite was the brand name of an explosive used for making explosive targets in weapons training exercises. Sarge knew it had many potential uses. Another explosion was heard, but they couldn't discern which team made the hit.

"Okay, nail one of the tower legs and see if it will be sufficient," said Steven. "Knowing Brad, it will be the back-side target."

Sarge stared through the rifle's scope. "It will take all three," said

Sarge. "They have the structure cross-braced. Let's do this." Sarge was fully focused in his own sniper bubble. He fired.

"Hit!" exclaimed Steven. "Left support down."

Sarge operated the bolt action for his fourth shot. He fired.

"Miss, right a few inches," said Steven. "The wind has stopped."

Sarge quickly prepared himself for another shot.

"Hit, two down," said Steven. The sound of explosions permeated the background. Sarge remained focus. *Play the course.* He drew a bead on the final strut located at the rear of the sniper hide. *Send it.*

"Hit, fuckin' A!" shouted Steven as he hugged his brother. "Nailed it, bro!" The brothers walked back up the hill to where a grinning Brad stood.

"Well, Sarge," said Brad, "do I need to personally deliver you to the JBCC recruiter's station? Nice shooting."

"Thanks, Brad," said Sarge. The team of Falcone and Shore came up to them a moment later followed by the team of Bergman and Rosenberg out of Fort Drum. Shore shook Sarge's hand.

"Where'd you train?" asked Shore.

Sarge couldn't tell him the truth. "Oh, our family has a little place west of Boston near Prescott that works as a pretty good practice facility," said Sarge. Sarge caught Brad and Steven exchanging a knowing glance.

"Well, it's paid off for you," said Shore. "I'm guessing that puts our two teams neck and neck at this point."

"Listen up everyone," interrupted Brad. "We started with a total of seven teams, but we now must reduce this to four. The following three teams have been eliminated: the Military Police Team from Devens and the two teams from Fort Dix." All of the teams exchanged handshakes with each other. There was no shame in being eliminated from this competition. Clearly, all of the participants were highly skilled soldiers.

"Round three is up next. There is nothing more primal than hand-to-hand combat. In urban campaigns, it is not unusual to find yourself in very tight quarters. There may be times when your only weapon is a knife," said Brad. "One wrong move could decide your fate. In this challenge, the first-place team will face off against the fourth-place team. You will be provided an electrically charged training knife delivering around seventy-five thousand volts. This is substantially less than a stun gun, but it will hurt you nonetheless. Also, the knife has been coated with simulated red blood for scoring purposes."

A makeshift ring had been created in the middle of the road. It was covered in mud, sand and loose gravel. Sarge had to be aware of his footing. He knew some Krav Maga training, which placed an emphasis on footwork. Krav Maga was a self-defense system developed for the Israeli military, and combined a variety of martial arts techniques into one discipline. It stressed threat neutralization together with combined offensive and defensive maneuvers. The key to Krav Maga was to either attack preemptively or to counterattack as soon as possible.

"We have to go up against Rose and Dodge," said Steven. "I'll take Dodge so you won't have to worry about beating a girl."

"Listen, Steven," said Sarge. "Don't underestimate her. In fact, Brad made a comment about her earlier. He called her a *third-degree ball buster.*"

"Bro, maybe so," said Steven. "But she's still a girl. Trust me, I know!"

"No, listen to me," said Sarge. "He said third degree. I think she has martial arts training. She won't fight the way you're used to. I have." Sarge waited for Steven to answer.

"Yeah, you're right," said Steven. "Plus, Rose seems to be a douche. I might just kick his ass for the hell of it."

Sarge and Steven watched as the other two teams squared off. The younger men from Fort Drum were clearly the aggressors against the remaining duo from Devens. Falcone held his own, but his opponent was determined to be the victor. Shore easily defeated Rosenberg from Fort Drum. Based upon Brad's tally of knife strikes and a consensus of the group regarding blood splatter, the Fort Devens team of Falcone and Shore were declared the winners. They would advance to the final round.

Sarge was first up against 2LT Dodge. Steven advised him to fight defensively. Let her come to him. Slashes were worth one point and stabs were worth two points. The brothers agreed to focus on slashes. Even an experienced fighter had a tendency to lunge when attempting a stab. Your opponent could use his arm to throw you off balance, resulting in a knife in your back. Sarge entered the ring to an awaiting Dodge. He immediately noticed she was using a forward knife grip, which would be expected from her military training. This was a traditional grip she chose to help overcome her reach disadvantage.

Sarge knew the disadvantages of the forward, traditional grip. First, the knife was far from the body, leaving the hand and arm vulnerable to being trapped or slashed by an attacker. Secondly, the forward grip naturally pointed the knife upward. A more powerful attacker could drive your arm upward, potentially stabbing you in the face with your own knife.

"Ready? Go!" shouted Brad.

Sarge stared in Dodge's eyes, trying to maintain continuous eye contact. While he entered the ring mimicking her grip, he quickly changed to a reverse knife grip. Were the knives real, Sarge would have placed the knife edge out. This was the preferred technique of a defensive, slash-style fighter. Because these knives were electrically charged, the blade orientation didn't matter. There were several advantages to this grip, all of which related to the ability to exert greater force on your opponent. The primary disadvantage related to reach, but Sarge already had a reach advantage due to his size.

For a moment, Sarge maintained a passive stance, feet spread apart and his knees locked. He waited for Dodge to make the first move. He saw her glance down to assess his posture for a brief moment and then she quickly moved toward him. In an instant, Sarge switched his feet to a classic fight stance—left foot forward, right foot back and his elbows in, minimizing the target. Dodge was caught off guard by Sarge's sudden reposition and her momentum carried her forward. She managed a glancing slash for one point, but Sarge slashed her right shoulder and quickly achieved a stab in her upper back. Dodge gathered herself, but Sarge was quicker. He quickly switched to a forward grip, allowing for maximum reach—executing a stab and a slash as he withdrew his knife. Dodge had no choice but to be the aggressor. Sarge switched back to the reverse grip and waited for Dodge to make her move. She was fast and executed a stab to Sarge's shoulder, but he slashed her arm as part of a block attempt. The match was over.

"Wow, look at you, bro," said Steven, slapping Sarge on the back.

"Don't gloat," said Sarge. "You've still got work to do."

Sarge knew Steven was an accomplished street fighter. Of all of the participants today, he was probably the only one who had been in a real knife fight. He had scars all over his body to prove it. This was different from a street fight, however. There were some rules of engagement and Steven didn't always follow the rules. Sarge looked over at Rose, who seemed to be determined.

"He looks pissed," said Sarge to Steven.

"It's probably because I banged his girlfriend." Steven laughed. Brad motioned for Steven to come into the ring. "This won't take long."

"Why's that?" asked Sarge.

"He's too emotional. Look at him. The veins are popping out of his neck. Also, his natural instincts will be to avoid getting cut. You always get cut in a knife fight. It's part of the fun," said Steven. *He's certifiable.*

Steven strolled casually into the ring. He had an added advantage. He was truly ambidextrous. He held the knife in his left hand using a forward grip, but with his hand dropped to his side.

"Ready, go!" shouted Brad.

Steven reached out to Rose as if to shake hands. Everyone could see this infuriated Rose. Rose charged Steven, achieving a slash on Steven's right bicep. Steven quickly responded with a stab to Rose's shoulder. As Rose passed him in the ring, Steven gracefully switched hands and stabbed him in the back.

"Four," shouted Steven. Sarge grinned. Steven was fucking with the man's head and it was working. Sarge watched Steven ready himself for the next attack.

Rose bull-rushed Steven. Ordinarily, the proper move was to sidestep and block the attacker. Steven didn't move. As Rose stabbed towards him, Steven grabbed the knife blade and ripped it out of Rose's hand. He then stabbed Rose with his own knife that was held in his left hand. As Rose struggled with his balance, Steve buried Rose's knife in his chest. Rose promptly fell backwards into the mud.

"Five, six, seven and out," shouted Steven.

Gripping both blades, allowing the voltage to shock him, he turned to Brad and offered him the knife handles.

"What's next?" asked Steven.

Rose was on his feet and walking straight toward Steven with his fists balled up. *Oh shit!*

Sarge didn't have to intervene. Falcone was on Rose immediately and held him back. Steven didn't help matters by asking *what, what* repeatedly with faux innocence. Technically, the rules did not prohibit disabling the attacker in the challenge, so Steven was clear to make the move. Further, no one said he couldn't taunt his opponent. Steve fought based upon his experiences, not some textbook definition of a knife fight. Sarge sensed Brad knew this, which explained why Steven wasn't admonished for the maneuver.

"The final round will be between the Fort Devens team of Falcone and Shore representing the 1st Battalion, 25th Regiment, and the boys from Boston representing," said Brad, his voice trailing off.

"The Mechanics," said Sarge. "You can call us the Mechanics." Sarge saw Brad smile.

"In the final round, the scenario will be an urban combat zone," said Brad. "You will be required to wind your way through a simulated Middle Eastern village, complete with a mosque, neutralizing the twenty hostiles without killing any friendlies. Then, you must locate and retrieve a hostage and return to this entrance within ten minutes. Is everybody clear?"

"Yes, sir," said Sarge.

"For this challenge, you will be issued a Beretta M9 sidearm and a Daniel Defense Mil Spec M4A1 carbine with two magazines for each weapon. Be judicious with your ammo, gentlemen," said Brad. "Fort Devens Team, you're up first."

Sarge and Steven were sequestered in a building around the corner, preventing them from observing the tactics used by the Fort Devens team. They could hear gunfire and muffled voice commands, but that was it. Sarge listened as Steven took this opportunity to brief him on some tactics.

"Do you hear those staccato bursts?" asked Steven.

"Yeah."

"First of all, do not select full auto on the M4," said Steven. "We don't have to worry about return fire, so we can preserve our ammunition—*maintain ammo discipline.*

"Second, let me lead with you staying to my left. You take red hostiles on the left side and I will take the ones on the right. Neither one of us will try to help the other or we'll fuckin' shoot each other. I guarantee there will be a decision point—a fork in the road. The course will require us to choose left or right. Most likely, the side of the road with the least number of hostiles will be the way to go. In a real battle, the enemy will try to lure you into a kill zone. We'll accommodate them this time, but only because they can't fire back— I hope."

"Okay," acknowledged Sarge.

"Voice commands are acceptable. Don't hesitate to speak up. The hostage will either be at the back side of the town or in a center square or structure. We'll know when we get in there. I expect the friendlies will be stacked in this area the most. Take your time. Shooting a friendly will be deadly—for us and for them."

"The Mechanics," yelled Brad. "Front and center."

As Sarge moved towards the door, Steven grabbed his arm. "Wait, last thing. Once inside the building, shoulder your M4 and switch to your sidearm. You'll have better weapons control in tight spaces. We will always enter a room together and quickly. The idea is to dominate the room. I seriously doubt there will be hostiles inside the building. Brad would not risk a ricochet taking one of us out. Even if you get a loose trigger finger, better for me to get shot with a 9mm than the 5.56 rounds."

"I'm not gonna shoot you, asswipe," said Sarge. "But Rose might."

Sarge and Steven jogged out of the building to the entrance. Sarge saw Steven wink in the direction of Dodge and Rose. He just couldn't help himself. Sarge wasn't sure who the wink was intended for.

"Gentlemen," said Brad, "the team from Fort Devens successfully completed the mission. You're up. Do you remember the requirements of this challenge?"

"Yes, sir," replied the Mechanics. Sarge and Steven moved through the makeshift village in a methodical, controlled manner. Just as Steven surmised, Sarge encountered four hostiles on the left side of the road to Steven's two on the right side. A fenced compound split the road into two forks. The men took the right fork as Steven suggested and the decision saved them considerable time. No friendlies were killed and they only had three misfires each. They learned afterwards the Fort Devens team went left and spent an excessive amount of time searching for hostiles that didn't exist on the left path. Sarge and Steven finished the challenge in just over seven minutes, well ahead of Falcone and Shore.

"Congratulations, gentlemen," said Brad. "Steven, as a retired Navy SEAL, you have shown your seasoned abilities and you have stayed in excellent battle condition. Sarge, I think I speak for everyone here in saying you have been quite impressive today. You could lead one of my platoons anytime." The other participants applauded their win. Brad addressed the group.

"Together, Steven and Sarge operated as a well-oiled, finely tuned machine befitting their moniker the Mechanics."

CHAPTER 25

June 6, 2016
The *Boston Herald* Editorial Conference Room
Boston, Massachusetts

"Good morning, people! We have a busy week on tap for this team of journalists and miscreants," said Joe Sciacca, editor of the *Boston Herald*. "I am sure *The Gray Lady's Younger Sister with an Inferiority Complex* is busy trying to spin a yarn or two." The editorial board of the *Herald* laughed at Sciacca's reference to the *Boston Globe*, their decidedly liberal counterpart.

"Tomorrow is primary day. Hillary is in town for a campaign event. The Bilderbergs invade our fair city. And last but not least, the Bronx Bombers visit Fenway at the end of the week. What more could one ask for?"

"Madonna is playing the TD Garden Thursday night," said an intern from the back of the room.

"Well, we are the center of the universe, aren't we?" asked Sciacca sarcastically. "Politics leads the way this week. Julia, you're up. Let's start with the primary."

"Thanks, Joe," started Julia. "As we all know, Massachusetts primary day is tomorrow, which is new for the state. For years, over many election cycles, state legislatures have attempted to consolidate the state's primaries to the first Monday in June. Previously, we have been part of an early March cycle. Tomorrow is being billed as *Decision Tuesday*. In past presidential primary years, the nominations have been sewn up by now. Several key states could sway the process. Besides Massachusetts, California and New Jersey hold primaries. New Mexico, although small electorally, has been determinative of the Republican nominee over ninety percent of the time."

"Doesn't Hillary have the nomination secured?" asked Sciacca.

"Not completely," replied Julia. "California should swing in her favor, but Biden is polling strong in New Jersey and here. Upset wins in these two states could make the numbers close. It explains why both camps are making appearances in the Bay State."

"Let's talk about that," said Sciacca. "Biden is campaigning in Boston today if I understand correctly."

"That's correct. He has strong union support here. His plans include a speech to MBTA workers in South Boston followed by a symbolic visit to the site of the Pumpsie Jones murder."

"What about Hillary?"

"She has a campaign event tomorrow at Quabbin Reservoir," replied Julia. She decided not to elaborate. There was no sense in creating additional interest in an important cog in the Loyal Nine's wheel.

"Okay, moving on," said Sciacca. "I understand there was a police-involved shooting overnight in Roxbury?"

"Yes, it happened at a Black Lives Matter event at Malcolm X Park following a 'get out the vote' rally held by civil rights leader and current congressman John Lewis," said Rene Petit, metro editor for the *Herald*. "The presentations were peaceful, but the trouble began after the congressman completed his remarks."

"What happened?" asked Sciacca.

"After Congressman Lewis closed his remarks, the crowd became raucous while shouting *Black Lives Matter* repeatedly. Police are still investigating, but reports indicate several plainclothes detectives identified a potential gunman in the crowd. As they moved in on the suspect, he fled on foot down Martin Luther King Boulevard. Turning south on Walnut, he was met by an unmarked van filled with Boston PD who were assisting with crowd control. A gunfight ensued and the young man was killed. The suspect has been identified as nineteen-year-old Tyrone Rockwell of Roxbury."

"Thank you, Rene, keep us up to date on this," said Sciacca.

Petit interrupted. "Wait, there is more. The deceased is the brother of Jarvis Rockwell."

"Why does that name ring a bell?" asked Sciacca.

"At Copley Square during the Boston Marathon, Rockwell's pregnant girlfriend lost their baby during a melee with police near the finish line. This escalated tensions between the black community and Boston PD. This will only exacerbate the strained relationship. In addition, my sources tell me the black gangs of Roxbury, Mattapan and Dorchester are consolidating their power under the leadership of Rockwell—street name J-Rock. My friend in the Boston PD gang unit tells me this is a precursor for increased gang violence."

"Does the presence of Congressman Lewis elevate this to a national story?" asked Sciacca.

"I think it does, depending on the angle we choose," said Petit.

"What do you mean?"

"Well, I have a theory, from a purely amateur sociologist's point of view, of course," said Petit. "It will be controversial and not necessarily PC."

"Go ahead, Rene, you're among friends."

"Julia might want to chime in here, from a political perspective. But here are my thoughts. The civil rights leaders of today are different than the era in which Congressman Lewis fought. Lewis was the son of sharecroppers who organized sit-ins at segregated lunch counters and businesses. In the era of the sixties, there was outward, blatant racism for which Congressman Lewis paid a price. He was beaten by police for his activism and lived with constant threats upon his life. He took up a cause that was personal to him and the result was the Voting Rights Act."

Julia looked around the room and gauged the reaction of her peers. Julia knew where Petit was going with this and she was anxious to hear the comments. Petit continued.

"Today, by all *legal standards*, blacks have the same rights as whites. Those barriers were taken down in the sixties. Today's civil rights leaders appear to stoke the flames of racism for the purpose of controlling their constituents. When bomb throwers like Louis Farrakhan and Al Sharpton stir up the black community with anti-white rants, the people who pay the price are the members of the black community. After they have fired up their followers, they leave for the comfort of their hotel suites in limousines, ignoring the bedlam they leave behind."

"Do you have examples?" asked Sciacca.

"Consider the two incidents discussed today—Copley Square and Malcolm X Park," replied Petit. "The Copley Square event was organized by Reverend Sharpton, using black gang leaders from the inner city to lead the procession of Black Lives Matter protesters. The protest was designed to create a confrontation with police, who are always mindful of a potential terrorist attack associated with the Boston Marathon. Where was Sharpton? He left town earlier that morning.

"Yesterday's event was slightly different because Congressman Lewis is an icon and a symbol of peaceful protest. But the day before, Farrakhan issued a rant that called for a race war. I believe these leaders are having a profound effect on young black men in particular by stirring passions to a fever pitch. The result is an unnecessary death like last night."

"Why would you say *unnecessary*? The reports say the deceased initiated a gunfight with police," said Sciacca.

"He did, and paid the ultimate price," said Petit. "However, there was no indication he intended to use the gun during the Lewis speech. He was followed *out of* Malcolm X Park by police and then sandwiched by an oncoming police van. My guess is he felt trapped.

"My point is this. Today's black leaders are creating a climate of anger and fear within black Americans that necessarily results in senseless tragedies like last night. Perhaps a series could be developed around this story, which would then bring the Boston tragedies to national prominence."

"Or, the *Herald* could be labeled racist for its approach," said Sciacca. "As editors, it is our job to provide opinion in addition to delivering the news. Ordinarily, I could see a series such as this generating a Pulitzer nomination, but not in today's liberal media environment. The subject of race relations in this country is taboo unless you are on the *enlightened* side of the discussion. While I may agree with your premise, writing a series of articles pointing out the unintended consequences of black protests would get hammered in the industry. We'll need to think this through very carefully."

Sciacca was right. *Freedom of Speech is dead in America.*

"Thank you, Rene. Sandra, what do we have on the economic front?" asked Sciacca.

"The story of the week is part political and part economic," replied Sandra Gottlieb, business editor of the *Herald*. "The Bilderbergs are coming to town."

CHAPTER 26

June 7, 2016
The Hack House
Binney Street
East Cambridge, Massachusetts

Lau left the world of reality and entered hackerspace with a sack full of Egg McMuffins for the Zero Day Gamers. It was going to be an interesting day for the Gamers. Lau was contacted two days ago via HackersList by an unknown client, as was typical. They were more selective after cashing in on several lucrative paydays. Lau laughed to himself as he realized they now had *standards* to follow. One of the things he enjoyed most about this enterprise was the diversity in its projects. Today could be trailblazing if the results were successful.

"Good morning all!" Lau announced as he saw the sleepy faces of Fakhri, Malvalaha and Walthaus.

"Good morning, Professor," replied Malvalaha with a slight tone of sarcasm. "Bright eyed and bushy tailed, as they say."

"I've downed half a pot of coffee," said Fakhri. "It's starting to give me the shakes."

"C'mon, you guys," said Lau. "It's not that early. This time a year ago you were getting ready for class at this hour. Are you getting soft on me?" Lau noticed Walthaus was quiet and looked disheveled.

"What's wrong with him?"

"He had a late night," replied Malvalaha.

"Really, Walthaus?" asked Lau. "I sent you guys home early yesterday to get some rest, not to party."

"I wasn't partying," mumbled Walthaus.

"He has a girlfriend," interjected Fakhri.

"Shut up!" said Walthaus.

"Her name is Wendy, like the burger girl," added Malvalaha. "Looks like her too. She has the freckles, red hair and ponytails." Fakhri and Malvalaha were having a good laugh at Walthaus' expense, who was now turning fifty shades of embarrassment.

"Shut up, guys, really!"

"Okay. Good for you, Walthaus, but wake up and smell the McMuffins," said Lau. "We won't tell *Wendy* you cheated on her with Ronald McDonald!" The room busted with laughter and Lau effectively woke them all up accordingly. It was time to get their game on.

"Quick summary of the project, please, Mr. Malvalaha," said Lau as he assumed his role of Professor of Hacktivism 101.

"The client would like to affect the outcome of today's Democratic primaries in New Jersey and Massachusetts," started Malvalaha. "They have not provided us a stated purpose, but the results will certainly favor candidate Biden."

"That breaks your heart, I'm sure," chimed in Walthaus. Malvalaha was a Biden supporter and despised Clinton. Walthaus was a political agnostic, believing neither party represented the best interests of the common guy.

"He speaks!" exclaimed Lau. "If Clinton has this nomination in the bag, as the pundits claim, how will a good showing or win help Biden?"

"We can only speculate, but perhaps Biden's people are trying to show his strength in order to gain him another VP slot," said Fakhri. "Or maybe the Republicans are trying to make Hillary look weak."

"Regardless, he who pays—wins. Right?" asked Lau.

"You betcha," replied Fakhri, using her best Arabic impersonation of Sarah Palin.

"The client has provided us targeted precincts in both states where vote manipulation will be least likely to draw attention," said Malvalaha. "A five percent increase for Biden will naturally reduce Clinton's advantage in a like amount. This will create a Biden win in most cases yet still be within the margin of error of the aggregate of polls."

"In New Jersey, for example, precincts in the south from AC towards Trenton share a border with Pennsylvania, a Biden stronghold," added Fakhri. "These voting precincts are our main target. Populated areas around the Newark area are Clinton dominated. The client chose the Pennsylvania contiguous precincts to show Biden's ability to carry that state if chosen as VP. But that's our theory."

"Walthaus, tell us about the hack," said Lau. After two McMuffins, Walthaus was back to the land of the living.

"There are two options," replied Walthaus. "A publicized option actually opened the door for our course of action. Many states used the AVS WinVote touch screen voting machine for years. Its state-of-the-art design was a direct result of the 2000 presidential debacle in Florida where lawyers with bad eyesight fought over hanging chads and voter intent."

Lau recalled visions of attorneys scrutinizing every punched ballot with magnifying glasses. The vote count went well into December and it took the Supreme Court to bring the dispute to a conclusion.

"After an expose` was published showing the ability to enter the encrypted WEP wireless system with the password *ABCDE*, the machines were abandoned," said Walthaus. "Further, as we have found repeatedly in our *work*, the Windows-based operating system was either out of date or inadequately protected. Any high school kid could sit in the parking lot of the voting booth and insert low-sophistication code to change voting outcomes."

"Believe it or not, this was still an option available to us," said Fakhri. "It would require a ZDG army to canvass all of the precincts. That's too much work."

"Let's talk about our plan." Lau enjoyed the process of walking through the hack and having all of his assistants provide their contribution or opinion. Despite his newfound *profession*, he was an MIT professor and every job was a learning experience for his trusted graduate assistants.

"We are going to play on two typical weaknesses in any government-run operation—complacency and a false sense of security," replied Walthaus. "Once the WinVote scandal broke, many state governments quickly threw money at the problem and purchased all new voting machine units. Massachusetts and New Jersey were no exception."

"As luck would have it, New Jersey and Massachusetts, like many of their northeastern neighbors, use a new Direct Recording Electronic voting machine without a paper ballot," said Fakhri. "We researched the Federal Election Commission website to study the different machines in use by our target precincts. While many states use the new DRE technology, some have not incorporated the VVPAT accompanying hardware."

"What is VVPAT?" asked Lau.

"VVPAT stands for voter verified paper audit trail printers," replied Malvalaha. "There are only eight states which utilize this configuration for voting—Jersey and Massachusetts are included."

"The selling point of the DRE-VVPAT voting system was their accessibility, usability, and efficiency," said Fakhri. "The machines allow for both the casting and tallying of a vote internally. At the end of the day, the votes are downloaded for tallying. It was a simple solution to the complex problems experienced in both the 2000 and 2004 elections."

"Companies like AccuVote TSX, Optech Insight, and Populex produced their own versions of the DRE-VVPAT," said Malvalaha. "But they all have one thing in common—a Windows-based operating system."

Lau smiled. "Our favorite. Won't they ever learn? Microsoft Windows is a hacker's dream."

"We've had great success entering Windows operating systems through the back door in the past," said Walthaus. "Today is no exception." Walthaus stood and walked to his desk where his monitors awaited his commands.

"I am ready to enter the Secretary of State website for both states when we are ready to go. I did some research on the hack of the

WorkSource Oregon site from last year. Anytime a state agency gives the public a portal to interact with, such as filing an unemployment claim, a window opens for us—pardon the pun."

Lau admired the great strides this young man had made in his analytical abilities and on a personal level. Walthaus went from a chubby geek with low self-esteem to one of the best in the business—with a girlfriend.

"By accessing the Department of Labor and Workforce Development, we can enter the Secretary of State's servers," continued Walthaus. "The Secretary of State department includes the Division of Elections."

"In the interest of government efficiency, all of the DRE units are interconnected to the Division of Election servers," said Fakhri. "We will insert the code into the targeted precincts via the Secretary of State's servers. While the poll watchers concern themselves with a hacker in their parking lot, we'll be here remotely modifying votes all day—completely undetected."

"Are you using a worm or a Trojan?" asked Lau.

"Both," replied Walthaus. "We all agree a Random Access Tool, a RAT, is necessary. We need a method of modifying real-time data and controlling user activity. Fakhri developed the worm for Massachusetts, and Malvalaha created a Trojan horse for the New Jersey voting machines."

"My focus will be on New Jersey," said Malvalaha. "Being from Brooklyn, it will be my pleasure to stick it to the New Jerseyites. We will use the njRAT Trojan, which is also known throughout the Middle East as *Bladabindi*."

"Blah, blah, blah," interrupted Fakhri. Lau laughed with the trio of hackers both for the humorous interjection and their ability to make jokes during a serious, technical conversation.

"Does *nj* stand for New Jersey?" joked Lau. The term njRAT was ironically coincidental and had nothing to do with the state.

"njRAT was developed using Microsoft .NET framework and, like many RATs, provides us complete control of the infected system," said Malvalaha. "It will deliver us an array of features that will allow us to manipulate votes by changing them or deleting them altogether. Variety is the spice of life."

Lau turned to Fakhri. "Tell us about your worm."

"For Massachusetts, I came up with an H-worm using a visual-based script variant of the njRAT source code," replied Fakhri. "It provides us similar controls to the njRAT, but it also uses dynamic DNS, allowing us to post requests as well as extract information. I like it because we can monitor vote totals as the day progresses. It is very popular with the Chinese."

"Why are we using both?" asked Lau. "Why are we using one for each state?"

"The Trojan and the worm use different parameters," replied Walthaus. "If some state IT guy gets lucky and discovers our intrusion during the course of the day, we can quickly flip the script—run njRAT in Massachusetts and vice versa."

"An additional benefit is later discovery," added Fakhri. "Should the manipulation come to light down the road, these particular hacks are peculiar to foreign nations. The Syrians or Iranians will be blamed for New Jersey while the Chinese will be blamed for Massachusetts. It provides us cover."

"Well done, everybody!" exclaimed Lau. "Polls are opening soon. Shall we get to work?"

"In we go," replied Walthaus.

Voting is the cornerstone of democracy and every vote counts—in theory.

CHAPTER 27

June 7, 2016
Quabbin Reservoir, Prescott Peninsula
Former town of Prescott, Massachusetts

Sarge and Julia leaned against the hood of the Mercedes G-Wagen and watched the festivities. They arrived early in order to avoid the traffic snarl along Highway 202, which runs for two miles from west to east along the entrance to Prescott Peninsula.

The campaign event was confined to the area where Cooleyville Road and Hunt Road intersect—by design. This very public event was orchestrated to insure the privacy of what would be going on farther down on the peninsula.

"It's beautiful up here," said Julia. "After we turned off the Mass Turnpike, it was like a different world. I loved the winding drive through the trees after we passed through Belchertown."

Sarge continued to observe the crowd and marveled at the levels of security. Originally slated as a ribbon-cutting ceremony to boost Abbie's senatorial campaign, it quickly devolved into a three-ring circus when Clinton's presidential entourage inserted itself into the festivities.

"Hey, Professor Sargent, are you in there?" asked Julia. She knocked on his head.

"Ouch, yes. It's a beautiful day," replied Sarge.

"That's not what I said," replied Julia. "What's on your mind?"

Sarge had a lot of things on his mind lately, including the herculean task of turning this pristine land into a well-fortified bug-out facility for the Boston Brahmin.

"Abbie's campaign event was supposed to be a lightly attended dog and pony show for the media," said Sarge. "The idea was to secure the privacy of the surrounding residents and looky-loos."

"I think the premise is still good, despite the rude interruption of—*this*," said Julia, gesturing to dozens of media satellite trucks, police vehicles and military Humvees. "How did Hillary become involved?"

"One of the platforms of her campaign is the whole War on Women thing."

"That's such a false premise," said Julia. "How does anyone buy into that?"

"I don't know, but it must be working for her. When her campaign found out Abbie was instrumental in creating a protected sanctuary for abused mothers and their children, it became a natural campaign stop for her."

"How does Abbie feel about the encroachment upon her time to shine?" Julia was fishing. Sarge thought Julia would always wonder about any lingering feelings he had for Abbie. *Maybe I'm putting something out there?*

"I don't know, but politically it helps her," replied Sarge. "She gains the added benefit of sharing the national stage with Hillary while showing her constituents she can swing both ways."

"Sarge!" Julia punched him—hard.

"What?"

"You can't say a woman *swings both ways*. One might get the wrong idea!"

"What? No, you know what I mean. Whatever. I think there is a War on Men around here. This place is full of man haters."

"Zip it, Sarge," said Julia.

"Look, there's someone I want you to meet." He gestured for one of the security men wearing a dark suit to come over to speak with him. As the man approached, he was smiling.

"How do you like the new uniform?" said Drew Jackson, Steven's Aegis team member with the code name Slash.

"You look like you're going to a funeral, Drew." Sarge laughed. "I want you to meet Julia Hawthorne. Julia, this is one of Steven's associates, Drew Jackson." Julia and Drew shook hands as he worked his Southern charm.

"Nice to meet you, ma'am," said Drew.

"It's nice to meet you as well. Steven's work is always mysterious, but you don't look too threatening." *If she only knew what a deadly operative he was.*

"Sla—I mean Drew has been assigned to Abbie's security detail for the remainder of the campaign," said Sarge. "She'll be in good hands and well protected."

"Senator Morgan's safety is my number one priority," said Drew. "I am glad, however, that she is not a presidential candidate. This whole operation is FUBAR."

"That it is, Drew. We were just talking about that," said Sarge. "Are you travelling with her campaign full time?"

"I am," said Drew. "I received specific instructions to live on the motor coach that accompanies her campaign stops. It's not quite as nice as the senator's, but I've slept in worst quarters."

"I can imagine," Julia said. "I detect your Southern accent, Drew. Where are you from originally?"

"Yeah, the country boy can't leave the way of talkin' behind," replied Drew. "I was born and raised in a farmin' community called Muddy Pond. It's located about halfway between Nashville and Knoxville, Tennessee. My folks and family still live there. I'm the only one who ventured out into the *real world.*"

"Do you miss it?" asked Julia.

"I do," he replied. "Listen, I better get back. It was nice to meet you, ma'am. Sarge, I'll see you around, I'm sure."

"Definitely, Drew. Be safe!"

Drew headed towards Abbie's motorhome.

"He seems like a good guy," said Julia.

"First class. Steven trusts him with his life," said Sarge. "I would too."

"Abbie's in good hands. Was this her dad's idea?"

"Yes. Mr. Morgan is not paranoid. Let's call it *hyperaware.* When you deal on his level, you become privy to things the rest of us don't know about until later. Prescott Peninsula is a part of the planning he takes so seriously. He is always one step ahead of the curve, it seems."

As Sarge and Julia continued to take it all in, a clean-cut guy wearing a white shirt and khakis approached. As he got closer, Sarge could see a blue *I'm Ready for Hillary* T-shirt underneath his shirt.

"What does this guy want?" asked Sarge. "I'm not *Ready for Hillary*. Not now, not ever."

"That's Robby Mook, her campaign manager."

"Great. I'm not donating to her either." Clearly, Mook was headed to see them, so Sarge stood a little taller to meet the Clinton interloper.

"Hi, my name is Robby Mook. I believe you are Henry Sargent," said Mook.

"I am. This is my friend Julia Hawthorne—political editor of the *Boston Herald*," replied Sarge. *Careful what you say, Mr. Mook, you're on the record.*

"Of course. Hello, Julia," said Mook. "You may not recall, but we met ten years ago when I worked with Senator Ben Cardin's campaign in his race against former GOP chair Michael Steele. You interviewed Senator Cardin after a debate that fall."

"Yes, I remember," replied Julia. "We were both much younger then."

"And idealistic," said Mook. "Listen, I don't want to take much of your time. Mr. Sargent…"

"Call me Sarge."

"I was told that, I'm sorry for the formality. Sarge, I will be brief, as the speeches will begin soon and then I'll need to spend a half hour explaining to the media what my candidate meant to say. You know how that goes, right, Julia?"

"I do."

"Sarge, may I ask you about your relationship with Senator Morgan?"

"Why?" Sarge got his hackles up. Julia moved closer to him and wrapped her arm in his to give Mook a clear signal—this is my guy.

"I understand you two had a closer relationship ten years ago, is that correct?"

"You don't waste any time, do you?" Sarge was incredulous. "This is really none of your business, but we did have a relationship many years ago. We are still *friends* today. That's it."

Mook held both hands up in a gesture requesting peace. "I don't mean to offend you, Sarge. My job is to conduct opposition research. Frankly, out of respect for you and the senator, I chose to ask you in person since I was told of your presence here today. Normally, a team would conduct the inquiry. My apologies to you as well, Julia."

"We understand," replied Julia. She was trembling.

"I'll leave you guys alone. Sorry for the intrusion." The head of *Team Ready for Hillary* disappeared into the crowd. Sarge and Julia watched in silence for a moment.

"Politics is dirty business," said Sarge. Julia was quiet. Sarge could feel the tension. Obviously, a stranger asking about his past relationship with Abbie struck a nerve.

"That was bullshit," said Julia. "Why is he conducting oppo research on a senatorial candidate?"

"Her name has been bantered about for a VP slot," replied Sarge. "If she makes the short list, there will be more questions about her past."

"I get that, but maybe their guy should have scheduled an appointment or something." She understood the process. She just didn't want to be included in it. Sarge turned her to face him and he held her face in his hands.

"Agreed. Now listen, don't doubt me. I love you. My—*our* relationship with Abbie is one built upon trust, friendship and common interests. Abbie is *our* friend. Right?" Sarge watched Julia tuck her chin into her chest. He suspected she felt silly.

"Yes, I'm an idiot," she said.

"No, you're brilliant. It seems you are properly protecting your investment. Obviously, you think I shoot the moon. I am the cat's meow. I'm the greatest thing since sliced bread. You do worship me as king, my Lady Hawthorne!"

Julia was smiling now as she reached down and grabbed him firmly by his privates. "Don't make me hurt you—King!"

Chapter 28

June 8, 2016
The Liberty Tree Hotel
The Bilderberg Conference
Boston, Massachusetts

John Morgan's Cadillac Escalade, retrofitted by Bentley, made a wide turn as it entered the courtyard of The Liberty Hotel. Completed in 1851, The Liberty is considered to be one of the best examples of the Boston Granite style of architecture prevalent during the mid-nineteenth century. Morgan admired the structure because it exuded strength and dignity and was symbolic of Boston's importance in the history of America.

By the mid-nineteenth century, The Liberty was transformed into the fabled Charles Street jail. Housing some of Boston's most notorious criminals for 120 years, the building, as well as its prisoners, was liberated and underwent a one-hundred-fifty-million-dollar transformation to become one of the top luxury hotels in the world.

Today, The Liberty Hotel would house a group of criminals of a different sort—the Bilderbergs. Officially, the Bilderberg Group was a private, annual conference of roughly one hundred fifty political leaders and experts from banking, industry, academia and the media, who were expected to foster dialogue between Europeans and Americans. Unofficially, the attendees of this conference formed a shadow world government with globalist intentions. Their goal was to supplant nation-state sovereignty with an all-powerful global government controlled by power brokers and kept in line through the use of military power.

Their names were synonymous with the world's power elites—Rockefeller, Soros, Kissinger, Merkel, Bernanke, Murdoch, Clinton and Morgan. The organizations they represented were always well represented, including the Trilateral Commission, the Council on Foreign Relations, the Federal Reserve and the World Bank.

For over fifty years, the attendees, sworn to secrecy, shaped world events via agendas and discussion topics that never escaped the confines of the conference location. No press was allowed, and as a result, conspiracy theories abounded. *For once, the conspiracy theorists are right.*

The real power brokers within the Bilderbergers held positions on the Steering Committee. The Bilderberg Group was the world's most exclusive club. Money would not buy you attendance. You must be invited. Only the Steering Committee decided whom to invite and they were carefully screened. Each year, long-standing members had the opportunity to request an invitation for one of their associates or family members.

In 1991, David Rockefeller secured an invitation for a relatively unknown former Arkansas governor named William Jefferson Clinton. Clinton began his primary campaign for President and adopted a Rockefeller affinity for a major trade agreement tying the economies of Mexico, Canada and the United States—NAFTA. Clinton made this a major platform of his presidential campaign, and the next year he became President.

Morgan fostered no interest in being named to the powerful Steering Committee. He didn't want to get his hands dirty. He was able to shape the agenda of the Steering Committee by determining the composition of its members. The Aegis team assisted in that regard over the last several months.

He was a planner. When Abbie won her senatorial campaign, Morgan arranged for the Bilderberg Conference to be held in Boston in 2016. When objections were raised about The Liberty's inner-city location, Morgan convinced the Steering Committee to create an illusion of transparency by avoiding the typical conference locations in remote parts of Europe.

The 2016 conference was going to be more important in other respects. Abbie would attend and be introduced to the members. She would become a part of the brain trust that shaped geopolitical affairs. As Morgan's sole heir, Abbie was being groomed to succeed him and continue the work of the Boston Brahmin.

This year's conference was fortuitous in one other respect. The wife of Morgan's close friend Bill Clinton was running for President. She would need a strong running mate—one that would complement her politically and draw voters from the middle of the political spectrum. Morgan was going to assist with that determination. He was meeting with the former President and it was time to call in a marker.

"This way, sir," said the member of the secret service entourage protecting both Mr. and Mrs. Clinton. Morgan and his assistant, Malcolm Lowe, followed the agent down the hall lined with a contingent of campaign personnel and security. The men entered through the red brick portico into the twenty-two-hundred-square-foot luxurious suite, the finest in the hotel. Designed with floor-to-ceiling windows, the suite's view over the Charles River and Beacon Hill would impress anyone—except a man who enjoyed this view every day.

Morgan saw Hillary huddled over a desk with her longtime assistant, Huma Mahmood Abedin. Abedin, a pro-sharia sociologist of Muslim faith, was the wife of former New York congressman Anthony Weiner. She was Hillary Clinton's most trusted confidante. When she noticed him, she interrupted her conversation to greet her guest.

"John! What a pleasure it is to see you. I truly enjoyed spending my day with Abigail yesterday." The two shared a brief, somewhat tepid hug.

"The ribbon-cutting ceremony was an excellent opportunity for both of you to show your commitment to the protection of women," replied Morgan. "It appears the campaign is going well, despite yesterday's surprise results in New Jersey and in our fair state."

"You know, John, you can't take anything for granted," she

replied. "Joe is still running a strong campaign although the electoral numbers are against him. His wins in those two states just stiffen my resolve to win this primary race. I just stick to my message that I am the right leader at the right time with the right plan."

"You certainly are on the home stretch," said Morgan. *She better not squander his support. But the timing couldn't be more perfect.*

Morgan continued. "I am sure you are aware that Abigail will be introduced at the conference this year."

"I am," she replied. "It's been twenty-five years since David invited Bill to attend—at your suggestion, if I recall." *Good memory. Let's hope your husband has retained some as well.*

"It was my honor, and naturally I appreciate the support you have shown Abigail. I know you are busy and I need to spend some time bending the ear of your husband. I look forward to hearing your closing remarks on Friday."

Hillary leaned into Morgan to whisper, "Thank you, John, and I could use a little more financial support. This extended primary has become very expensive."

"I understand. I'll see what I can do." *Yes, money can buy elections.*

Morgan made his way to the large open-air terrace where Bill stood alone overlooking the river. Morgan waited until the former President noticed him and waved him outside.

"Sheila honey, I will only be in Boston for a few days. Then I'll fly back to Chappaqua," said Bill. Morgan waited patiently while Clinton finished his phone call with his longtime mistress, Sheila McMahon. Clinton's trysts with McMahon were so frequent, the secret service gave her the code name *Energizer*. Morgan would call in this marker as well.

Clinton ended his call and embraced his old friend. "John, it has been too long."

"Very true, my friend. How have you been since your recent bypass surgery?" asked Morgan. Two months prior, Clinton, while in Chappaqua purportedly with the Energizer, began experiencing chest pains. In 2004, he successfully underwent quadruple-bypass surgery together with a follow-up procedure to insert stents. The Clintons feared a relapse.

"Oh, I'm fine. It's not so much my health as it is the optics. I'm still dedicated and have the energy to help with the campaign, but I find myself wanting to spend more time at home."

"How is your relationship with Sheila? I hope the grant I provided Energy Pioneer Solutions was adequate." Morgan intended to remind his old friend of several secrets the two shared.

Clinton laughed and spoke in his instantly recognizable croaky timbre voice that had coarsened with the passage of time. "Yes, it was more than adequate and she sends her thanks. She's doing fine. Sheila worries about me. The boys call her the Energizer. Sometimes my ticker can't take all of her *energy*, if you know what I mean."

No, not really. Time for the next reminder. "Bill, my old friend, if I remember correctly, your heart surgery in '04 came after quite a few visits down to Epstein's little island paradise. Perhaps it's time to act your age, my old friend." Morgan was making clever reference to the former President's frequent visits to the private island of Jeffrey Epstein in the U.S. Virgin Islands, known for its lavish sex parties.

Clinton laughed heartily. "I don't know if there is a correlation between my infamous libido and heart health, but I'll go out with a smile!" The men laughed, but Morgan knew Clinton's libido would become the brunt of late night jokes during the fall campaign.

"It has been twenty-five years since you first attended the conference," said Morgan, starting to get down to business.

"I remember when you first approached me about attending," he replied. "I was exploring my options when I came to a Boston meeting with Teddy. We had lunch at the Union Oyster House. Three days later I met with David Rockefeller and a few months later everyone in America knew my name."

"We've done great things together over the years," said Morgan. "Bill, I know you have limited time. I've spoken with Hillary about campaign finances."

Clinton interrupted. "She didn't spend enough time here or in New Jersey. Mook took this state for granted and didn't allocate the requisite financial resources either. Biden pulled out two close wins, which are irrelevant electorally, but make Hill look bad. Republicans pounced on the results as a sign of weakness in her electability."

"I have always been here to help you both," said Morgan. "Let's help each other this time."

"What do you have in mind, John?"

"Abigail, as an independent, holds a twenty-point lead in one of the most left-leaning states in the country. She has excellent appeal to young people and the ten percent undecided voters who comprise the middle of the political spectrum. She also has a financial war chest that is unsurpassed, as you can imagine."

"I can't disagree," said Clinton. "Her reelection is assured."

Morgan decided to be blunt. "I want her on the ticket."

Clinton took a step back and looked out across the cityscape. Morgan caught him off guard. *Good.*

"John, you know the VP slot isn't up to me. Hillary will make the final decision during the convention next month with feedback from hundreds of political operatives. You know how that works. Of course, I will put in a good word for her."

Morgan expected this response. "I do know *how that works*," replied Morgan with emphasis. "I elect Presidents every four years. You'll do more than *put in a good word*, my old friend. Hillary will become President, but in name only. You and I both know this is your opportunity for a third term in office. There is *unfinished business*, am I right?"

"Yes, there is. Look, John, I will get push back. The politicos will want to pick a Hispanic or a Black—someone to play to the base. Your daughter will be a tough sell because she caucuses with the Republicans and isn't far enough left to suit some."

"Abigail will deliver the middle, Bill. You and I both know the GOP and the Democrats can each count on forty-seven to forty-eight percent of the vote. They simply have to turn out their base. But elections are won by convincing those four to five percent unaffiliated, sometimes apathetic voters to swing in your direction. Abigail's libertarian leanings can deliver the college-age vote in a big way. Hillary doesn't appeal to them at all. Abigail will also siphon off the libertarian support currently in Rand Paul's camp."

"All good points." Clinton turned and rested both hands on the rail. He looked deep in thought as he surveyed the Boston landscape.

"I will solve the campaign's money problems. Also, you know the financial and geopolitical issues important to us." Morgan made his case without bringing up the nuclear option—Benghazi. Morgan had damning evidence of Hillary's involvement in the entire Libyan embassy disaster, which, if released, would sink her chances of winning. He would save this for a later date, if necessary.

"Okay, I will make it happen. We'll need one hundred million donated to the Clinton Foundation, delivered immediately after the announcement in Philadelphia next month."

"Thank you, Bill. Take care." Morgan turned and left, smiling.

CHAPTER 29

June 8, 2016
White House Situation Room
Washington, D.C.

The White House Situation Room is a five-thousand-square-foot complex of rooms located on the ground floor of the West Wing. It is commonly referred to as *The Woodshed.*

The Situation Room was born out of frustration on the part of President John Kennedy after the Bay of Pigs debacle in Cuba. President Kennedy felt betrayed by the conflicting advice and information coming in to him from the various agencies that comprised the nation's defense departments. Kennedy ordered the bowling alley built during the Truman presidency removed and replaced with the Situation Room.

Initially, before the age of electronics, President Kennedy required at least one Central Intelligence analyst remain in the Situation Room at all times. The analyst would work a twenty-hour shift and sleep on a cot during the night.

Other Presidents, like Nixon and Ford, never used the Situation Room. In most cases, a visit from the President was a formal undertaking, happening only on rare occasions. President George H.W. Bush, a former CIA head, would frequently call and ask if he could stop by and say hello.

When there had been a foreign policy failure, such as when the shoe bomber boarded a flight on Christmas Day in 2009, the Situation Room became a forum for a tongue-lashing of top-level intelligence and national security personnel.

Katie had not experienced a tongue-lashing, nor had she seen the

President in the Situation Room. But the President's top two advisors, Susan Giles and Valerie Jarrett, were regulars and had the full authority of the President to berate and castigate at will. The tension in the room indicated this briefing would be one of those mornings.

"The President has had enough!" barked Giles, looking over her reading glasses, piercing eyes blowing holes through the attendees skulls. "Not only are the cyber attacks of the Pentagon email system a serious matter of national security, they are goddamn embarrassing!"

Katie glanced around the room and noticed she was the sole female in attendance besides Jarrett and Giles. The men were squirming. Katie was not. She had been sounding alarm bells about cyber terror for many weeks.

"General Dempsey, how are you and the Joint Chiefs going to deal with this?" asked Giles.

"The DoD, through the United States Strategic command, is working closely with USSTRATCOM in defending the global information grid," replied General Martin Dempsey, chairman of the Joint Chiefs of Staff. "In conjunction with the United States Cyber Command, the DoD turns away hundreds of thousands of attacks on our governmental facilities a day. The cyber attacks are continuous and relentless."

"O'Shea!" snapped Jarrett. "You are the liaison between the Cyber Threat Intelligence Integration Center and the President's Intelligence Advisory Board. Well, advise us."

Katie glanced at Giles, trying to remember her prior admonishment about the political aspects of her analysis. She wondered how Giles would react to this. *I'm on the hot seat.*

Looking at General Dempsey, then back to Jarrett, Katie started, "We're at war, and we are losing." She allowed the words to permeate the twenty-first-century whisper walls—glad they couldn't seep out into the corridors or upstairs to the Oval Office.

"Tensions continue to escalate between our country, Russia and China. Reports of cyber warfare are now commonplace in the media. Politically, a cyber war doesn't get the attention of the American people like a militaristic war with tanks, guns and troops. But it is a war nonetheless.

"The perception of which countries are most likely to be in the wrong certainly differs greatly depending on one's geographic location. Our media reports portray China and Russia as the bad actors. However, reporting in these two eastern nations is significantly different. In fact, Putin stated the other day the United States has initiated a cyber war against both Russia and China. He used this as justification for his troop movements to the Arctic." Katie had command of the room.

"The Chinese are the bullies of cyberspace. They have an army of hackers covertly gathering intelligence on every nation. Of course, this is denied by the Chinese authorities as well as Chinese embassy spokespersons. It is clear that each of the three major world superpowers is ramping up its attempts to attack one another in cyberspace."

"Do you think we are underestimating the threat?" asked Jarrett.

"Not internally, but we are in public," replied Katie. "I believe cyber warfare is the beginning of a distinctive period in history that will define future conflicts between the three countries. We have substantial economic and geopolitical disagreements with Russia and China. There are increased territorial disputes, which could escalate to military conflict.

"Cyber war has remained physically peaceful thus far, although the potential for future conflict between the three nations, and others, remains significant."

"What would you have us do? Should the President ask Congress for a declaration of—*cyber war*?" asked Giles. Katie again glanced at General Dempsey, a decorated military man nearly forty years her senior.

"I suggest the DoD consider a variety of retaliatory measures in order to respond in kind. For political purposes, it is important for the President to continue playing the victim card. Let's face it. The United States is the most powerful country in the world militarily and we have the most advanced cyber technologies. Let's use our abilities to hit the bullies in the nose."

General Dempsey spoke up. "We have to be careful here. If we stubbornly retaliate with measures in cyber space, we will be known for being a cyber bully and will have to shoulder responsibility for escalating confrontation. There will be consequences."

"If we don't retaliate, then we will lose the confidence of the American people," replied Giles. "How do you suggest we proceed, O'Shea?"

"I will leave the mechanics to the political advisors," started Katie. She was reminding NSA Giles that she was cognizant of the ramifications of her suggestions. "The essential framework for our public response centers around five principles.

"First, we need to raise awareness in our country that there is a new domain for warfare—cyberspace.

"Second, the White House should continue its successful campaign of claiming victim status. Outwardly, stress to the American people we are strengthening our passive defenses such as firewalls and other protective measures. Let it be known our cyber-defense agencies will implement proactive defenses using available sensors to provide a rapid response to detect and stop a cyber attack on the nation's computer networks. Within the confines of government confidentiality, but made available via strategic information leaks, establish military protocols and tactics to back trace, hunt down, and attack an enemy cyber-intruder."

"Let me interrupt right there," said Dempsey. "Are you suggesting we use military force against hackers?"

"We use drones to destroy ISIS targets," replied Katie dryly. "Why not state all options are available? We have to accept cyber war as a real war. Just because the enemy comes at us in the cyber domain doesn't mean we have to respond in the cyber domain. Our adversaries need to know that a military response is a part of our national defense strategy. The goal is to convince them not to engage in escalatory behavior."

She continued. General Dempsey was clearly not happy with her. "Third, let's recruit the best and brightest computer minds throughout the country and dedicate them to this task. It is an urgent matter of national security to maintain and enhance our advantage in technological and artificial intelligence capabilities.

"Fourth, we need to enlist the support of our allies. America is not the only country under attack. By establishing a collective defense against these rogue nations and bad actors, we can share information and react quickly to enhance our cyber warfare defense structure."

Now, for the real wake-up call.

"Finally, our country needs to move quickly to protect its critical infrastructure. A cyber attack can destroy our power grid, leaving an energy-dependent nation in the dark. The attack itself may not kill anyone, but the aftermath will."

Katie paused to let this soak in. It took twenty years to convince Congress to protect the grid from the catastrophic effects of electromagnetic pulse weapons or coronal mass ejections. They still had not acted. *How long will it take them to protect the power grid from a cyber attack?*

Katie instinctively knew it would be too late.

CHAPTER 30

June 8, 2016
Quabbin Reservoir, Prescott Peninsula
Former town of Prescott, Massachusetts

"I could live here," observed Susan Quinn as Donald maneuvered the SUV down the gravel road towards the center of Prescott Peninsula.

"Someday we may have to, Suze," replied Donald. "We really have our work cut out for us. Mr. Morgan expects this entire project to be complete by the end of summer."

"Well, I must say, he has provided us with an incredible canvas to create this work of art," said J.J. from the backseat. "We've been going over the plans night and day now for a couple of weeks. I couldn't imagine the beauty of the Quabbin Reservoir by staring at those maps."

"When I first came out here with Sarge and Steven a week ago, we realized this location was idyllic," said Donald. "Of course, Steven just complained about how we were going to defend it. Despite being surrounded on three sides by water, the two-mile-wide entrance is a problem."

"Does Steven have a plan for that?" asked Susan.

"He met with Brad last week and they have a solution," replied Donald. "The solution will require manpower, which raises a new set of concerns—operational security. It will be incumbent on Steven and Brad to recruit like-minded military personnel who are one hundred percent on board with the intent and purpose of what we are doing here. They have to be careful who they approach."

"Makes sense," said J.J., pointing towards two vehicles in a clearing ahead. "They're already here."

Sarge, Steven and Brad were reviewing a large set of drawings on the hood of Sarge's car. Steven was pointing from one side of the drawings to the other. Donald guessed the fence was the topic du jour.

"Hey, guys," said Susan through the window as Donald pulled the SUV alongside their friends. "Fancy meeting you here."

"Susie Q, how are you?" asked Steven. "I see you let DQ drive this time."

"Don't bust my balls from the git-go, Steven," said Donald. His constant ribbing did get old sometimes.

"Relax, old buddy. We're taking another look at this damn two-mile opening we need to secure. Brad has it covered, though."

"Hey, Brad," said Donald, shaking the military man's hand firmly. "Susan baked you a couple of pies to take back to the boys."

"Thanks, Susan. Apple, I hope?" asked Brad. Susan felt the need to give Brad special attention because he was single, estranged from his family and surrounded by military guys. A touch of home cooking always warmed Brad's heart.

"You got it!" replied Susan. "You'll need your strength to build that fence." Susan and Donald moved closer to the plans as Sarge greeted J.J.

"Hey, Doc, how's Sabs?" asked Sarge. "It was really nice of her to watch the Quinn monsters while we spend the day out here."

"She actually looked forward to it," replied J.J.

Susan leaned back to give Sarge a little hell. "You know, Sarge, there will be a time when you'll settle down and quit playing Indiana Jones," interjected Susan. "Who knows, you might even get married and have your own *monsters*."

"That's right, bro. Let their uncle Steven show them a thing or two."

"Marriage, children and the thought of an uncle Steven? Have I offended you guys in some way?"

Brad forced the current contingent of the Loyal Nine to focus.

BOBBY AKART

"At ease, soldiers. We've got a lot to talk about."

Brad continued. "You did a great job creating a private environment for us to work. The campaign event went well and I believe our construction efforts will go largely unnoticed."

"Thanks, Brad," said Donald. "We had to create an illusion that was also a good cause. Curiosity seekers will not want to intrude on the lives of abused women and children. Further, the fast-track construction will hopefully fly under the radar of Brad's friends at nearby Fort Devens and the prying eyes of the NSA's satellites."

"The next step is creating a secured perimeter," said Brad. "It will require some extra effort and expense, but we will stretch fencing across the entire northern border." Brad drew a line with his finger stretching from the inlet to the west across the peninsula entrance to the east at the largest part of the reservoir.

"The fence won't stop a determined intruder," added Steven. "To be effective, any barrier must be augmented with security force personnel and other means of protection with intent to comply with the five Ds."

"What are the five Ds?" asked Susan.

"Preparation without security is meaningless," replied Brad. "The five Ds include deter, deny, detect, delay and defend."

"I would also add a sixth D," said Steven. "The sixth D is deceased if you don't keep these factors in mind when creating your perimeter security."

"In a nutshell, the five Ds of perimeter security can be summarized like this," said Brad, who directed everyone's attention to the blue-lined drawings on Sarge's Mercedes. "First, by defining the perimeter as a restricted area, we provide a physical and psychological deterrent to unauthorized entry while serving notice that entry is not freely permitted.

"Second, a properly constructed security fence will deny accidental entry to wayward hunters or adventure seekers looking to hike or camp on the peninsula.

"Third, our security personnel will be able to detect and apprehend intruders.

140

"Fourth, this detection element will enable us to delay anyone who is making their way to our compound, which will enable us to put into effect the last D."

"Defense," said Steven. "Anyone who intends to cause us harm will have to go through several layers of defensive measures, which will reduce their element of surprise."

"Finally, we are going to establish a series of choke points using the existing road system," said Brad. "If a substantial force does manage to break through our first lines of defense, we'll have something for them."

"Brad, this sounds very good on paper, but defending this place will take a battalion-sized security team," said Sarge.

J.J. stepped forward and put his hands on the shoulders of his military compatriots. "We've been working on this issue for some time. Donald is the money man, so this will require his, or at least our benefactor's, approval."

"How much?" asked Donald.

Brad, a student of military history, knew the cost of a standing army was substantial. The defense of Prescott Peninsula could take more than a hundred highly trained men working around the clock.

"Finding the soldiers necessary for the defense of Prescott Peninsula is just half the battle," said Brad. "First we have to recruit based upon ideology. After that, we must be convinced of their commitment. When the shit hits the fan, we can't have our security forces run for home. They have to become a part of the community."

"Let's address the issue of ideology first," said Sarge. "How do you approach potential recruits?"

"The three of us have spent our careers establishing friends and contacts in the military, and in the case of Steven, private contractor work," said J.J. "In the last three years we have stepped up our efforts to identify individuals who think like we do."

"For example?" asked Sarge.

"Let me start with a brief history lesson," said Brad. Donald admired Brad for his passion of studying war and military history. Although the tactics may have changed somewhat due to advanced technology, the principles of warfare and military science were the same.

"We all know the history of the original Loyal Nine because of our families' lineages," said Brad. "During the War for Independence, the colonists who actually fought on behalf of freedom amounted to no more than three percent of the population. They were the true patriots who were willing to lose their lives for the creation of our nation. They stood up against tyranny and chose freedom."

"As military personnel, we took an oath to support and defend the constitution," said Steven. "The oath is sacred and as such we have formed certain beliefs. As oathkeepers, we will not obey any orders that infringe upon the rights of freedom-loving Americans."

"After our service ended, we met hundreds of Americans who, like the colonists, did not have a military or law enforcement background," said J.J. "Yet they believed in the constitution and their rights to freedom and liberty. Many of them took the same oath and joined organizations identifying with the three percent."

"We've kept a black book of sorts," said Brad. "Our contacts extend throughout the military and law enforcement around the world. Like us, when we gave the oath of enlistment, we wrote a blank check made payable to the United States of America for an amount that may include our lives. The three percent swore a similar oath and we would stand shoulder to shoulder in the event tyranny or a hostile foreign nation threatens our country."

"In the event America takes a drastic turn for the worst—in the form of a catastrophic collapse event, will your contacts stand with us?" asked Sarge.

"Absolutely," replied Brad. "When the time comes, they will form a worldwide unit using the moniker the Mechanics in honor of the Loyal Nine and the colonists who fought insurgency battles as part of the Sons of Liberty. They will also be identified by the rebellious stripes flag, again symbolic of those brave colonists who risked their lives for our freedoms."

"So we'll have our own army?" asked Susan.

"In a sense, yes," replied Brad. "Should the country experience a catastrophic event, we will be able to gauge our government's intentions in the first several days and weeks. If the politicians are opportunistic—using the catastrophe to infringe upon the constitutional rights of Americans—then we will be able to mobilize quickly to protect ourselves and others."

"At some point, we knew a decision would have to be reached that sets our plan into motion," said Steven. "We think the time is now. The signs are all there. The very nature and existence of this project screams *wake up!*"

"What do you need from me?" asked Donald.

"We have to build this facility and protect its privacy," replied Brad. "I have identified a small cadre of two dozen soldiers from Fort Devens who will stand with us and help make this operation a reality. They will want assurances, which I can provide. They will need pay for themselves and their families."

"Done. I don't need to ask."

"Also, we will need equipment," added Steven. "This will include weaponry, tactical gear and security gear."

"Make a list and I'll get it for you," replied Donald. "What else?"

"That's it from the defense side," replied Brad.

"I think this operation needs a name," said Donald. "Something that doesn't scream *bug-out location.*"

"I've got it, DQ," said Steven. "Welcome to the Quabbin Reservoir, designed and constructed by DQ and Susie Q—the Triple Q Ranch."

CHAPTER 31

June 30, 2016
100 Beacon
Boston, Massachusetts

"Julia, what can I do to help?" asked Katie as she set her wineglass on the kitchen island.

"You're fine, Katie," replied Julia. "Just keep the boys drinking. Maybe we can loosen them up and take advantage of their bodies." They both laughed.

"Wait, isn't it supposed to be the other way around?"

"We're part of the new liberated women of America," replied Julia. "Pretty soon we'll dictate the terms of sexual interaction." Their laughter drew the attention of the guys.

"Hey, bro, I sniff a conspiracy brewing in the kitchen, along with something else incredible," said Steven as he hugged Katie around the waist and smelled her neck.

"Get off me, you beast!"

"You don't mean it," he replied.

"Listen up, you two, dinner first, then we will negotiate the terms of dessert," said Julia. "Hey, Sarge, what has you engrossed over there?"

"Same shit, different day. I was just watching the footage from a protest gone wild in Manhattan. Social unrest is happening all over."

"Sarge is right," added Steven. "My buddy Ray Bower is a hedge fund guy and was in the conference hall when the melee broke out."

"What happened?" asked Julia.

"It's like Sarge said, same shit, different day. Out of nowhere,

144

protestors crammed their way into the Waldorf ballroom, where a hedge fund conference was under way. They shouted the usual drivel about increasing the minimum wage and jail the bankers."

"I had the same experience during my trip to Nashville last week," said Sarge. "It didn't interrupt my presentation at the Opryland Hotel, but the protestors invaded the Garden Observatory, where several of us were having drinks that night. Supposedly they were brought in by rented school buses and entered the hotel by the hundreds. It was chaos."

"When does peaceful protest become outright harassment?" asked Katie.

"Interesting you bring that up, Katie," replied Sarge. "As the protestors bullied their way through the hotel guests, a young girl became frightened and fell down an escalator. She was injured and taken to a hospital. It did not, however, stop the protestors from disrupting the entire complex."

"What can be done?" asked Julia.

"Just shoot 'em!" exclaimed Steven. "I mean, enough is enough already."

"This may sound out of line, but I almost get the sense they want that to happen," said Sarge. "These protests are growing in intensity and frequency. The demonstrations are no longer confined to the top ten metro areas. Nashville is a typical Southern city in Tennessee, not exactly a hotbed of social outcry."

"I'm just saying, it's gonna blow at some point," added Steven.

"Here is what else I learned," continued Sarge. "This is especially true in the South, it appears. Normally quiet white suburbanites are becoming more active. The military's Jade Helm activities have expanded from the Southwest throughout the Southeast. State and local politicians are being extremely vocal about why the Jade Helm exercises are confined to their regions and not the Northeast or Midwest. The soccer moms are up in arms. Local Tea Party organizations are putting together counterdemonstrations when the Black Lives Matter crowd shows up. There was a significant physical altercation between protesting groups at the Perimeter Mall in Sandy

Springs, Georgia, an affluent white suburb of Atlanta. As the demonstrators are emboldened by their leaders and the lack of government intervention, they begin to disrupt the lives of Americans who ordinarily don't give a shit."

"It's gonna blow," said Steven dryly.

Katie poured Sarge another glass of wine. Julia looked at him and saw he was unwinding. His travel schedule was hectic and he was burdened by what he saw around the country. He also expressed his concern about getting the Triple Q Ranch operational. Collectively, the Loyal Nine felt the trouble coming at them like a freight train.

Sarge continued. "As I travel around the country promoting the book, the venues are filled with people chanting *Choose Freedom* and waving the Rebellious Flag. I know a book cover can be inspiring, but I am humbled at the response."

"But it's more than that, right, Sarge?" asked Julia. She gestured for everyone to take a seat at the dining table.

"It is. *Choose Freedom* has become a rallying cry. The Rebellious Flag is a symbol of America's desire to support the constitutional principles established by our Founding Fathers."

"Sarge has become a recognized expert on the concept of American and state sovereignty," said Julia. "But it also appears he is becoming a renowned spokesman for personal and economic freedom. Honey, you are becoming a leader."

"Put Sarge in charge! Sarge for President," hollered Steven, raising his glass to toast.

"Fuckin' forget it! I've got enough trouble." Sarge had enough on his plate, including a salad that Julia just served to her guests. He poured on the chipotle dressing.

"But I will say this. Like we discussed the other day, when the shit hits the fan, we will need allies—true patriots who will work with us to put this humpty dumpty of a country back together again. As I travel, I have established a network of folks who will help us when the time comes. They are oathkeepers, three percenters, NRA members, tea party supporters and average joes from all walks of life who believe in a better America."

"He sounds like a politician to me." Steven laughed, just before a cherry tomato bounced off his forehead.

PART THREE

CHAPTER 32

July 4, 2016
The Hack House
Binney Street
East Cambridge, Massachusetts

"How can you call yourself a hacker and not be a student of Greek mythology?" asked Walthaus.

"C'mon, man, I'm a computer geek, not a philosopher," replied Malvalaha. "When I grew up, the only thing I associated with Trojans was that pack of rubbers my father gave me when we had *the talk*."

"That's gross, Leo," chimed in Fakhri.

"What's gross about it? It's a guy thing."

"Seriously, the Trojan horse was a game changer," said Walthaus. "It put an end to a war that completely caught the enemy off guard."

Lau listened in amusement from his office as the Zero Day Gamers killed time waiting for tonight's fireworks. As always, their project and its implementation was thoroughly researched. Walthaus always took it a step further.

"The Greeks and the Trojans fought a bloody war for a decade. After one particular epic battle, the Greeks appeared to be in retreat. Achilles, the great Greek warrior, was dead. So was his contemporary, Hector, leader of the Trojans. This left the two sides evenly matched."

Lau entered the room to join the conversation.

Walthaus continued. "Eventually, the Greek ships were seen leaving Troy, although they hid just out of sight. Before they sailed, the Greeks delivered a giant wooden object made to look like a horse. The Trojans, believing victory to be in hand, thought the wooden horse was a parting gift from their enemy—a present to the gods."

"Odysseus designed it," added Lau. The three soldiers of the Zero Day Gamers turned their heads toward Lau in amazement. "He was not a warrior, but Odysseus was very clever. He proved wars could be won using brains instead of brawn."

"You know this stuff, boss?" asked Fakhri.

"Like Walthaus, I like to know the why—as well as the how. Continue, please."

"The Trojans celebrated their victory and contemplated burning the wooden horse as a tribute. However, their celebration lasted late into the night and the drunken party took its toll. While they slept, the Greeks climbed down from the belly of the Trojan horse, opened the city gates and ushered in the rest of the Greek army. They pillaged and burned Troy."

"The moral of the story is *beware of Greeks bearing gifts*," added Lau.

"If you put this into the context of what we do, it makes perfect sense," said Malvalaha. "Viruses and Trojan horses are both destructive programs that masquerade as a seemingly benign application. Both programs enter the network by *invitation*. Unlike viruses, after a Trojan horse enters the network, it does not replicate. It waits. It is triggered by an event or instructions or the passage of time."

"My freshmen commonly misuse the terminology," said Lau. "The most common mistake people make when discussing computer viruses is to refer to a worm or Trojan horse as a virus. The terms are used interchangeably, which is a mistake. Right, Walthaus?"

"Yes, sir. A virus attaches itself to a program or file, enabling it to spread from one computer to another, leaving infections as it travels. Almost all viruses are attached to an executable file, which means the virus may exist on your computer but it actually cannot cause damage until it is activated by a malicious program."

"I prefer worms," said Malvalaha.

"Of course you do," replied Fakhri. Lau watched the interaction between the two and wondered if they'd stepped up their relationship.

"No, really. Worms do all the work and have the ability to replicate themselves on the system. A worm can send out thousands of copies of itself. For example, a worm delivers a copy to everyone in someone's email address book. Then, the worm replicates and sends itself out to everyone listed in each of the receivers' address books, and the process continues down the line. It's exponential."

"Then there's Vegas," said Walthaus.

In February, the Zero Day Gamers executed an incredible hack of the Las Vegas power grid. Hired by the local unions, their task was to create a power outage on the famed Las Vegas Strip, giving the unions cover for a massive work stoppage. The stoppage enabled the unions to gain the upper hand in some contentious contract negotiations with the casinos. The implementation was complex, but flawless. Within the hacking community, the Gamers became legendary. To everyone else, they were quickly becoming public enemy number one.

"Vegas was epic," said Malvalaha. "The GIF-and-INF cocktail was the perfect blended threat. Very sophisticated. As far as I know, no one has publicly disclosed the details of how we pulled this off."

"Blended threats are considered to be the worst risk to security since the introduction of the virus," said Fakhri. "Rather than a predetermined attack on a specific EXE file, the blended threats will do multiple malicious acts like modifying EXE files, HTML files and registry keys at the same time."

"They wreak havoc, which brings us to tonight's fireworks," said Lau. "It's time to play."

Lau approached the wall adjoining his office and opened two curtains to reveal a large-screen television. Using the remote, he changed the monitor's input until it reached hdmi. He brought up the NASA live stream for the International Space Station on uStream.

"It's Independence Day, but only by coincidence," started Lau. "We chose this day because it is a new moon, which reduces the amount of ambient sunlight reflecting off the Moon. It creates ideal conditions for viewing from the ISS. We will get to watch the fireworks right here." Lau pointed to the monitor.

"The ISS will fly over the facility for five minutes this evening," said Walthaus. "They will have a bird's-eye view, as will we."

When Lau was contacted by Greenpeace via HackersList, he took a moment to consider the consequences of their request. When Greenpeace was founded, the group actively opposed nuclear power. Their position softened under the suggestion of Canadian ecologist Patrick Moore. Nuclear power was considered as the lesser of two evils, causing some leaders of the group to recognize nuclear energy as a viable alternative to fossil fuels and greenhouse gases. Moore was forced out, and the group was again on an antinuclear rampage. They were looking for an opportunity to raise awareness about the dangers of nuclear power, and they found one.

The Callaway Nuclear Power Plant is located near the state capital of Missouri, Jefferson City, and services almost the entire state. Greenpeace monitored the facility for over a year and successfully shut it down twice due to nonemergency leaks in a reaction control system. Now, Callaway faced a new issue. After a recent transformer fire, thousands of gallons of oil leaked into the surrounding monitoring wells. Residents called in the Environmental Protection Agency to investigate and Callaway promptly contained the spill and cleaned up the transformer fluid. Greenpeace demanded additional testing of the wells, and radioactive tritium was found.

Tests of the exterior monitoring wells were normally run on a quarterly basis. The Nuclear Regulatory Commission, at the insistence of the EPA, ordered Ameren Missouri, the utility that operates Callaway, to conduct the tests on a monthly basis.

The additional testing was insufficient to satisfy Greenpeace, so they contacted the Zero Day Gamers. Initially, they wanted Lau to create a breach, resulting in the permanent shutdown of the facility. After Lau discussed the project with the rest of the Gamers, they concluded a risk of nuclear meltdown along the lines of Fukushima was too great. Lau provided Greenpeace an alternative to raise awareness of the vulnerability without causing potential harm to innocent residents in Missouri or wherever the prevailing winds may take the fallout.

The importance of cyber security for nuclear plants had been addressed for years. The goal of Greenpeace was to successfully attack the facility, which would undermine the confidence in the ability of the utility to operate Callaway in a safe and secure manner.

Contemporary nuclear power plants relied extensively on a large and diverse array of computers for a host of tasks. Some computers might play a role in monitoring or controlling the operation of the reactor itself, as well as ancillary systems. Operating and technical support staff commonly used a computer network within the facility to perform these tasks.

Following the terrorist attacks of 9/11, the Nuclear Regulatory Commission mandated that all nuclear plants become closed networks in order to protect them from potential intrusions via the Internet. Callaway, which came online in 1984, complied with this requirement by 2005.

"Let's walk through the sequence," said Lau. Wearing his signature Boston Red Sox jersey and cap, Lau paced from one side of the loft to the other. He was nervous about this operation because a mistake in their calculations could kill tens of thousands of innocent people.

"Greenpeace provided lots of intelligence and we supplemented their information with our own research," said Fakhri. "The Callaway facility is operated by Ameren Missouri. As part of their normal operations, they contract with GZA GeoEnvironmental to conduct the tests upon the monitoring wells. The details of the NRC monitoring mandate, Commission Order CLI-16-15, were obtained from the NRC website." Fakhri held up several pages of the NRC order.

"The order required testing of the outside monitoring wells and internal temperatures, particulates, and water quality," said Malvalaha. "All of the testing must be performed between the first and fourth day of the month."

Fakhri continued. "GZA assigned the project to its subsidiary in Oak Brook, Illinois—Huff & Huff. The environmental engineers at Huff & Huff will act as our Trojan horse."

"Every utility which operates a nuclear power plant must submit a Cyber Security Plan to the NRC," said Malvalaha. "We found the detailed plan in pdf format on the NRC.gov website. It was submitted by AmerenUE for the Callaway facility four months ago. The plan prohibits the entry of flash drives, cell phones, etc. into certain parts of the facility. Because their network is closed to outside Internet connections, their primary concern was the introduction of a malicious program via an employee's handheld device."

"The argument for a closed network is that isolation of a utility's network from any external communication makes it secure," said Lau. "But we all know it is very difficult to *air gap* a system by keeping it electronically isolated. An air gap makes a system subject to physical access or electronic compromise."

An air gap was a network security measure employed within a computer network to physically isolate it from unsecured networks such as the Internet. Typical uses included government servers containing *high-side* classified information and life-critical systems such as nuclear power plants. The Gamers learned the Hoover Dam utilized air-gapping to insulate its internal servers from intrusions. One option to circumvent this protocol was to use cellphone-based malware to remotely access any data stored in the targeted system. The Ameren cybersecurity plan prohibited the use of cell phones in the Callaway facility.

The Gamers were provided with another option courtesy of the EPA.

"The security dynamic changed when the EPA insisted upon this extraordinary monitoring regiment," said Walthaus. "By requiring both external monitoring of the water quality as well as internal comparisons of particulates, the EPA inadvertently created an opportunity for us—an air gap."

"The EPA's good intentions have resulted in unintended consequences for the cyber security of the Callaway facility," added Fakhri.

The television screen flashed darkness—momentarily catching everyone's attention. In unison, the Gamers looked at their watches.

Too early.

"Must have been a solar flare." Lau laughed. "This program better hurry up before a CME beats us to the punch."

"A solar flare would be ironic," said Walthaus. "Anyway, this is our most sophisticated project to date because it involves all of the aspects of the blended threat we discussed earlier. Tonight, our weapon of choice is the Aurora vulnerability."

"Ironic indeed." Lau laughed. "How did we exploit the opportunity so graciously provided by the EPA?"

"Recently, Huff & Huff received an award from the American Council of Engineering Companies at a conference in Chicago," said Malvalaha. "We were there, sort of."

"One of Huff's biological engineers was asked to give a PowerPoint presentation on some type of environmental waste project," said Fakhri. "He used the Wi-Fi system at the McCormick Place convention center—the conference venue. We infected their network by burying a keylogger Trojan in a rootkit on his laptop the moment his presentation began."

"Very stealthy," said Lau.

"Yes. Once he returned to the company's office in Oak Brook, we monitored his keystroke activities and easily gained the information necessary to access the Huff & Huff servers," said Malvalaha.

"What was the next step?"

"We did not know for certain which of the Huff & Huff personnel would be conducting the Callaway testing, so Malvalaha created one of his beloved worms to infect all of the Huff computers with a Trojan carrying the Aurora code," replied Fakhri. "Every laptop in the company became our Trojan horse."

"When the inspector entered the facility numerous times this weekend, he connected to the Callaway internal network," said Walthaus. "Once he accessed the main servers to gather data, our Trojan was carried from servers to stations throughout the nuclear power plant. Aurora is waiting on the clock to hit 11:11 Central Daylight Time."

"Why 11:11?" asked Lau.

Walthaus sat up in his chair to note the location of the ISS on the NASA live feed. "From Missouri's perspective, the International Space Station will appear at twenty-three degrees on the north-northwest horizon and five minutes later it will disappear at ten degrees above the east horizon. The ISS will have maximum exposure over Callaway at 11:11 CDT."

"At 11:11, Aurora will be unleashed," added Fakhri.

Lau was very familiar with Aurora. The Aurora Project was a 2007 research effort led by the Idaho National Laboratory, demonstrating how easy it was to hack elements in the nation's critical infrastructure such as power and water systems. In 2015, in response to a Freedom of Information Act request about Operation Aurora, an unrelated cyber attack initiated by the Chinese, some government official inadvertently released more than eight hundred pages of detailed documents and schematics related to the Aurora Project.

The Aurora Project exposed a vulnerability common to many electrical generators, water pumps and nuclear power facilities wherein an attacker remotely opened and closed key circuit breakers, throwing the internal machinery of the facility out of sync with other timed functions within the utility.

Lau recalled a report on the release of the details of Aurora. The word used by the head of Homeland Security was *breathtaking*. The Aurora report included three pages of critical infrastructure locations that could bring the United States power grid to virtual collapse. The report revealed, for example, which Pacific Gas and Electric substations you could shut down to create a cascading collapse of the entire West Coast power grid.

"Perpetrating an Aurora attack is not easy," added Malvalaha. "Based upon our research of publicly available information, this will be the first. I suspect it will send shockwaves throughout the world."

"It will certainly please our client, who has paid handsomely," added Lau. "What happens when Aurora is activated?"

"After the June visit by the inspector, we analyzed the internal power system interconnections of Calloway," replied Walthaus. "The data downloaded onto the Huff & Huff servers for reporting purposes provided all the information we needed on load and impedance conditions, access alarms and their passwords."

"It's 11:09 local time," said Lau. "Let me start the recording."

"The Aurora malware is set to shut down the generators connected to the Calloway turbines shortly," said Walthaus. "When it does, most of Missouri will go dark, leaving a huge black void in the middle of the United States. In about ten minutes, the malware will release control of the system pending a reboot by Callaway's engineers."

"We also have developed a calling card for you, Professor," said Malvalaha. "A surprise."

"What did you do?"

"We created a hybrid of the Prism Software used by Revival Control Systems," replied Malvalaha. "Revival Control is the company that developed the software for the computer-generated Christmas light shows set to music."

"Okaaay," said Lau as his voice trailed off. *It's Christmas in July.*

"You'll see."

Lau heard Fakhri's watch alarm go off and immediately drew his attention to the television monitor. At night, the view of the United States is very telling of its population density. The lights illuminated the majority of the eastern half of the country and the extreme West Coast. The western half of the U.S. and Mexico was predominantly dark. As the clock struck 11:11 in Missouri, an irregular dark shape appeared on the screen. It gave the appearance of a black hole in a sea of lights. Lau watched in awe as the ISS made its way across the central United States.

Suddenly, after a minute of pitch blackness, the lights began to flicker in a slow, methodical pattern. The flashing pattern repeated itself until there was darkness again. The pattern seemed familiar to Lau, but he couldn't pinpoint it.

--.. . .-. --- / -.. .- -.-- / --. .- -- . .-. ...

"Do you see the pattern, Professor?"

"I do, it's repeating," he replied. "Tell me what it means."

"It's Morse code, sir," said Walthaus. "It reads *Zero Day Gamers*."

CHAPTER 33

July 9, 2016
100 Beacon
Boston, Massachusetts

"I'm sorry the Sox-Yankees game got rained out," said Sarge. "I am not sorry about the alternative festivities." Julia draped her leg over Sarge as the two lay in bed next to each other. Her nakedness felt good against him, as always.

"We were both soaking wet and the bed looked inviting." She laid her head on his chest.

Sarge rubbed his fingers through her still-wet hair and stared mindlessly at the start of *Justice with Judge Jeanine* on the Fox News Channel.

"They're playing a doubleheader tomorrow, but I think I'll pass," said Sarge.

"I'll play a doubleheader with you." Julia was still wound up and ready to play ball. Sarge paused the television and enjoyed Julia for a little while longer. After they both finished, she left to get them a glass of wine. He followed her silhouette as she walked away. *I am one lucky guy.*

Sarge stared at the screen for a moment. When Sarge first started following Jeanine Pirro's program, she annoyed him a little bit. Perhaps she was too brash and combative. He couldn't put his finger on it. Over time, she grew on him, especially for her raising awareness of the threats to our power grid.

Tonight her special guests included retired General Thomas McInerney, the founder of a consulting firm dealing with high-tech companies, and Frank J. Gaffney, founder of the Center for Security

161

Policy. Both of these men repeatedly sounded the alarm of the fragility of our power grid and its susceptibility to terrorist attack. These two men, along with former Speaker of the House Newt Gingrich, were instrumental in the formation of the EMP Commission, which brought before the public eye the threats we face to the grid.

Now, a new threat to America's critical infrastructure emerged in the form of cyber terror. The President made a major policy speech at the NATO summit in Warsaw, Poland, today. Julia returned with the wine.

"I see you forgot all about me," said Julia. She handed him his glass with a kiss on the cheek. He patted her lovingly on the rear.

"I'm busted. I traded you in for my pal Judge Jeanine."

"I know better. What did the President say in Warsaw today?"

"If you'll hold me, I'll let you watch."

"What a guy," she said. Sarge pushed play.

"This summit comes at a crucial time for the Alliance as the tectonic plates of Euro-Atlantic security have shifted both in the East and the South. We are already implementing the biggest reinforcement of our collective defenses since the end of the Cold War. While in Warsaw, the member states of NATO will chart the course for the Alliance's adaptation to the new security environment so that NATO remains ready to defend all Allies against any threat from any direction.

"We will build on our valuable work with partner nations to keep all of our neighborhoods stable. We will strengthen the bond between Europe and North America on which our Alliance is founded. Since joining in 1999, Poland has been a staunch ally of NATO and I thank them for hosting our meeting."

Sarge paused the television.

"He sounds like he's justifying a build-up of NATO forces in the region," said Sarge. "Did you notice the phrase *biggest reinforcement of our collective defenses?*"

"I did. I also caught the caveat *against any threat from any direction.* Katie tells me the White House is fed up with these cyber attacks. They tried to diminish them once as cyber *vandalism.* Cyber terror escalated to new levels Monday night when the hacker group Zero Day Gamers took over the computers of a nuclear power plant."

"Very brazen and arrogant," said Sarge. "They threw their abilities in our faces with the Morse code stunt."

"Katie tells me the President ordered an entire task force to hunt them down. She has been named to head it up."

"Good for her! She'll keep us posted, I'm sure." Sarge continued the show.

"In cyberspace, where the risk of getting caught is low and the rewards are potentially great, these hackers are driven by simple economic forces. Breaking into computer networks, whether public or private, generates a payday. I intend to up the consequences and penalties for this activity. The member nations of NATO will make bad actors pay a price that will far outweigh the benefit.

"Let me be clear. What might be recommended for one scenario is not necessarily recommended in another. But from this point forward, there are many options on the table, including the use of conventional military weapons.

"Today, I am urging my fellow NATO leaders to order a ramp-up of their cyber-defense capabilities. Make no mistake, a cyber attack against a NATO member state will be considered military aggression and could trigger a collective military response."

"Well, there you have it," said Sarge. "I've always asked the question *when does a cyber attack become an act of war?* The President just said it depends on the scenario."

"That's pretty nebulous."

"Well, it was a speech, but you always have to question the man's intentions. I don't trust him. When he talks tough militarily, I believe he has ulterior motives."

"His biggest problem is proof," said Julia. "These computer hackers are shrewd and easily cover their tracks. A particular cyber attack may have all the markings of the Chinese, but it may simply be initiated by a pimple-faced teenager in mommy's basement."

"This is a new era, Julia. For the first time in history, the correlation between the capital spent and the military power it produces is undermined. Cyber attacks are low-cost alternatives to physical attacks, providing lesser nation-states a coequal ability to bring a superpower to its knees."

"For what purpose?" she asked.

"Never underestimate the power of jealousy and envy to destroy what others have."

Never underestimate that.

CHAPTER 34

July 16, 2016
Triple Q Ranch, Prescott Peninsula
Quabbin Reservoir, Massachusetts

Steven and Brad walked the entire fence line in about an hour. As part of a military training exercise, Brad used 3rd Battalion's Logistical Support Regiment and their Caterpillar D5 bulldozers to clear a two-mile-long, thirty-foot-wide swath through the forest about a half mile south of Highway 202.

Brad suggested a company called Fiber Fence to Donald. After the Homeland Security boys paid their visit several months ago, Brad learned the Fort Devens perimeter fence was deemed inadequate to protect the base in the event of social unrest. The bid specifications for the project were released by the GAO, but Brad knew it would take years to come to fruition. After reviewing the specs, he researched the fiber-optic perimeter fencing systems.

A fiber-optic system could detect and locate intruders anywhere along a fence up to ten miles long. The two-mile span and limited availability of personnel was a concern for Brad. The opti-mag sensing system generated an alert to the guard shack when something caused a disturbance to the optical fiber or the trip devices, which were attached at varying heights.

As an added security measure, fiber-optic cameras were installed along the perimeter, which provided live feeds to both the guard shacks and to a control room located within the main facility. Donald designed a dedicated solar array for the perimeter security system and encased all critical electronics in hardened compartments for protection against any form of electromagnetic pulse.

"DQ gets things done," said Steven. "You know I bust his balls a lot, but I have a shit ton of respect for him. His dedication to preparedness and attention to detail will save all of our collective asses one day."

"I agree," said Brad. "Donald studied every aspect of the Triple Q before he started. He envisioned every contingency and tried to account for it. He once said to me, 'Every morning I wake up and ask myself, if the shit hit the fan while I was sleeping, what prep do I wish I had?' Then he gets it. He's applied the same commitment to benefit us."

The men left the entrance and drove along the western shore of Prescott Peninsula and admired the serenity of the woods. Closed to the public for almost ten years, the woods of Prescott Peninsula began to overtake the gravel roads bearing names like Rattlesnake Den and Sunk Brook. The west side of the Quabbin Reservoir hugged the shoreline but was only a thousand feet across.

"I'm comfortable with our security at the front of the peninsula," said Brad. "Securing the miles of shoreline will be a challenge. Too many patrol boats will attract attention from across the shore." The men waved to three of Brad's men who were on patrol. By design, they wore hiking gear but carried concealed sidearms. It was not time for uniforms and heavy firepower—*yet.*

"I've given this some thought and talked to my friend Drew about this," said Steven. "He's from Tennessee and fishes a lot. He recommended a company called Stroker Boats near Knoxville. We've acquired a dozen nondescript bass boats custom designed to suit our purposes. The Triple Q Ranch has its own navy."

"Well, Admiral Sargent, tell me more."

"These all look like typical bass boats, painted in various shades of camo. They have a large open bow, which will allow for gear storage, and the boats can easily handle four personnel. In place of the customary pedestal-mounted boat seats, we retrofitted the pedestal to allow for a Ma Deuce to be attached."

"Light 'em up! That .50 cal will make the fish jump out of the water and into the boat."

"I don't know about the fish, but I hope it doesn't come to lighting up unwanted visitors," replied Steven. "These boats will cruise at ninety miles per hour with only the driver, but easily hits seventy fully loaded. After they arrived, a buddy of mine retrofitted them with Armorcore bullet-resistant fiberglass panels. Together with the standard Kevlar braided hoses and hydraulic system used by Stroker, we have a pretty decent gunship that passes as your run-of-the-mill bass boat." Steven wheeled into the construction site.

"Good work, Steven," said Brad.

"There's our director of procurement now," said Steven.

Donald was walking with a set of plans, holding his hands up asking them to stop. Pointing to his left, a large Lull was approaching with a twenty-two-thousand-watt Generac attached to its forks. Donald waved Steven towards the newly constructed main building of the Triple Q Ranch complex. He approached the car.

"Gentlemen, this is a restricted construction area," quipped Donald. "Brad, do you have your combat helmet?"

"Of course I do."

"Lieutenant Commander Sargent, do you have your hard head with you today?" asked Donald.

Steven spilled out of the truck and gave chase. "Fuck you, DQ! I was just saying nice things about you, asshole!"

Susan emerged from inside the building as Donald ran past her. "Boys! Boys! Take it easy!"

"Mommy, Donny was mean to me."

"I'm sure you can handle it just fine, little Stevie," replied Susan, giving her man-child friend a hug. "Brad, how do you deal with this—*ten-year-old.*"

"I have a whole base full of them, Susan," replied Brad. "In fact, several should be roaming the woods today."

"They are. Like well-trained soldiers, they check in with me hourly to provide a sitrep," said Susan.

"Sitrep! Listen to you, Susie Q!" said Steven. "That is so sexy. If DQ wasn't my friend, I'd have to—"

Susan swatted him with a set of plans and interrupted his banter.

"Life is just one long pussy crawl for you, isn't it?" The entire group busted out in laughter at Susan's completely out of character use of the p-word. "Behave or I will put you in the stockade!"

"Wait. We have a stockade?" asked Brad.

"We do, fellows, wait 'til you see our progress," replied Donald.

The Triple Q Ranch was a construction marvel only made possible by the wealth of the Boston Brahmin and the organizational skills of Donald. Although the facility was closed to the public and secured from curious intruders, hikers and bored fishermen, it still had the outward appearance of a shelter for abused women and children. The property contained twelve freestanding bungalows, which housed six each and contained fully equipped kitchenettes. Each bungalow had its own solar array and water source in the form of a well.

The main structure had two primary components. Aboveground, Donald designed an Indiana-farm-style structure with a three-hundred-sixty-degree wraparound covered porch and a large cupola-enclosed widow's walk. The widow's walk provided an excellent observation post as the main building was built on the highest point of Prescott Peninsula.

"Welcome to 1PP," said Donald as the group ascended the stairs onto the porch. "One-P-P stands for one Prescott Peninsula. Each of the bungalows and the guard stations has a similar code name. Outwardly, the design looks like a typical clapboard-siding building with upper level dormers. But I assure you, the appearance of a nostalgic farmhouse ends there." The group entered what appeared to be a large living room and reception space.

"We've constructed the first and second levels on top of the original belowground bunker using concrete block poured with shredded rebar-infused concrete. Then the entirety of the perimeter is fortified with twenty-four-gauge steel panels. These ballistic-proof walls will easily stop a fifty-caliber-round and most mortar rounds. The fortified walls also enabled us to use steel I-beam construction for the roof and a fortified poured-concrete slab."

"It's a fortress," interjected Susan. "Yet it will function as a residence and headquarters after TEOTWAWKI."

"The five-thousand-square-foot first level contains an exercise room, laundry facilities, multiple bath rooms, storage and mechanical rooms," added Donald. Donald walked them to the rear of the building through an open fortified door. The door lent the appearance of two open bookcases. "These are the stockades."

The group filed in and walked through a hallway filled with several small rooms sealed with steel grate doors. Each space resembled a jail cell.

"Looks like a jail," said Steven. "Where are the stretching racks and thumbscrews?"

"You watch too much *Game of Thrones*," replied Susan. "One of the things we haven't talked about as a group is the disposition of intruders or marauders."

"Just shoot 'em," chimed in Steven.

"That's your response for everything," said Susan.

"It's efficient," said Steven. "Dead men don't talk."

"Susan is right. We will have to address this at some point," added Brad. "After the shit hits the fan, our perimeter security may take someone into custody. We can't let them go if they catch a glimpse of this. Donald made the right decision by building a way to house them while a decision is made. At some point, they will have to be disposed of."

Steven sat on one of the bunks. "They'll like it here. Do we have to feed them?"

"Of course!" replied Susan.

Steven got up and walked out of the stockade's hallway. "Then just shoot 'em."

"Jeez," mumbled Susan.

Donald continued the tour. "The entire building is equipped with vaults for firearms and ammunition. There are hidden compartments and sliding bookcases for precious metals, cash and other valuable preparedness assets."

"How do we get downstairs?" asked Steven.

"You tell me," replied Donald.

Steven walked through the day room, pulling on bookcases and stomping on the wooden floor, listening for a hollow sound. He was unsuccessful. "Is there an outside entrance?"

Donald gestured for the group to follow him. "There is, but its three hundred yards into the woods towards the docks where Egypt Creek dumps into the reservoir.

"This is the mechanical room. You'll see the two large air-handling units, which ostensibly are part of the air-supply ductwork."

Donald walked around the room and allowed the group to inspect the air handlers. "They're identical in every respect except for what's inside."

He opened the access panel to one of the units, which revealed another panel that he easily removed.

"Wow," exclaimed Brad. "This takes you to a spiral staircase below. Ingenious."

"I got the idea from a Batman movie."

"Of course you did," said Steven. "This is first class, DQ. You've thought of everything."

"Thanks."

"Has anything changed in the bunker?" asked Brad.

"It's complete except for outfitting it with electronics and gear," replied Susan. "I'll need your wish lists." Brad and Steven both fumbled through their pockets to provide a list of suggested equipment and weaponry.

"Before we installed the exterior walls for the new structure, we reinforced the bunker with a burster slab engineered to handle most ordnance," said Donald as the group exited the mechanical room. "The bunker is EMP proof and its entries are protected with military-grade CBRE equipment, including air filtration, blast doors and blast valves. In the event of a sophisticated attack on the facility, the occupants will be protected against chemical, biological, radiological, and explosive threats."

"Speaking of occupants, have you provided a tour to any of the Brahmin?" asked Steven.

"Not yet, although I do provide Mr. Morgan constant updates.

His response is always the same—*Ahh know yahh awn top of it, Mr. Quinn*," said Donald, using his best Thurston Howell III accent.

CHAPTER 35

July 28, 2016
Democratic National Convention
Philadelphia, Pennsylvania

The noise inside the Wells Fargo Arena was deafening with the excitement of twenty thousand plus rabid democrats. Abbie could not make out the words of fellow Massachusetts Senator Elizabeth Warren's speech placing Abbie's name into nomination for the vice presidential spot on the ticket with Hillary Clinton. Abbie knew the majority of the crowd wanted her senior senator from Massachusetts at the top of the democrat presidential ticket. She endured more than a few grumbles when she was formally announced as the VP choice because of her libertarian leanings and her choice to caucus with the Republicans. Abbie would have been surprised at her choice as well had she not known her father's political clout.

"Abigail," John Morgan interrupted her thoughts, "you will do fantastic tonight and I am very proud of you."

"Thank you, Father, I am a little nervous," she said.

"Do not let the crowd distract you. You have an excellent speech prepared and your personality will win them over. The nation is polarized as Americans have adopted this *us versus them* attitude. It's a no-win situation for most politicians, who view our society through the prism of racial, cultural and religious politics. You will transcend this divide and the independents will love you. As you know, independents win elections."

"I assumed that's why I'm here."

"Yes, Abigail. You are here because you deserve it and you will be instrumental in dragging this dinosaur of a political dynasty across the finish line. Your time will come to lead this great nation sooner than you think. First, you must capture the world's attention with your speech."

"No pressure, right?"

"There is always pressure, but you have been groomed for this moment. When you begin, many world leaders will view you as a woman and scoff. When you are finished, they will fear and respect you." Morgan, in a rare show of affection, gave his daughter a hug and a peck on the forehead. He whispered in her ear, "I'm proud of you Abigail."

After he exited the room, she was momentarily alone as she took in the spectacle via the production facilities of Comcast SportsNet Philadelphia. She was provided an advance copy of Warren's nomination speech, but she didn't have time to read it. It was probably edited several times by DNC staffers. Her own speech was heavily scrutinized and became the first of many battles she would have with the DNC. If her policy positions didn't comport with Hillary's, it was removed from the speech and she was admonished to refrain from discussing them on the stump. After the first edit, half of the speech was missing and Abbie became disgruntled. Debbie Wasserman Schultz, Chair of the Democratic National Committee, consoled Abbie and gave her advice.

Abbie recalled the conversation. *Pick a sensible metaphor and stick with it.* President Clinton used *bridge to the 21ˢᵗ century* twenty-six times in his acceptance speech. The President used *hope and change* too many times to count. Abbie would co-opt the title of Sarge's book—*Choose Freedom.*

The second piece of advice Debbie gave was to downplay her differences with the top of the ticket—*KISS, Keep It Simple and Secondary.* Abbie would focus on foreign policy issues on the minds of the American people. The country would be introduced to the phrase *World War C.*

She was reminded to not forget the new voters. Every presidential election cycle, millions of Americans became voter eligible either by achieving the age of eighteen or through recent citizenship. These voters were especially impressionable.

Lastly, she was exhorted to *negatively define your opponent without name-calling*. This was the most difficult aspect of her entire speech. Abbie was a libertarian, but her political ideology leaned more right than left, and everyone knew it. It would be difficult for her to provide red meat to the democratic base by railing against Republicans. *Those people were her friends.* Rand Paul, the GOP nominee, was one of her best friends in the Senate.

Abbie knew how to address the last two suggestions by creating a captivating speech in both style and substance. She would articulate a very populist message, appealing to the hopes and fears of the general population, especially the middle of the political spectrum. Despite her background, she would try to connect with the American people in order to bridge the gap of the two major parties.

Abbie did not realize how tense she had become until Drew Jackson entered the studio alone to provide her a two-minute warning.

"Madame Vice President *nominee-in-training*, or whatever I'm supposed to call you," said Drew. "It's almost time for you to knock 'em dead, so to speak."

"Okay."

"Here, let me rescue these." Drew took Abbie's crumpled notes from her tight-fisted hands, causing her to relax at his touch. He looked down into her face and smiled. "This will be a piece of cake. I've been watching this drivel for three days. They're all a bunch of phony politicians. You're real, Abbie, and everyone will know it when you finish your acceptance speech tonight."

Abbie didn't want Drew to stop holding her hand. She missed a man's touch. Tonight, many of the words she would speak were written by Sarge at her request. They would comfort her as they came across the teleprompter. But it would be this moment, Drew's touch that would give her strength to persevere.

"Where will you be?" she asked.

"Right behind you, as always." The convention hall erupted in applause as Senator Warren finished her nomination speech.

A DNC staffer opened the door and interrupted their moment. "Senator, we're ready for you."

Abbie smiled and laughed with Drew. *It was going to be all right.*

CHAPTER 36

July 28, 2016
Democratic National Conventions
Super Box #13, Wells Fargo Center
Philadelphia, Pennsylvania

"I made sure they had Glengoyne for you," said former President Clinton.

Morgan took a sip of the exquisite single malt whisky from Scotland. *I see his memory hasn't faded.* "Thank you, Bill. This is a big night for Abigail and your wife. A toast to great things." The men clinked glasses and finished their cocktails before settling into their seats. Senator Warren was just finishing her nomination speech and the two men grabbed a drink as they awaited Abigail's acceptance speech.

Morgan read the final draft of Abigail's speech several times before it was ready for her. He could almost recite it from memory. Asking Henry to help was his idea. He and Henry saw eye to eye on everything except his involvement with Abigail and his insistence that he be referred to as Sarge. *Sarge* was his father's nickname, given to him by Morgan when they were boys growing up together on Beacon Hill. He would always look at Henry as his dearly departed friend's son.

As Abigail spoke, Morgan's mind wandered to the conversation he had late last night with the President. He was furious with the DNC and the Clintons. The President provided assurances Abigail would not be the subject of his wrath, but the very public feud with the Clintons would escalate after he was slighted in his speaking role. Relegated to a second-day speech was outrageous in his mind. *I am a sitting two-term President*, he'd said repeatedly. Morgan got the sense the President was becoming unhinged as this last term neared its end.

Abigail appeared very confident on stage and was receiving exuberant rounds of applause. She completed the domestic policy portion of her speech and was now in the middle of her foreign policy presentation.

"What is the difference between cyber terror and killer terror? Nothing, my friends! We cannot stand idly by as China and Russia escalate their military activity around the world and use cyber warfare against us. The Russians claim the Arctic belongs to them. But the Chinese think our computer servers, intellectual property and user data belongs to them! Why? Because we don't do anything to stop them!

"I submit to you cyber warfare is the fourth dimension of conventional warfare alongside our military's land, air and sea capabilities. Cyberspace enables our enemies to attack us without declaring victory or leaving fingerprints. If China, Russia, Syria or ISIS was running around America strapping explosives to the desktop computers of our nation's businesses, governmental offices or critical infrastructure, the media and the American public would be screaming for retaliation.

"My fellow Americans, cyber attacks are every bit the existential threat as nuclear proliferation because every rogue state possesses this capability. A well-coordinated cyber attack would cost trillions of dollars to our economy and, more importantly, significant loss of life. It is a double-edged sword that favors the weak over the strong. It is a matter of time before our enemies use their cyber capabilities to move beyond identity theft or espionage. A devastating attack could cause damage to our power grid and bring our nation to its knees. Therefore, I submit to you we are in the midst of a twenty-first-century war—World War C. We need to come together as a nation and stand strong against our enemies!"

Morgan was enjoying the spectacle. Abigail was a superstar and the naysayers would come around. Bill Clinton leaned back and smiled. He mouthed one word, *wow*. This was a pretty good endorsement from one of the best orators in the modern era.

"I believe in an America where all individuals are in control of their own lives and no one is forced to sacrifice his or her values for the benefit of others. As a freedom-loving people, we should not be restrained from expressing or

communicating our beliefs in front of others. Further, our economic liberties should not be infringed upon as we all try to make a better life for ourselves. We should never be restrained from advancement."

Morgan knew Abigail was in her element now as she entered into her stump speech.

"Our country was founded upon principles we all hold true in our hearts today. The Constitution is our only protection against a heavy-handed government. If the Constitution is not followed and honored, then the power of the federal government goes unrestrained. Once the federal government gains a foothold, it is extremely difficult to reverse that trend. Freedom is the bedrock of our society. Freedom is what makes our great nation exceptional—and our freedoms are under attack, both here and abroad!

"I believe all of my fellow Americans should be free to live their life as they want to live it. It doesn't matter what the color of your skin is or who you want to marry. As Americans, you should have a choice free from governmental interference or the judgment of others. When given a choice, my fellow Americans, I urge you to Choose Freedom!"

Morgan looked around the arena and noticed everyone standing. The crowd was electrified and with every mention of the phrase *Choose Freedom*, the crowd amped it up and repeated the phrase until Abbie calmed them down. She had command of the crowd.

"Finally, and most importantly, our Founding Fathers would be appalled at the state of legislative affairs in Washington. I am a direct descendant of John Adams and John Quincy Adams, and I believe they would call upon our nation to achieve unity as Americans. In 1789, John Adams, the second president of the United States, predicted today's sad state of affairs in Washington." Abigail looked in his direction. Morgan was extremely proud of his daughter—and so would their Adams ancestors.

"He said, 'There is nothing which I dread so much as a division of the republic into two great parties, each arranged under its leader, and concerting measures in opposition to each other. This, in my humble apprehension, is to be dreaded as the greatest political evil under our Constitution.' Wise words spoken by President Adams over two hundred years ago are frighteningly accurate today.

"If we could set aside our political differences and simply talk to each other, we might realize our distinctions aren't as vast as we have been led to believe. I firmly

believe our divisiveness comes not from our disagreements about policy, but from our attempts to force those beliefs on those who don't agree. The pundits talk about the big tent—a coalition that accommodates people who have a wide range of beliefs. I submit to you, unless all of us find a way to live together under such a big tent, our country will continue to suffer.

"I stand with all of you in this fight. I hope to continue together in the task of repairing and revitalizing our great nation. So, with the support of my family, my colleagues and the lovely people of America, I proudly accept your nomination to become the next Vice President of the United States!"

Morgan watched as Abigail stood back from the microphone and waved to the crowd, who were on their feet, roaring with approval. The chant of *Abbie, Abbie, Abbie* intensified around her. Team Clinton was all smiles and seemed very pleased at *their* choice.

My daughter will make an excellent president someday—*soon.*

CHAPTER 37

July 29, 2016
The *Boston Herald* Editorial Board
Conference Room
Boston, Massachusetts

"So what's the good news?" Joe Sciacca asked a decidedly sleepy group of editors. After a moment, there was no answer, so Sciacca continued.

"Throughout my career, numerous individuals have approached me with the question—*why doesn't the media report any good news?* Have you guys noticed that?"

Julia watched a few attendees nod their heads.

Sciacca continued. "I can honestly say, for the first time in my career, there is very little good news to report."

"The Red Sox won both games of the doubleheader yesterday," replied a voice from the back of the room.

Julia squirmed in her chair a little bit as the butterflies flew in her abdomen. *So did I. She really loved Sarge.*

"There is that. Otherwise, let's take a look at some facts." Sciacca opened his laptop and produced a series of facts and figures and projected them on the wallboard.

"First category is world financial. That's you, Sandra. Go!"

Sandra Gottlieb began to read the list of figures. "Ratio of world debt to GDP is three hundred forty-eight percent, up from one hundred eighty-six percent the year before."

"This figure has doubled," interrupted Sciacca. "Continue."

"Puerto Rico, California and New York defaulted on their bond obligations," read Gottlieb.

"They requested a bailout," said Sciacca. "They didn't get one because the federal government can't afford it. California is, excuse me, *was* the sixth largest economy in the world. Now the state is bankrupt." He paused, so Gottlieb continued.

"The stock market is down to a little over ten thousand, off from its nearly eighteen-thousand-point high a year ago."

"Think about what this means to the capital structure of this nation. Corporations were not expanding and hiring when the market was on a roll. Now they've lost a third of their value and are downsizing across every industry. Please, Sandra, just one more."

"Unemployment is eighteen percent. The labor participation rate is forty-nine percent."

"That, my friends, is the lowest in history. Half of the American workforce can't find work or has given up completely. We are a welfare state. The unemployment rate number is completely bogus."

"What does this mean for the collective attitude of our nation, Rene?" Sciacca switched screens to provide a new list.

"In a word—malaise," replied Petit. "This reminds me of the famous speech by President Jimmy Carter in which he talked about the invisible threat America faced in the form of a crisis of confidence. America is going through the five stages of grief. Last year, the country denied the dire circumstances we faced. Perhaps many still believed in *hope and change*. Now, Americans are angry. They feel betrayed and let down by their leaders."

Sciacca held his hand up to interrupt. "Rene, you followed the racial tensions in Boston and around the country. Do you get the sense Americans are pointing fingers of blame at each other?"

"I do, Joe. Americans are engaging in class warfare as well as a race war. It just hasn't escalated to actual gunfights, yet."

"I've identified the next item on my societal unrest list as lawlessness," said Sciacca. "Doesn't any government agency want to enforce the law anymore?"

"I've talked extensively with local law enforcement about this," replied Petit. "Cops are afraid to act. Every time they make an arrest, dozens of people crowd around the scene with cameras, taunting them. They see their hands as being tied, and as a result violent crime and murder rates are soaring in the urban areas."

"Societal unrest is at an all-time high, wouldn't you all agree?" asked Sciacca. Julia joined the room in nodding affirmative. "Is this confined to urban areas?"

"Mostly," replied Petit. "Smaller metropolitan areas are starting to experience these phenomena as well. But let me add, the social unrest is not limited to members of a certain class and race. People who are not normally politically active have joined in the fracas."

"Good. This leads me to my third point—gun ownership," said Sciacca. "There are more guns per capita in the United States than any country in the world. A Japanese naval commander, Admiral Yamamoto, supposedly said at the start of World War II that the United States mainland could not be invaded because there would be a rifle behind every blade of grass."

Julia spoke up. "I know the quote, Joe, and some have questioned the attribution to the Japanese admiral. But it does not obfuscate the premise. There are reportedly three hundred million guns in America, and more being bought daily in primarily rural areas of the United States. Ammunition shelves in stores and online have been empty for many weeks."

"What caused the shortage?" asked Sciacca.

"Every time the federal government makes a statement that alludes to gun control or confiscation, sales skyrocket," replied Julia. "Recently the EPA administrator made a policy speech in which she advocated following California's new laws limiting the lead content of bullets because of the environmental hazards lead poses. The result was record sales of weapons and ammunition together with massive increases in production by American manufacturers. Sources tell me the EPA is putting these regulations on a fast track for implementation prior to the end of the President's term."

"Oh yes, thank you for reminding me about that," said Sciacca. "The dems bad blood spilled over in gushes as a result of the Clintons' snub of the President."

"It was the news story of the convention and completely

overshadowed Hillary's pick of our own Senator Morgan as her running mate," said Julia. "The President never publicly endorsed Mrs. Clinton's candidacy during the primary season, which infuriated her entire camp and many prominent democrats. He was clearly not welcome at the convention and was relegated to a second-night time slot for his speech."

"Is there any fallout?"

"The President still has supporters, some of which have been very vocal about the snub. There was a protest of sorts when several prominent members of the delegation walked out of the hall during former President Bill Clinton's introduction of his wife."

"Will the two sides come together?"

"I doubt it, and a bill introduced in both houses of Congress today will make matters worse," replied Julia.

"What's the purpose of the legislation?"

"Of course, the President still has plenty of supporters. Last year in Kenya, he told the African Union he felt he'd been a pretty good president. If he were allowed to run for a third term, he'd probably win."

"I remember that."

"It was possibly tongue-in-cheek, but the legislation to repeal the 22nd amendment introduced on the heels of the Clinton nomination suggests otherwise."

"Is that the Presidential term limits amendment?"

"Yes. Not only does the President think he could win a third term, it appears he desperately wants to try."

"He's delusional."

CHAPTER 38

July 30, 2016
The Hack House
Binney Street
East Cambridge, Massachusetts

Herm Walthaus was on top of his game. He'd met Wendy at a meeting of a social club at MIT—Improv-a-Do!—where students participate in impromptu computer and engineering challenges. They were paired together by random draw and instantly hit it off. As they worked on the project, they found a lot of things in common besides computing, namely weed and sex.

"C'mon, Herm, let's smoke another one," said Wendy. "I'm soooo chill—hashtag horny too." Wendy was half dressed and rubbing her breasts on Herm's shoulders as he studied the computer monitor.

"Okay, Wendy, but let's have some fun first."

"Yeah, I'm sooo ready!"

"No, we'll do that again in a moment. I want to mess with somebody." Wendy continued to rub on Herm and the distraction might soon pull him away from the task at hand—but teaching that pompous senator a lesson or two temporarily took priority.

Walthaus watched the vice presidential acceptance speech of Abbie a couple of days prior and inexplicably took her remarks on cyber war as a challenge. Foreign countries were receiving all of the praise for advancements in cyber intrusions. The accomplishments of the Zero Day Gamers were underappreciated.

"Who?"

"It's Senator Morgan's computer."

"Yeah, fuck with that do-gooder. What are you going to do?"

"Watch."

Wendy was now rubbing her hands down his chest and biting at his ears. His loins were feeling the urge. *Pot really makes me horny. Hurry up, big boy.*

The day after the DNC speech, Walthaus sent Abbie an email purporting to be a reporter requesting an interview for the UK *Telegraph*. He planted a miniscule one-pixel-by-one pixel image in the email. He *fingerprinted* her computer, which provided him the identity of her operating system, browser and security software she was using. When an email contains an image, despite its size, the receiver's email client has to contact the sender's email server in order to fetch the image. The exchange of data provided Walthaus the technical details of Abbie's computer.

Later that day, he sent another email, which appeared to be a LinkedIn request from another journalist at the UK *Telegraph*. A button was provided to confirm or deny the request. Abbie chose to deny the request because she didn't know the reporter. Walthaus designed the email so any form of interaction would result in further fingerprinting in addition to automatically triggering the download of a RAT—a remote access Trojan.

Walthaus now had complete administrative control of Abbie's laptop. At this point, he was able to see everything Abbie did on the computer. He was able to open up folders, operate the webcam and download her computer files. He was now ready to launch his attack.

Walthaus quickly moved icons around on the screen of Abbie's computer. He took a peek at the pictures folder—just for fun. He intended to install a version of keylogger, but Wendy was growing impatient.

Walthaus navigated to the settings icon and changed Abbie's desktop wallpaper. He uploaded an animated gif—a cartoonish donkey copulating with an elephant. *There, done.*

"I hope you enjoy that, Miss High and Mighty Senator." He spun his chair around, leaving the screen open. He grabbed Wendy by her ponytails as she straddled his lap.

"Now, missy, what's it gonna be—smoke or poke?"

CHAPTER 39

July 30, 2016
2723 N Street NW
Georgetown
Washington, D.C.

Abbie was enjoying a rare evening at home in Georgetown. By all accounts, including from right-leaning pundits, her acceptance speech Thursday night was a huge success. The last forty-eight hours had been a whirlwind of congratulatory phone calls, pressers, and meetings with campaign staffers. She kicked off her Alexander McQueen heels and poured herself a glass of wine.

She loved her home. Built in the early 1800s, her Federal-era townhome underwent a major renovation by Alaska Senator Lisa Murkowski in 2003 before she moved to northwest D.C. The size was much more than she needed, but her father insisted upon the prominent location.

Resisting the urge to change into some oversized sweatpants and a T-shirt, Abbie quickly settled on the sofa with her wine. Despite warnings from everyone not to look, Abbie instinctively had to look. She pulled her laptop out of the briefcase and propped her feet on the mahogany and glass coffee table.

Not too bad. The majority of the criticism of her being selected came from the far left. Abbie knew they would vote for the ticket anyway. *Where else would they go?* She set the laptop aside and went to the kitchen to pour another glass of wine. She also took a moment to change clothes.

As she walked back into the living room, she noticed her cursor moving on the screen. Her icons were being shuffled. She ran to grab her laptop, but then remembered the reports of former CBS reporter Sharyl Attkisson's computer hacking allegations. Despite a detailed report by an independent technical team substantiating the intrusion, the Department of Justice's inspector general would not substantiate the allegations of FBI or government personnel involvement. The whole affair had been covered up and expertly buried using the White House press machine. Knowing there was nothing of informational value on the laptop, Abbie decided to let it play out.

But she did call Katie immediately.

"Katie, I'm watching someone remotely access my laptop as we speak. They are opening folders, moving icons and now they have uploaded an image to my desktop screen. It's a donkey fucking an elephant!"

After the two shared some nervous laughter, Katie advised Abbie to leave her computer alone. Steven was in town for the weekend and they would both be over shortly. Reassured, Abbie hung up and let her secret service team know to expect visitors. She invited Drew inside.

Since her father had assigned Drew to her personal security detail two months ago, they became friends and he became her confidant. At this level of politics, Abbie knew trustworthiness and confidentiality were in short supply. She could always count on her friends within the Loyal Nine, but it was nice to have someone like Drew as a constant companion.

"Is everything all right, Senator?" asked Drew, still in earshot of the assigned secret service team. He and Abbie were well beyond such formalities.

"Please come in. I need to discuss something with you." Not just because of Steven's recommendation, but based upon her own observations, Abbie knew she could trust Drew Jackson with her intimate secrets—and her life. She closed the door behind him.

"Am I a vision of loveliness or what?"

Drew laughed at Abbie's self-deprecation. "You don't think I'd love to throw on a pair of shorts and a Vols T-shirt?"

Abbie immediately contemplated allowing Drew to keep some

clothes in a drawer. *Whoa, Nellie!* "Trust me, I know wearing a suit all day and night is grueling."

"Appearances are important. When we campaign down South, maybe I can loosen up on the collar."

"I'll insist upon it. Drew, I have a problem. I've called Steven and my friend Katie over to take a look. This has to be kept quiet, okay."

Drew immediately searched around the townhouse, looking for threats. Out of habit, he placed his hand on his sidearm. Abbie noticed his heightened awareness.

"No, nothing dangerous. My computer has been hacked."

"Shouldn't we call the FBI?"

"I don't know who is behind this, and I only trust Katie and her team to find out. This could be our government or a foreign nation. This could be political espionage from the GOP. Hell, it could have come from the Democrat side. Who knows?"

"I understand. Trust no one. Is there anything on there that's *embarrassing?*"

"Embarrassing? Like what?"

"You know. Embarrassing, like photos or videos."

"You mean sex tapes?"

Drew blushed. "No. Well, I was making sure…" Drew's voice trailed off.

Abbie would let him off the hook. Using her best *Gone with the Wind* Southern belle voice, she said, "Why, Mr. Jackson, how dare you impugn my character. I am a proper lady and would never consider videotaping my romp in the hay with my beau."

She teasingly led him by the arm to the sofa, where they stared at her laptop with the continuously moving gif of the copulating donkey and elephant.

"Does this do anything for you?" she asked.

"Reminds me of stump trainin'."

"What's stump training, Drew?"

"Really? You've never heard of stump trainin'?"

"No."

"Well, down on the farm, it's when a guy stands on a stump and backs a large farm animal up to him so he can…"

"STOP! I get the visual!"

"It's really common in some parts. Here's what they do…"

Abbie's intercom system announced the arrival of Katie and Steven while saving Abbie from the detailed explanation of stump training.

"Thank God," said Abbie. She stood and threw a pillow at Drew. "You, sir, are no gentleman, speaking to a proper lady in such a manner." Abbie adjusted her sweatpants as she met her guests at the door.

"Hi, guys."

"Abbie, are you okay?" asked Katie.

"Pretty nice digs, Abbie," said Steven.

"Thanks. Katie, I was doing fine until this brutish friend of Steven's forgot his manners."

Steven and Drew gave each other a bro hug. "Are you taking good care of the next Vice President of the United States?"

"I guess. Sometimes I wonder if I should rejoin your unit."

"Hey!" objected Abbie.

"Just kiddin'. Look at this, buddy." Drew pointed to the constantly moving image on the laptop.

"Nice," said Steven. "Shouldn't it be the other way around?"

"Abbie, has this been in your possession the whole time?" asked Katie.

"Yes."

"Even while in Philly?"

"Yes."

"You've probably been hacked from a remote source," said Katie. "We'll have to analyze it to determine if they left a passive digital footprint."

"What does that mean?" asked Abbie.

"A digital footprint is the data left behind by users of the Internet," explained Katie. "Active digital footprints are created when personal data is released deliberately by a user for the purpose of sharing information, like on Facebook or in chatrooms."

"What about passive?" asked Drew.

"A passive digital footprint is a little more complicated," Katie replied. "It is created when data is collected at the moment the owner downloads or uploads data. I will have my people take a look."

"Okay."

"Have you touched anything?"

"No. Katie, we have to keep this quiet. I want to find out who is behind this before they can cover it up."

"Tomorrow is Sunday. I'll call in my most trusted assistants. We'll get to the bottom of it, Abbie, I promise."

Abbie gave Katie a hug. Two days into her VP nomination and someone was rifling through her laptop. *This sucks.*

PART FOUR

CHAPTER 40

August 1, 2016
27 O Street SW
Washington, D.C.

It was 3:00 a.m. when Katie entered her rented townhome and found Steven asleep on the couch. He immediately woke up and gave her a hug. She felt his *morning wake-up call.*

"Either you were dreaming about me or watching porn when you fell asleep," she said, playfully pushing him away.

"I was dreaming about us—making a movie."

"Forget it! After what Abbie went through, you'll never film us having sex!"

"Okay, forget the filming part," Steven said as he reached to pull her back.

"Can I put my briefcase down first?"

"Sure, let me help you with that."

Katie squirmed out of his grasp. "Listen, horn dog, this is important. I've got something."

Steven, looking like a little boy who just had his G.I Joe taken away, let her go.

She walked through the open floor plan to the kitchen and grabbed a bottle of Evian. She'd been awake for nearly twenty-four hours. In just five hours, she was expected in the Situation Room for the daily briefing. She'd feel *and look* like death warmed over.

"I have to get a few hours' sleep before work, but let me tell you what I know. Come to bed and we'll talk." Katie led Steven to the bedroom, leaving a trail of shoes and various forms of apparel. Once in bed she kissed him and relayed her findings.

"I need to explain this to you and then I need you to set up a meeting as soon as possible with Mr. Morgan, okay?" she asked.

"Yes, but how bad is it?"

"I think I know the who, but I am unclear as to the why?" replied Katie. "You've read about the hacktivist group called the Zero Day Gamers. They took responsibility for the Callaway Nuclear Plant attack and the hijacking of the American Airlines flight back in May."

"Weren't they also suspected in the Vegas Casino deal when Sarge and Julia were in town?" asked Steven.

"Yes. They're ghosts. No agency has been able to pin down their location or their intentions. So far, their activity has been referred to by the President as cyber vandalism. But I have noticed their cyber attacks have escalated and become more sophisticated." Katie exhaled and relaxed as she was finally able to let her two worlds meet. Steven caressed her face and put her more at ease. She really liked him and was amazed at how caring and loving he could be considering his occupation—and boyish ways.

"Do they have something to do with Abbie's computer?" asked Steven.

"I think so, but this is what is confusing about the whole situation." Katie rolled over on her back and stared upward. After catching her breath, she continued.

"The Zero Day Gamers, as they call themselves, are very talented and, so far, remain stealth. The hack of Abbie's laptop used malware designed in such a way to avoid being flagged by any of the mainstream antivirus products. This particular RAT malware used numerous reverse connect-back mechanisms that provided remote access."

"Isn't that typical of what the Chinese use to steal financial data from someone's computer?"

"Yes, but this was different. The hacker used three different connect-back mechanisms built in to improve the likelihood of establishing the command and control channel necessary to access Abbie's computer. In addition, the malware was also *packed* to help avoid detection at rest."

"What does *packed* mean?"

"At some point, Abbie must have interacted with an email containing the remote access Trojan malware. In the process, she probably received an innocuous-looking message box which displayed an error or some type of prompt. This inserted the malware into her computer system while encrypting the data to avoid detection. Very sophisticated."

"Espionage?" asked Steven.

Katie sat up and propped herself against the headboard. She took another sip of Evian. She contemplated a glass of wine to relax but was too tired to get it. Katie continued.

"That was my first thought. The detail associated with this malware delivery screamed Chinese or Russian government spy agencies. Then I found the hacker's error."

"What was it?"

"The key to successfully hiding your identity when undertaking a hack is to make sure you pass through enough interim sites—proxy servers—to conceal your point of origin permanently."

"Makes sense."

"Hackers go through these extraordinary efforts, but this time a mistake was made. We were only successful because Abbie contacted us immediately and the hacker didn't cover his tracks."

"What did you find?"

"We searched Google and found the animated gif uploaded to Abbie's computer. It was created on a community weblog called MetaFilter by a user named ZDG. We analyzed the MetaFilter weblogs and found the IP address of ZDG. I immediately performed a back trace on this IP address and found it still connected to Abbie's computer. Apparently, the hacker failed to terminate his remote access program. Stupid mistake."

"The two computers were still talking to each other?"

"They were."

"Did you find a physical location for the IP address?"

"Yeah. Each IP source tool uses a different geolocation database and tries to find the Internet router that's closest to the target IP. The accuracy of the result depends on the database used and the number of known routers in the target IP area. I pinned it down to within a two-mile radius—in Cambridge."

"Our Cambridge or England?"

"The Cambridge in Boston, right in the heart of MIT."

"Fuck me."

Katie swatted him even though she knew it was Steven's favorite figure of speech.

"Then I had a hunch."

"What was it?"

"I went to two prominent hacker websites—hackers for hire and hackers list. I cross-referenced the IP address, Cambridge, MIT and ISP records for Internet service providers in the area with the metadata found on the hacker websites. I've isolated the IP user's physical address to the Lofts at Kendall Square on East Binney Street. Ironically, the building is located next to a white hacker group known as Hack/Reduce."

"Do you think they're related?"

"I hope not. They were founded by a friend of mine."

"So what's the next step?"

"I need to inform Mr. Morgan. He's wanted me to locate the Zero Day Gamers for months. I'll need you to set up the meeting right away, okay?"

"Yes, ma'am. Anything else, ma'am?"

"Well, I am still a little wound up. Please help me fall asleep, sir." She pulled his head toward her as she closed her eyes.

"With pleasure, ma'am."

CHAPTER 41

August 3, 2016
1st Battalion, 25th Marines HQ
Fort Devens, Massachusetts

"That was an excellent presentation, General Drier," said Brad as he offered the commander of the 4th Marine Division a seat in his office. "May I offer you something to drink? I have my own stash."

Major General Paul Drier was a highly decorated combat vet who received a silver star and a legion of merit for his service. His duty assignments, before being given command of the 4th Marines, included the Pentagon, where he acted as the commandant for Plans, Policies and Operations. P, P & O is instrumental in organizing the military training exercises known as Jade Helm.

"Thank you, Brad, I will. Further, please call me Paul. You and I have a lot to discuss beyond the formality of rank."

Brad handed him a glass of whiskey and settled in his chair. *This should be interesting.* "Cheers."

"Brad, I'll cut to the chase," started General Drier. "Jade Helm has been on the drawing board for some time and was intended to resemble past realistic military training exercises like Bold Alligator and Robin Sage. These two exercises were barely noticed in the media or by the public. Jade Helm is different." Drier took a sip of whiskey.

"Special Operations Command made a critical mistake last year by releasing the hypothetical map of the exercise, which identified Southern California, Utah, and Texas as hostile. These regions are typically considered politically conservative. The remainder of California, Colorado and Nevada—all leaning liberal—were identified as permissive. Doubling down on that map and increasing the exercise to include the Southeastern states has the conspiracy theorists stirred up, which is why P, P & O sent me on this dog and pony show around the country."

"I understand, sir," said Brad. "This year, when Special Operations Command tripled the military presence in both personnel and equipment, citizens grew concerned. On the surface, it appears our country is being conditioned for the appearance of the military in our streets. Social unrest in our major cities is being met with a military response, in addition to local law enforcement." The Jade Helm activities screamed martial law in Brad's mind.

"It started with the mishandling of the Ferguson, Missouri, riots two years ago," said General Drier. "Law enforcement was ordered to stand down and not intervene as the unrest escalated out of control. Finally, the National Guard was called in, giving the appearance of a military clamp down. The same thing happened in Baltimore."

Brad spent a considerable amount of time studying the government's reactions to civil unrest. "A few decades ago, the thought of martial law in America was absolutely unthinkable, but today the increased intensity of societal unrest is causing a number of citizens to embrace the idea of troops patrolling our cities. It makes them feel safe."

"Brad, there are some Executive Orders being signed in the coming days that should concern all of us. The President will use the EPA to limit the lead content in the manufacture of ammunition. He has instructed several agencies to purchase all available supplies of ammo for training purposes. He is also issuing regulations through the Bureau of Alcohol, Tobacco and Firearms to limit the magazine capacities of long rifles to ten and pistols to seven, effective immediately. All magazines in capacities larger than ten and seven are deemed unsafe under Department of Health and Human Services guidelines and subject to confiscation. Finally, he is announcing a mandatory gun registration law, which will be a condition of receiving any federal government benefits or contracts. Failure to register all of your weapons will result in criminal and civil penalties—including civil forfeiture."

"You mean they will confiscate your guns if you don't register?" asked Brad.

"Yes, and also the real estate where the weapons were located, under civil forfeiture," replied General Drier.

"Damn."

"It gets better. In the past, the National Guard acted as a military support tool to the governors in the event of natural disaster or extraordinary social unrest. As you know, this is happening with regularity. The President, relying on an opinion from the U.S. Attorney General, is declaring the Posse Comitatus Act as inapplicable in the event of foreign hostilities against the United States. He plans on using all branches of the military to restore order on the streets if a catastrophic event occurs."

The Posse Comitatus Act was a federal law limiting the power of the federal government in using the military as domestic law enforcement. The act specifically applied to the Army and Air Force, but the Navy adopted the provisions via regulations. Posse Comitatus did not apply to the National Guard or the Coast Guard. *That's why they send a team to Camp Edwards.*

"What type of catastrophic event?" asked Brad.

"It will be up to the President's discretion. I believe this is the first step towards the implementation of martial law if deemed necessary."

"General, our troops are not trained to operate under circumstances like martial law. In our policing role in the Middle East, the enemy was difficult to define, but at least their ethnicity was different. Soldiers are trained to be warriors, not peace officers. Putting full-time warriors into a civilian policing situation can result in serious collateral damage to American life and liberty."

Brad recalled a GAO report after 9/11 when the suspension of Posse Comitatus was suggested. According to the report, while on domestic military missions, combat units were unable to maintain proficiency because these missions provided less opportunity to practice the skills required for hostile combat. The GAO concluded domestic unrest should fall under the purview of the National Guard as directed by a state's governor. Disaster relief and responding to civil disturbances were core missions for the Guard, not active-duty combat soldiers.

"I agree, Brad. There are like-minded soldiers around our military who are staying in contact as this develops. Something is coming, we just don't know what it is."

Brad absorbed the words—something was coming. The Loyal Nine sensed this as well and were preparing accordingly.

"General, the globalists are racing toward World War III before people notice. I refuse to give up the freedoms of America to a group of New World Order architects and instigators behind the formation of a single, global state."

"Then you and I see eye to eye, Brad. Now, let's talk about how we can work together to save our country from its downfall."

CHAPTER 42

August 13, 2016
Grand Floridian Hotel
Walt Disney World
Orlando, Florida

Sarge walked through the lush gardens of Disney's Grand Floridian Resort, the site of this year's annual Cato Institute conference. In May, Morgan insisted Sarge form a think tank on the matter of America's sovereignty. As the research organization came to fruition, Sarge struck up a friendship with executive vice president of the CATO Institute, David Boaz. As a result, he was invited to be the keynote speaker by Boaz, the recognized voice of Libertarians nationwide. Cited often in Sarge's best-selling book, *Choose Freedom*, Boaz was very supportive of Sarge last year as he conducted his research.

Boaz invited Sarge to join him and several Libertarian party leaders for drinks and dinner at Narcoossee's, a spectacular waterfront pavilion overlooking the Seven Seas Lagoon fronting the Magic Kingdom. Sarge loved the Victorian feel of the Grand Floridian and it made him miss Julia. Six months ago, he gave a speech at the Republican governor's conference at the Hotel del Coronado in San Diego before their ill-fated trip to Las Vegas. Julia joined him on the trip and they had lived together since. It was one hundred days until the Presidential election and Sarge suspected he would see Julia only sparingly. Perhaps a vacation getaway would be in order.

Sarge spotted the group of seven seated at a large window-front table facing the lagoon. Boaz waved to get his attention. He recognized Governor Mike Pence of Indiana.

"Sarge! Pull up a seat and join us," said Boaz. "There are some folks I want you to meet."

"Hi, everybody," said Sarge. He immediately shook Governor Pence's hand. "Governor, we've made a habit of meeting in Victorian-style hotel bars. Imagine what the media would think?" When Sarge and Julia arrived at the Hotel Del in February, they immediately went to the lobby bar, where they struck up a conversation with several republican governors, including Mike Pence."

"Of course I remember, Sarge, we had a great conversation that afternoon, which I relayed to David," replied Governor Pence. Boaz confirmed Pence was instrumental in Sarge's invitation to speak at the Cato Institute conference.

"Folks, as you know if you paid attention during today's incredible keynote speech, Professor Henry Sargent, Sarge to his friends, is a professor at the prestigious Harvard Kennedy School of Government," said Boaz.

"Hi, Sarge," said Nicholas Sarwark, chairman of the Libertarian Party. "You teach in the den of the lions, my friend."

Sarge shook his hand and sat next to him. "Now that I'm tenured, I don't have to hide in the shadows." Sarge laughed. "I am clearly in the minority. But I am pleased to tell you, my students are less liberal than one might think—at least in my class." Sarge observed the ferryboat crossing the lagoon, transporting guests to see their beloved Mickey Mouse.

"Sarge, I would like you to meet Governor Sam Brownback of Kansas," said Boaz. "He's a big fan of your book."

"That's right," said Governor Brownback. "In fact, I have several questions about the concept of state sovereignty as it relates to the Keystone XL pipeline, but I won't bore the rest of you with my headache."

"We'll get together before I head back to Boston tomorrow night," said Sarge.

Sarge spent the next hour speaking about the interrelationship between sovereign nations and the global institutions transcending their boundaries. Without cooperation, the global economy would come to a halt.

"What would it take to reach a level of cordial cooperation across political boundaries in this country?" asked Boaz.

"These concepts apply within the United States at the state level as well," said Sarge. "As you all know, we have a republic form of government in which the power was intended to reside in the hands, or votes, if you will, of the people. In a republic, sovereignty rests with the people. In a democracy, the sovereignty is in the group. There has been a trend to mislabel our form of government as a pure democracy in which fifty-one percent beats forty-nine percent, leaving the minority with no rights. This contravenes Article Four of the Constitution.

"There are those who wish to exert their political beliefs across the entire nation rather than limiting their influence to the particular state in which they reside," continued Sarge. "A person who resides in California, for example, votes there. His right to vote is limited to the State of California. However, that person may vehemently disagree with a law passed in Indiana. While this person may have the absolute right to express his opinion anywhere in America, he does not have the right to vote in Indiana for elected officials who might agree with him on that particular issue. Only Hoosiers in Indiana, a sovereign state, are granted the privilege to challenge representatives standing for, or against, a particular set of laws."

"Technically, under the Constitution, that is all very true," said Governor Pence. "But we all know that politics is an intricate and convoluted maze we as elected officials must navigate."

"A very good point, Governor, so let's bring the concept close to home, shall we?" said Sarge. He appreciated the intensity with which Governor Pence engaged in the conversation. He decided to use an example particular to his state.

"Last year, you joined twenty other states and signed into law Indiana's version of the Religious Freedom Act," said Sarge.

Governor Pence tensed but was deeply engrossed, nodding acknowledgement.

"This ignited a firestorm, especially from the left, who decried the legislation as bigoted. Certainly, the citizens of Indiana could vote against you in your reelection bid this fall, but a large majority of those against the legislation may be from another state, like California."

"Indiana was inundated with out-of-state special interests who flooded the capital," said Governor Pence. "It wasn't quite as bad as what Governor Walker experienced in Wisconsin with the unions, but close."

"Precisely. Californians, for example, who cannot vote against you, may try other methods, including putting pressure on businesses in Indiana and encouraging them to leave the state," said Sarge. "Sound familiar?"

"Oh yes," said Governor Pence. "I was blasted from all directions. All I wanted to do was preserve the rights of any business owner to act in a way that comports with their religious beliefs. The law immediately became labeled as antigay, which was totally ludicrous."

"This brings us to the quandary faced by any government," said Sarge. "Do you stand by your laws as a sovereign state, or do you capitulate to the political pressures exerted by outside forces, including businesses and organizations who have threatened to leave you? If you are principled in your beliefs and not ashamed of the law you enacted, then I believe you will choose freedom—sovereignty— as opposed to capitulation."

Sarge was commanding the attention of the leaders of America's Libertarian Party because they wanted to listen to what he had to say, not because he was a speaker on their agenda. By the end of the evening, Sarge was a part of their inner circle. By the end of the conference, the libertarian faithful were asking why Henry Winthrop Sargent IV wasn't their 2016 Presidential nominee.

CHAPTER 43

August 14, 2016
73 Tremont
Boston, Massachusetts

For almost four hundred years, Boston Common belonged to the people. Originally part of the farm of clergyman William Blackstone, it was sold to the City of Boston for today's equivalent of forty-seven dollars. Once rolling scrubland with three ponds, it is now the vibrant hub of activity in the most historic city in the United States. *At least it was.*

Morgan surveyed the Common from the gold-leaf-domed Statehouse towards his left and Brewer Fountain. The fountain, a replica of the original featured at the 1855 Paris World Fair, was a gift from nineteenth-century philanthropist Gardner Brewer. Brewer advanced the industrial revolution throughout the United States and was known for his charitable giving for the benefit of the public. Brewer was also an advocate of Protectionism—the policy of government intervention in international trade to protect the business of their country. In the short term, protectionist policies might protect U.S. companies from foreign competitors. It also temporarily created jobs. But it was a matter of time before foreign nations retaliated by erecting their own protectionist policies.

The wealth of the Boston Brahmin was built on a global marketplace. Their political power was derived from the careful placement of assets into positions of power in foreign governments and industry. When the President was first elected in 2008, he began to espouse protectionist policies as a form of payback to his union supporters. Morgan shut that down—*immediately*. He worked very hard to orchestrate the adoption of the North American Free Trade Agreement. It took three presidents and millions of dollars before NAFTA and a comparable European Union treaty were signed in 1993. Last year's Trans-Pacific Partnership laid the groundwork for a rapid expansion of the Boston Brahmin's military-based industries across the globe.

Protectionist policies are bad for our business.

Yet, Hillary Clinton had openly defied Morgan's directives and adopted the protectionist rhetoric first espoused by Donald Trump during the GOP primary process. In fact, the moment the check cleared following the DNC convention, Hillary adopted policy positions contrary to their agreement. Suddenly, the campaign staff became unavailable to him and Bill wasn't returning his phone calls. Her political operatives repeatedly impugned Abigail as the running mate choice. Above all, the ticket's post-convention bounce in the polls had evaporated and Hillary was sinking under the weight of previously undisclosed scandals.

Morgan felt his blood pressure rise. Against his doctor's advice, he poured himself a Glengoyne to calm his nerves. His mind snapped back to attention as he awaited the arrival of William Holmes, his former law partner at Morgan-Holmes. He noticed how devoid Boston Common was of activity—except for the homeless pushing shopping carts from one previously pillaged trash bin to another. There were no families enjoying the beautiful day with a picnic or on bicycles. The scene was almost apocalyptic.

Where are the good people? How had our great nation descended into an abyss filled with degenerates and parasites? Our government had created a dependency class that now constituted the majority of Americans. The takers outnumbered the makers, and it was unendurable. America would collapse under the weight of those with their hands out.

As he took another sip of scotch, his thoughts were interrupted by the intercom. "Sir, Mr. Holmes is here to see you."

Morgan pressed the button and replied, "Show him in, please, Malcolm." Morgan picked up a folder and thumbed through the pages. He had outlined nineteen Executive Orders and Policy Directives. Executive Orders were a matter of public record and, to be legal, must be published in the Federal Register. Policy Directives, like Clinton's infamous Secretary of State emails, were considered *born classified*—classified from the moment of its creation. Therefore, they were typically maintained in the files of National Security Council staff. They both had the same legal effect. In the 1990s, Morgan and Bill Clinton made use of directives liberally.

"Good afternoon, John," said Holmes as Lowe showed him in. "This is a rare meeting on a Sunday. I hope all is well." The men shook hands and Morgan offered his old friend a seat.

"Malcolm, we won't be long. Have our guests arrived?"

"Almost everyone, sir. I've made them comfortable in the conference room as requested. Sir, Mr. Lowell and Mr. Cabot insisted upon opening the bar," said Lowe. "I hope that isn't a problem."

"Not a problem at all, Malcolm. Besides, who's going to stop them from an afternoon cocktail? The National Guard has their hands full nowadays." Morgan reached for the Glengoyne to pour his friend a drink as Lowe quietly exited the room.

"Thank you, John," said Holmes. "How can I help?"

"William, we have a President who needs some direction."

"Don't they all?" The men laughed and toasted the statement. Every President had a hot-button issue, an agenda. Morgan supported them when the policy didn't conflict with his agenda. Over the last forty years, there had been numerous times when a President needed to be reminded of certain *matters of importance* to the Boston Brahmin.

"The President has lost his way somewhat," said Morgan. He slid the file folder full of notes across the table to Holmes. As Holmes thumbed through the paperwork, Morgan continued. "These policy directives will strengthen the President's power in times of military conflict and will lay the groundwork for our best interests to be implemented. Our relationship is built on a codependency of interests. These policy directives will protect our interests while assisting the President in his goals."

"I see that," said Holmes.

"The President will be staying at my vacation home in Martha's Vineyard for a few weeks. We have a meeting on the twenty-third. I have a series of Executive Orders and Policy Directives for you to draft. The President will sign and implement them immediately."

"This is serious stuff, John—all dealing with the same issue. Is something looming on the horizon?"

"Perhaps, William. When I know more, you will be contacted. Get these back to me by Wednesday for my review. I will deliver them to the President." Morgan finished his drink and pushed up out of his chair, which was a signal for Holmes to do the same.

"I will take care of this immediately, John. You look troubled, old friend. If there is anything else I can do to help, let me know."

"Thank you, William." He patted Holmes on the back as he escorted him towards the front of the office where Lowe was waiting.

"Sir, everyone is here."

"Thank you, Malcolm." Turning to Holmes, he said, "Handle this personally, William, understood?"

"Of course," replied Holmes as he left.

"Malcolm, no interruptions, please," said Morgan.

"Yes, sir."

Morgan, ever-present in a traditional three-piece suit, steadied himself with a deep breath and approached the conference room. *It's for the greater good.*

"Good afternoon, my friends, and thank you for coming in on short notice."

"You've interrupted my golf game today, John," said Samuel Bradlee, a former Secretary of Defense who hadn't broken a hundred on the links in fifteen years.

"So what, Samuel?" interjected Henry Endicott. The two former military men were always sparring, especially during the week of the Army-Navy football game. "Golf is just a good walk spoiled by stress and vulgarities." The men chuckled at the comeback.

"Gentlemen, I need everyone to get settled, as we have serious business to discuss," interjected Morgan. He looked into the faces of the Boston Brahmin. They relied upon him in these matters and he could feel the weight on his shoulders. The culmination of events over the next few weeks would result in a more powerful America. The dependant class would be eliminated. His friends would become wealthier and politically powerful. More importantly, the downward spiral this country was taking would stop.

He hated duping his friends, but it was necessary—for the greater good.

"I'll get right to the point. As we discussed in May, the social and economic direction of this country is unsustainable. I have received actionable intelligence from my sources in Washington. The day of reckoning is upon us. A reset is imminent." Morgan sat back in his chair and allowed the significance of his statement to resonate in the room.

"John, what the hell are you talking about? Are we going to war?" asked Lawrence Lowell.

"I don't know, Lawrence. I will be meeting with the President in a week or so to discuss it." *Of course I know, sorry to deceive you, my friend.* Morgan was committed to the deception now. He continued.

"Gentlemen, here is what I know. The intelligence community has determined that our enemies are lining up against us. Russia, China and now ISIS have formed an alliance of sorts to bring our country to its knees."

"How?" asked Walter Cabot from across the table. "We have the strongest, most sophisticated military on the planet. They wouldn't risk a blood-soaked war."

"I would add *why*," said Lowell. "Why in God's name would these countries attack us?"

This was Morgan's opportunity to identify an enemy. "We all know the Russians and Chinese have been moving in this direction—economically and militarily. This President is weak and our enemies recognize this. They have five months before a new Commander-in-Chief is sworn in. I believe they will act now."

"Do they think Hillary will be a tougher President?" asked Bradlee. "She *loathes* the military as much as her husband did." Several of the Brahmin nodded their heads in agreement.

"It is hard for me to question their motives, especially in this unholy alliance they have established with the heathen ISIS group," replied Morgan. "I do know we will be prepared for the events and their aftermath."

"Our country is in shambles," said Cabot. "America has never faced so many internal problems. The economic situation for average Americans is dire. Social unrest is out of control. The nation is dominated by the weak, poor and unproductive. There is no unity."

"I agree with Walter," said Endicott. "We've discussed this ad nauseam. Sadly, our country is in need of a reset. Our politicians don't have the balls to make the tough choices to set us on a proper course. Perhaps our enemies will force our hand."

"I agree with Henry," said Bradlee. "Sometimes a cataclysmic conflict is necessary to change the direction of a wayward nation. Except for Vietnam, this nation has always taken a turn for the better following a war."

"Wars certainly benefit all of us financially," added Lowell. Morgan knew the Boston Brahmin shared a commonality of purpose—wealth and power. Regardless of the methods employed, the end result was tantamount.

Morgan continued. "After every shock to America, whether by war or economic calamity, our connections within the government grow stronger and our ability to expand wealth into public-sector assets grows. I am not just talking about the military and industrial advancements. I am referring also to the acquisition of previously owned government assets like bridges, buildings and land."

"Quabbin Reservoir," said Cabot.

"Exactly," replied Morgan. "The acquisition of Quabbin Reservoir and Prescott Peninsula was the result of political maneuvering, but the divestiture was deemed necessary due to government overspending and budget deficits. The timing of the Quabbin matter has proven fortuitous." Morgan hoped his friends would enjoy a short stay at their new home away from home. Surely they could handle a week or two of *roughing it*.

Morgan leaned forward and looked each of the Boston Brahmin

in the eye. "Gentlemen, I believe we have a short time to get our personal and business affairs in order. In the next two weeks, without raising any alarms that might attract public scrutiny, have your families get ready for a period of unrest and instruct your businesses to prepare for a rough ride."

"How bad will it get? Do you seriously think our enemies plan to invade the United States?" asked Lowell.

Morgan had raised a sufficient level of concern in all of his associates without causing panic. He needed to keep them on alert. Morgan drove home his point. "It's coming. We won't know from where or from whom, but we'll certainly know when."

"God help us," muttered more than one of the Boston Brahmin.

Morgan allowed his fellow Boston Brahmin to reach the conclusion he sought—*America needs a cleanse, a purge, a reset.*

They just didn't need to know who was sweeping the broom or pushing the button.

CHAPTER 44

August 15, 2016
The *Boston Herald* Editorial Conference Room
Boston, Massachusetts

"Julia, how does Senator Morgan's people feel about the campaign so far?" asked Sciacca. Julia shifted in her chair as she addressed her chief editor. The morning meetings of the editorial board now stretched for two hours. On any given day, a single major news story might be the topic du jour, but America was experiencing signs of collapse on many levels—complicated by a Presidential campaign deep in the gutter. Of all the candidates, Abbie had the least baggage although she had a major skeleton in her closet—John Adams Morgan. *If the media only knew the reach of his many tentacles.*

"Joe, Senator Morgan's campaign people are thrilled that the mudslinging hasn't tarnished her reputation. She has the highest favorability ratings of any candidate running."

Sciacca sat in his chair and propped his feet on the table. "What are they saying about the slipping poll numbers?"

"They are puzzled," replied Julia. "The post-convention bounce enjoyed in past elections quickly evaporated. Some Democrat faithful are blaming the choice of Senator Morgan. Pundits cite her lack of liberal bona fides and question her loyalty to Mrs. Clinton's vision for America."

"Some of that is true, is it not?"

"It is, Joe, but on the Republican side, Senator Paul has plenty of reason to demand a departure from the political status quo. He has effectively co-opted the President's campaign mantra from eight years ago—*change.* The decline in the democrat ticket is more from a rise in the republican ticket's popularity than it is from the choice of Senator Morgan. Her popularity proves it."

Sciacca brought his feet down with a clap on the floor and immediately jumped up to the whiteboard. He scribbled *Economy* on the board. "Her husband once famously said—*it's the economy, stupid.* The White House does an excellent job of manipulating numbers to protect this President, but both Wall Street and Main Street know better." He drew an arrow pointing downward.

"As Sandra can attest, all world economic indicators are headed south. Ordinarily, the bond market will increase its value to the detriment of the stock market. One nation's currency devaluation will increase another nation's. These things tend to have an inverse effect. Over this summer, everything of value has decreased substantially while the price of consumer goods and precious metals has skyrocketed. The stability of the world's economy is untenable at best."

Julia interrupted. "This is a major issue in the campaign and the GOP ticket has successfully driven the narrative. With the President nearly out of office and losing support of his own party, they have laid blame at his feet but hung his legacy around Mrs. Clinton's neck."

Sciacca addressed Sandra Gottlieb. "What is all of this telling you, Sandra?"

"Joe, the decline of the global economy is unprecedented," replied Gottlieb. "In 1929, the United States economy fell into a deep recession six months prior to the infamous October stock market crash. The effects of the U.S. recession were being felt in Europe prior to the crash. After World War I, the two economies became increasingly dependent upon each other. We became the primary financier and creditor in postwar Europe. When our economy collapsed after October 1929, Europe and the rest of the global economy followed suit."

Sciacca leaned against his chair with both hands. "The economies of the world are even more dependent on America's consuming ways today, are they not?"

"They are, Joe, and the financial collapse of '08 proved that. Economic collapses happen gradually. I believe we are witnessing the beginning of a major worldwide calamity. Unfortunately, all this fragile economic climate needs is a precipitating event to send it over the cliff." The room remained silent and Julia looked at the faces of her peers. *They know something is coming.*

Sciacca walked back to the whiteboard and wrote the words *societal collapse.* "Speaking of a gradual collapse, is there any doubt our society is disintegrating before our eyes? I'm not speaking rhetorically either. Julia?"

"There is a general destabilization across America," replied Julia. "The anger has been building for some time but has accelerated in the last six months. Patience has worn thin and adults are responding like petulant children to adverse events affecting them."

"What do you mean?"

"Here is an example from last Friday," replied Julia. She shifted through her notes. "As you know, I was interviewing all four nominees over the weekend while traveling with the campaigns across Ohio. On Friday, the Ohio Treasurer halted its EBT payments system due to a cyber attack. Hackers penetrated state servers on the QUEST network that administers the majority of states' online electronic benefits to recipients. QUEST notified the affected states of the data breach, which included Alabama, Louisiana and Ohio. Alabama and Louisiana were back online within hours, causing only minor inconveniences. Ohio was a different story, and I watched the aftermath first hand."

"What happened?"

"I was traveling with Senator Morgan's entourage to a morning rally at Case Western University in downtown Cleveland when the state announced a glitch in the system would cause the EBT payment system to shut down for the day. Within hours, the streets were filled with protestors. They stormed the Ohio Department of Job and Family Services and ransacked the building, injuring four staff members. East Cleveland and Shaker Heights had several out-of-control fires. By nightfall, Governor Kasich was calling in the

National Guard."

Sciacca underlined societal collapse on the whiteboard several times. "This sounds like the riots we experienced following the Boston Marathon this spring. These outbursts have grown in intensity and frequency."

"You're right, Joe, the thin veneer of civilization is beginning to crack," said Julia. "The EBT situation in Ohio was a temporary inconvenience to the state. One can only imagine the impact a major catastrophe would have under the present mindset of Americans."

Sciacca wrote *Cyber Attack* on the whiteboard and circled it several times. He poked it with his knuckle. "This has become daily news and no country or entity is immune from it. In my opinion, we are in the middle of a world war—a *cyber world war*."

"And everyone is in the act now," added Julia. "Reports out of the Pentagon indicate ISIS now poses a direct threat to America in the form of its rapidly developing cyber warfare capabilities. Its model is different from that employed by other terrorist groups, the Russians or Chinese. Through their effective use of social media, ISIS has developed a cyber army within the United States capable of using cyber attacks to shut down America's critical infrastructure, including the power grid."

"How concerned is the Pentagon about their capabilities?" asked Sciacca as he sat back into his chair.

"Intelligence sources tell me they are trying to track the movement of several key individuals who studied computer science in top British and European universities," replied Julia. "Do you remember Jihadi John, the British national responsible for several high-profile beheadings a few years ago?"

"Yes," replied Sciacca.

"It wasn't widely reported in the American media, but Jihadi John had an advanced computer science degree. The Pentagon's primary concern is the ability of ISIS to use social media to marshal attacks from within the U.S. by these talented sympathizers who have created a diffuse and unconnected network that is virtually untraceable."

Julia knew the threat of cyber attacks was growing exponentially in America. This was the subject of many late night conversations with Sarge. Recently an ISIS recruitment document was obtained by cyber-intelligence agencies announcing a Cyber Caliphate to be used against the United States—*The Great Satan*. This had added a terrorist threat our counterterrorism approach was not designed to guard against.

Julia continued. "Their use of the Internet has been described as unprecedented for a terrorist group. The ISIS Cyber Caliphate has taken credit for several high-profile hacks including the email accounts of the British ambassador, the shutting down of a French television network, and the recent shutdown of Sacramento's smart grid." Julia caught her breath before dropping the next bombshell.

"My sources tell me the Pentagon has identified a credible threat by ISIS against most of the United States power grid. They want to put us in the dark. They want to provoke the end of the world."

CHAPTER 45

August 15, 2016
73 Tremont
Boston, Massachusetts

When Katie was instructed to bring information on the Zero Day Gamers directly to Morgan back in the spring, she assumed he had something in mind. During their brief telephone conversation almost two weeks ago, he was very excited to hear about her discovery. Then nothing, until yesterday when he summoned her along with Steven to his office for an urgent meeting.

"Please come with me," Lowe announced as he emerged from Morgan's office. Katie and Steven dutifully followed. Steven grabbed her ass, earning him a slap on the hand.

She whispered, "Don't fuck around in here. He is very intense."

"Yeah, yeah," replied her man-child. Over the summer, Steven had changed with her. He spent every available weekend in Washington with her and sent her text messages constantly. Whatever caused him to become more attentive worked for her. She too was ready to become exclusive. Her days of *Fifty Shades of Katie*, as Abbie put it, were behind her. She still enjoyed his playful ways, however, just not right now.

"Have a seat," Morgan said brusquely. "This is important business."

Katie and Steven settled into the chairs across the desk from Morgan while Lowe sat to the side on the couch.

"Hello, sir," said Steven. Morgan was Steven's godfather but not in the Mafioso sense. Steven told Katie the history of the Sargents and Morgans, so she understood the formality. She found herself acting more formal during her meetings with Morgan as well.

"Thanks to the excellent work of Miss O'Shea, we have located the hacker group known as the Zero Day Gamers," started Morgan. "An Aegis team has been dispatched to surveil their activities continuously. Malcolm, distribute the dossiers. This is to be shared with no one, understood?"

"Yes, sir," responded Katie. She knew this statement was primarily directed at her. It was a reminder as to who her real employer was.

"Malcolm, tell them what you have discerned about the good professor and his associates."

Lowe stood and opened a wall cabinet containing a whiteboard listing the names of Andrew Lau and his three graduate assistants who comprised the core of the Zero Day Gamers. He also listed several cyber attacks, some of which Katie was unaware.

"The package of materials will provide you the details," said Lowe. "Professor Lau formed the group a year ago with the help of Fakhri and Malvalaha. Walthaus is the newest member of the group. We have employed our own team of cyber-security experts to analyze the known activities of this group. While there have been more advanced hacking activities, this group appears to be particularly adept at covering their tracks."

"It was excellent cyber-detective work on your part, Miss O'Shea, to expose their identities," added Morgan. *Rare praise.* Steven unexpectedly squeezed her thigh under the desk, giving her a jolt in more ways than one. "Continue, Malcolm."

"The Zero Day Gamers have earned a reputation amongst their fellow hackers as being expert in attacking complex, secured servers like those associated with the Nevada Energy power grid and the Callaway Nuclear Power Plant in Missouri. Each of the cyber attacks they perform vary in scope and purpose. It shows versatility in methodology that can be of use to us."

Katie resisted the urge to ask—*what are you guys up to?*

"How?" *Thanks, Steven.*

"We will be hiring the Zero Day Gamers for a task that has a national security component," replied Morgan. "By its nature, it must be covert and carried out through Aegis. There can be no United States government involvement, or *knowledge*, Miss O'Shea."

Katie instinctively covered her ears, which drew a rare laugh from Morgan.

"The purpose of hiring the group is still yet undetermined," continued Lowe. "Our first goal is to make contact with them and get their attention. They are normally hired anonymously through hacktivist websites. Their payment is made via money transfers to a variety of offshore accounts. We will be taking a different approach."

Morgan stood and watched the heavy rain blow against the windows, obscuring their view of the State House.

"The term *Trojan horse* has changed its meaning over the years," said Morgan. "Initially, it had a military connotation. Today, it is more widely used in relation to cyber warfare. There is a variant of this concept called a Stalking Horse offer. Are you familiar with this term?"

Both Katie and Steven shook their heads.

"In the political world, a Stalking Horse candidate is used by a party to advance their choice of candidate by inserting another candidate into the race in order to split the vote of a rival. Arguably, the 1992 candidacy of Ross Perot acted as a stalking horse, insuring the successful election of Bill Clinton. In the present campaign, Donald Trump's run as an independent would similarly assist Hillary."

"Makes sense," said Katie. "We have employed similar tactics in setting up a mole within an organization or a successor to be used by the CIA during regime change."

"It is designed to conceal someone's real intentions under a false pretext. We will employ the Stalking Horse tactics in our approach to the Zero Day Gamers," said Lowe, turning to Steven. "You and I will walk in their front door and make them an attractive offer."

"One they cannot refuse," added Morgan.

Chills ran up Katie's spine.

CHAPTER 46

August 19, 2016
The Hack House
Binney Street
East Cambridge, Massachusetts

Steven and Lowe exited the elevator and made their way down the hallway to the Zero Day Gamers loft. Both men wore suits and were armed although they did not anticipate any need for their weapons today. A microphone and camera were hidden inside Lowe's tie clasp.

"Control, final radio check, copy," said Steven.

"Five-by-five."

"Radio check," said Lowe.

"Five-by-five, sir."

Steven stopped in the hallway. "Why does he get a *sir*?"

"He writes the checks. Move along."

"Roger that," said Steven as he and Lowe approached the entrance. Both men concealed their ear pieces. Only Lowe's microphone was important at this point.

During the briefing, surveillance located on the top floor of the Third Square Apartments confirmed Lau and his three assistants were in the loft. Steven and Lowe expected them to be surprised by the visit. Lowe would take the lead and attempt to separate Lau so they could talk privately. Eyes and ears were on from many directions. Aegis was very thorough.

"Allow me," said Steven as he opened the door for Lowe to pass into the loft. Fakhri, Malvalaha and Walthaus were working at computer stations and quickly spun around in their chairs. Lowe moved into the room and Steven quickly conducted a threat assessment. As expected, it was a bunch of harmless computer geeks. Steven observed Lau carefully as he emerged from a bedroom turned office.

"I believe you must be lost, gentlemen," said Lau. "This is private property and we don't accept visitors." Lau spread his arms apart as he approached as if to herd Steven and Lowe out of the loft.

"No, Professor Lau, we're not lost," said Lowe, handing Lau a bogus business card with his left hand while extending his right to shake hands. "We are here to see you. My name is Dennis Troutman and I'm here on behalf of the Center for Infrastructure Protection."

Lau was clearly caught off guard. His assistants looked frightened. *Good.*

"But, wait, I don't understand," said Lau. "What do you want with me? How did you know I maintained an office in this building?" Lau was sweating, obviously nervous.

"Perhaps we should speak in private," said Lowe. "Your office?"

"Yes, sure." Lau's eyes darted around nervously.

"May my driver wait out here with your associates?"

"Yes, of course. Would you like something to drink?"

Steven shook his head and moved against a wall where he had a full view of all the hands and activities of the Zero Day Gamers. He was playing the intimidating role well.

"This way, please," said Lau. He shrugged his shoulders and led Lowe through the doorway.

For the next twenty minutes, Steven didn't speak a word and the Gamers didn't tap a key. Lowe finally emerged from the office with Lau, who was all smiles.

"Professor, it has been a real pleasure." Lowe extended his hand and the men shook.

"Yes, absolutely," replied Lau. "I am sure my associates will be interested in hearing the details of your proposal. I will call you at this number as requested."

The Gamers still appeared to be nervous although a noticeable sense of relief appeared over the face of Walthaus when his professor emerged all smiles.

"Good. Oh, one more thing. I have something for each of you." Lowe reached into his pocket and handed a gold coin to each of the Zero Day Gamers.

"Hey, this is the new Denarium Bitcoin," said Walthaus. "They replaced the old defunct Casascius cryptocoin."

"That's correct, young man," said Lowe. "These are issued by one of the largest Bitcoin exchanges in the world and are considered the gold standard in cryptocurrency. Consider this a token of our gratitude for your assistance and a symbol of great things to come." *It also has a tracking device to help us keep up with your dumb asses.*

Steven was impressed with Lowe's skills as an undercover operative. He played the role perfectly and the body language of the four members of the Zero Day Gamers was telling.

"Driver, let's go."

I'm gonna kick his ass when we get out of here.

CHAPTER 47

August 19, 2016
The Hack House
Binney Street
East Cambridge, Massachusetts

"What the hell just happened?" asked Malvalaha. "Are those guys for real?"

"Were they feds?"

"I've never held a bitcoin," said Walthaus.

"How did they find us?"

Lau's head was still swirling. He had more questions than answers. Although he was being peppered with questions from the Zero Day Gamers, he was oblivious as he walked to the plate-glass windows in the loft and stared mindlessly across Binney Street towards MIT. Receiving the offer to teach at the famed technology institute was a pipe dream fulfilled. The job could be intense and consuming. The peer pressure was fierce. Over time he earned the respect of his faculty colleagues and thrived in their academic environment.

MIT was a famed research institution and its faculty was expected to produce innovative advancements in their field. Twenty years ago, the provost recognized the extraordinary expense associated with research endeavors as well as the time constraints placed on the faculty. The graduate students became an easily accessible labor pool for the professors. As Lau entered into his second job as a hacker for hire, the graduate students became integral in the expansion and success of the Zero Day Gamers. They were now going to receive a paycheck for their efforts which was retirement worthy.

"Professor, Professor, are you okay? What's wrong?" asked Fakhri as she gently shook him by the shoulders.

Lau snapped out of his trance. He cleared his throat. "Nothing, everything is good. More than good, actually. I think we have a new client." He was now beaming, which produced smiles on all of his loyal graduate students.

"Tell us!" insisted Walthaus as he flipped his bitcoin in the air—choosing heads or tails.

"I don't know where to start. There is so much to discuss from the short conversation."

Walthaus flipped the coin again. "How much? There's a good starting point." He had really matured since his first successful hack in the spring. Now it was all about the payday.

"Sure, why not," Lau started as he rolled the bitcoin through his fingers like a high-stakes poker player analyzing his hand. "One million dollars in Bitcoin, obviously."

"Wow!" exclaimed Malvalaha. "Nice payout. I'm going to buy that Porsche we talked about, Herm."

"Sweet," replied Walthaus. The two exchanged high fives.

"Each." Lau paused to gauge their reactions. This would generate some high fives.

"What? Each?" questioned Fakhri. She approached Lau as if about to cry.

"Yes, Anna. Each. We will each be paid one million dollars for this job." Then Fakhri cried. As did Walthaus, who fell into his chair with his face buried in his hands.

"Do you know what this can do for my family?" asked Fakhri through the tears.

"For all of our families," added Malvalaha. He and Fakhri were hugging while Walthaus continued to shake his head in disbelief. He was muttering.

"Are you okay, Walthaus?" asked Lau. He leaned over and placed his hands on the young graduate assistant's shoulders.

"Who do we have to kill?" he asked. A sudden look of apprehension came over the faces of Fakhri and Malvalaha.

"We're not going to kill anyone, guys. Relax. We are going to do what we do best—send a message. In fact, you could even say we are going to perform a valuable public service."

"White hat?" asked Malvalaha.

"You could say that," replied Lau. He rolled a chair from one of the computer stations and sat, indicating Fakhri and Malvalaha to do the same. "Let me give you the rundown of the project and let's brainstorm some ideas."

"I for one don't care what it is. If their money is good, I'm in," said Walthaus. He was now twirling his bitcoin on the desk like a kid's top.

"You are so greedy, Walthaus," said Fakhri. "It's the new girlfriend, isn't it?"

Malvalaha laughed with Fakhri.

"She has needs and wants," replied Walthaus. He puffed out his chest with pride.

"I bet she does," said Fakhri dryly. *She clearly didn't approve of Wendy.* Lau cleared his throat to get the Gamers back into focus.

"Listen up, everybody, if we are going to do this—" said Lau, who was interrupted by laughter. "What?"

"A million-dollar payday and you seriously wonder if we're in?" asked Walthaus. "Hell yeah I'm in."

"Me too!"

"No question."

"Then pay attention, we'll be on a deadline. Everything must be a go by no later than August 31 or we get paid nothing. Everyone good with that?"

"Yeah." Lau turned his cap backwards and laid out the details.

Their client, the Center for Infrastructure Protection, was in the process of securing funding for the Tres Amigas SuperStation. The purpose of the project was to tie the United States power grid together via three separate five-gigawatt superconductive high-voltage power lines. These power lines would permit the flow of energy throughout America via high-temperature superconductor wire. Tres Amigas would act as a power market hub of sorts, enabling the buying and selling of electricity between the three major power grids servicing the U.S. The entire cost of the project was in excess of two billion dollars but would generate many times that in profits for the owners of Tres Amigas.

"This all sounds like an interesting concept," said Malvalaha. "How would we be involved?"

Lau walked to the kitchen to grab a Barq's Root Beer. "Anyone?"

"No, thanks," replied Walthaus.

Lau paused to take a sip and let out a little belch. Discussing Congress did that to him.

"Tres Amigas, via our client's think tank, is going to lobby Congress this fall for funding," said Lau. "They want us to help raise awareness of the vulnerability of the U.S. power grid to solar flares, nuclear EMPs and cyber attacks. Ironic, isn't it?" Lau took another sip. His throat was dry.

"Fear is a great motivator. If we can scare Congress into acting, they will get their funding. Our job is to crash the grid."

"You mean like we did in Vegas?" asked Fakhri.

"Except this project will be for the public good," replied Lau. "It is very straightforward in its scope, but complex in its execution."

"Very white hat," repeated Malvalaha. He was chomping on Nicorette gum as part of his smoking cessation plan. His next step was electronic cigarettes. "In a way, we could redeem ourselves for the aftermath of Vegas."

"We couldn't predict how the public would react," defended Fakhri. "The unions made it worse and never disclosed their involvement in the plan." Lau was angry after the Vegas hack of the Nevada Energy servers. The hack was successful and received accolades online, but the union blindsided him with their staged walkout, leaving the casino patrons to fend for themselves. Lives were lost as a result and he vowed to be more careful. As a result, the American Airlines takeover and the Callaway Nuclear hack were of very short duration by design. He was toying with the targets. During his private conversation with Troutman, he insisted on brevity and Troutman agreed. *We just want to get their attention*, Troutman insisted.

"I voiced our concern and it was stipulated in the deal," said Lau. "Now, let's talk about what we know about the entire power grid before we throw out ideas on the intrusion. Walthaus, you've studied this more than any of us."

"After the Vegas hack, I became interested in the issues raised on the vulnerability of the U.S. power grid to various threats—including cyber," started Walthaus. "When we were contacted by Greenpeace, I thoroughly researched this in order to avoid a repeat of Vegas. This is why I suggested we execute the Callaway hack for a limited period of time to coincide with the Space Station flying overhead." Walthaus stood and approached a chalkboard recently installed by Lau. *Today, he was the professor.*

"On a national scale, how does the grid work?" asked Fakhri.

Walthaus began writing as he spoke. "Generally, the delivery of electricity has three main components—power plants, transmission lines and the distribution to the end user through local utilities. The Vegas project affected a local utility while the Callaway project attacked a power plant." He drew images of a nuclear plant's cooling tower and stick houses, connected by lines.

"In addition, the power lines between the power plants and the utilities pass through variable-frequency transformers, which permit a controlled flow of energy. Without these transformers, the flow of power moves through the lines uncontrolled as to source and load. The result to the utility network would be a massive destabilization from the rapid changes in power. The converter transformers at the utility would be overloaded and fail."

"Why isn't the grid interconnected?" asked Lau. "How many components are there?"

"The better way to look at it is by region," replied Walthaus. "The U.S. is divided into two major interconnected power grids. The Western Interconnection spans the entire West Coast from Canada to Mexico, and then east over towards the Midwest. The Eastern Interconnection includes all of the East Coast and extends to the base of the Rocky Mountains. Both of the major power grids exclude Alaska, Hawaii and Texas."

"I can understand how Alaska and Hawaii are separated geographically, but why Texas?" asked Lau.

"Partly because of their historical desire for self-sufficiency and partly because of their bumper sticker *Don't Mess with Texas*, the state maintained its independence during the early days of building the grid. During World War II, Texas was home to several factories vital to the war effort. Their utility planners were anxious to keep the assembly lines running and were concerned about the reliability of the power supply from other states. Texas continues to be the nation's number one gas producer and one of the top coal producers."

Lau interrupted. "Texas created its own island of energy. They didn't need the rest of us."

"Basically, yes," replied Walthaus. "It has served them well. As a result, the Texas grid is exempt from the majority of regulations imposed by the Federal Energy Regulatory Commission because they do not sell electricity across state lines."

"Good for them," said Malvalaha. "Texas is by far the largest user of electricity in the nation, yet their power costs are the lowest. Why would they submit to the federal bureaucracy?"

"It has worked out for them apparently," said Fakhri. "But you have to wonder if this Tres Amigas proposal will meet with resistance from Texas."

"What does that mean in Spanish anyway?" asked Malvalaha.

"Three friends," said Walthaus. "If they were friends, they would have connected their grids already."

"The client wants us to shut down all three of these grids at the same time?" asked Fakhri, turning her attention to Lau.

"Yes. He specifically said to avoid wasting time on Hawaii or Alaska. Their point will be made without the extra effort."

Lau approached the chalkboard and erased the drawing. He wrote *East – West – Texas* across the top. "Let's divide the research between the three *amigos*. Malvalaha will take the eastern grid, Fakhri will research the west, and Walthaus will try to crack the Republic of Texas." Lau underlined each region.

"Electric systems are not designed to withstand or quickly recover from damage inflicted concurrently on multiple components. Our client wants us to coordinate the hack to put the country in the dark for a brief period of time, and then bring it back online. We need to research if this can be done simultaneously or staggered. For this reason, each of us will handle a different interconnection and I will consider the simultaneous approach. If it can't be done as a coordinated effort, then I will tell our new client of the risks. I am sure they will understand."

Of all the questions Lau answered that afternoon as the Zero Day Gamers conjured up a plan, one was not addressed—*how did they find us?*

CHAPTER 48

August 21, 2016
The Hack House
Binney Street
East Cambridge, Massachusetts

Lau impressed upon the Zero Day Gamers the importance of privacy and hiding their digital footprint. They utilized several approaches to use the web incognito. First, they always browsed the web using privacy windows, preventing websites from planting tracking cookies to trace their whereabouts or follow their activities.

Second, they utilized a virtual private network—VPN. A VPN utilized advanced encryption to hide Internet use by creating a virtual data tunnel while the user's true IP address remained hidden from the rest of the world. Lau used the example of an author who was raided by Homeland Security based upon a warrantless NSA analysis of his online research. The author's computer was seized and he was detained indefinitely as a domestic terrorist. The author finally convinced DHS he was researching a novel and he was eventually released. The Zero Day Gamers would not be.

"I have to provide an update to Mr. Troutman this afternoon, so let's see where we are on our research," said Lau. He pushed himself up to sit on the kitchen island countertop, allowing his feet to swing beneath him. He was feeling good. The Red Sox were on their way to clinching their division early and the thought of bitcoins in his virtual wallet was alluring. "Fakhri, West Coast, talk to me!"

"We collectively researched the documents and filings contained on the Federal Energy Regulatory Commission website," replied Fakhri. "Based upon their latest classified filings with the Senate

Committee on Energy, FERC has identified nine critical substations out of fifty-five thousand in need of additional security."

"How did you access classified filings, or do I want to know?" asked Lau.

"It was actually simple, Professor," replied Walthaus. "One of the committee members is Senator Al Franken, the former *Saturday Night Live* comedian. In his 2008 Senate race, activists for Greenpeace were accused of helping Franken commit voter fraud to secure his election by a mere three hundred votes."

"So, he's a funny crooked politician," said Lau, his feet now beating against the kitchen island cabinets like a kid.

"It's more than that, Professor," said Malvalaha. "All three of us were amazed at the amount of detailed information Greenpeace had on the Callaway Nuclear Power Plant—some of which was not publically available.

"Fakhri spoke with her contact there, who admitted Franken was exchanging classified information on the nation's infrastructure in exchange for campaign support," said Malvalaha. She handed Lau a printout from her Greenpeace contact. "This report was generated by FERC for the Energy Committee. It identifies the nine critical substations."

Lau hopped off the island and headed to the chalkboard. He scribbled the names of the locations under each of the regions. Under West, he wrote Portland, Denver and Calgary. Under East, he wrote Philly, Albany, Indy and Chattanooga.

"Chattanooga is an odd location," said Lau as he looked at the report to confirm the location.

"Small city with a big impact on the Southeastern United States power grid," replied Walthaus. "It is the heart of the massive Tennessee Valley Authority network of dams and nuclear facilities."

"Okay. Then in Texas we have Austin and Waco," said Lau. "Is there anything about these geographic locations of importance other than their location within the various interconnections?"

"Yes," replied Walthaus. He stood and approached the blackboard. "These nine substations are in close proximity to the ten largest power plants in America. Only three of the top ten power plants are not nuclear—one hydro, one gas and one coal. Grand Coulee in the Pacific Northwest is a hydroelectric station and Plant Scherer—a coal-fired plant south of Chattanooga—are examples."

Walthaus wrote the number ten on the board. "Based upon our research, these ten power plants generate over eighty percent of America's electricity. If these nine substations identified by FERC were taken offline, the ten largest U.S. power plants would stop distributing energy and the entire nation would go dark."

"Are you telling me we have to undertake ten intrusions like Callaway and Nevada Energy at the same time?" asked Lau. He removed his cap and ran his fingers through his thinning hair. He was surprised it hadn't fallen out at this point.

"No," said Walthaus. "We're going to go after the substations. Because of the proximity of these nine substations to the most critical power generation stations, their failure will create a cascading failure across the three respective grids. There are a lot of factors to consider such as energy demand, weather and activity of the power plants themselves, but we believe for maximum effect, these nine substations will be our targets."

"Let's talk about timetable because I expect Troutman to ask," said Lau. "First, do you have a date in mind, and second, can you be ready?"

"We have a date, sir," replied Fakhri. "The images from the International Space Station were repeated throughout the international media for weeks. For that reason, we chose Saturday night, September 2. Like the Callaway hack on July 4, there will be a new moon and the ISS will have a complete view of the continental U.S. at approximately nine Eastern that evening."

"And, we can be ready," added Malvalaha. He sat up in his chair. "Don't get me wrong, we have identified several methods to access the respective servers. We are in the process of conducting penetration tests to gain insight into each system's structure. The next week will be very busy for us."

"There is good news," said Walthaus as he approached the

blackboard again. He wrote one word—Microsoft. "The common denominator so far is a Microsoft Windows–based operating system, *our old friend.* We should be able to use elements of the Vegas and Callaway hacks for this project."

"Good news indeed," said Lau. He hopped off the kitchen island, generating another belch.

"We have found some precedent for what we are trying to accomplish," said Malvalaha. "This is similar to the India blackouts of 2012." Malvalaha opened up a window on his monitor and pointed to a map of India.

"What happened in 2012?" asked Lau as he walked to get a better view of the monitor.

"Like the United States, India is demarcated into several interconnections," started Malvalaha, pointing at the screen. He circled the northern part of the map. "All of these regions were synchronously interconnected. This is what Tres Amigas is attempting to achieve. However, the southern regional grid is asynchronous—detached, like the United States power grid. When the country was hit by the cascading failures in 2012, the southern grid was spared.

"If the U.S. grid was interconnected, our job would be easier," said Malvalaha. "Like India, a cascading failure of the grid will occur, but it will be compartmentalized between east, west and Texas. Something our client is not considering is the ancillary benefit of asynchronicity. After Tres Amigas is built, a terrorist or foreign country could bring the entire grid down with one intrusion because all three regions will be interconnected. At least now, some parts of the country's grid would be protected."

"Give me an overview of the plan," said Lau.

Malvalaha switched to another map showing a picture of the continental United States with a series of red stars, blue dots and red interconnecting lines. The image resembled an airline route map you might see in the seat pocket in front of you while flying.

"We obtained this from a presentation given by the North American SynchroPhasor Institute last spring during a Homeland

Security Subcommittee briefing. We downloaded it off the SmartGrid.gov website. You'll notice the nine red stars. These represent the nine critical substations we identified on the blackboard. It wasn't difficult to put two and two together and confirm the grid's most vulnerable underbellies." *Impressive.*

"I'm surprised terrorists haven't figured this out," said Lau.

"They're too busy cutting off heads." Walthaus chuckled. "Idiots."

"You'll notice there are no lines connecting the dots between the Texas, east, and west regions," continued Malvalaha. "We will treat each interconnection separately, as its own country. By dividing up the responsibilities, we can formulate a plan quickly. Then we can coordinate our timing."

Lau drew lines under the word *west* on the blackboard. "Using the western grid as an example, walk me through the process."

"We haven't thoroughly studied each system to identify the mechanics, but basically, here's how it works," replied Malvalaha. "We create a failure of the Calgary substation, which will immediately overdraw more power than what was scheduled from the Portland and Denver facilities. This creates an unscheduled interchange, which is normally done when there is a surplus of power available from the grid. It is less expensive than purchasing power from local, independent power producers. The western grid could survive a failure of the Calgary substation alone, but within seconds, the Denver substation will be taken offline. This will force the Portland facility to shed loads and transfer power to both Calgary and Denver. While we will be prepared to deactivate Portland as well, we probably won't have to. The overdraw by Denver and Calgary will combine to trip the thermal plants at Portland beyond their capacity, leaving the entire system in the dark."

Lau envisioned the process like a ripple on a pond. Once a single point of failure was identified, then all of the elements in the power transmission system became compromised.

"How do you restore power?" asked Lau.

"We're still working on that detail," replied Fakhri. "Using the 2012 India blackout as an example, the system engineers were able to restore eighty percent of the power within five hours. We consider that to be the worst case here." *Five hours in the dark, worst case.* The blackout of 2003 in the northeast United States was largely restored within seven hours.

Lau studied the map. The Gamers had a viable, workable plan.

"Do you guys know what chaos theory is?"

"You mean like in the *Jurassic Park* movie?" asked Walthaus.

Lau instantly visualized dinosaurs roaming through Boston Common.

"I remember that scene as well," said Lau. "Chaos Theory is the science of surprises and the unpredictable. As Julie Chen on my favorite reality show *Big Brother* says—*expect the unexpected.* Our friends at MIT study predictable phenomena like gravity, electricity or chemical reactions. Chaos Theory is the study of unpredictable events and their effect on an experiment. In our case, a slight error or complication in our methodology could be amplified dramatically."

"Like what, Professor?" asked Fakhri.

"The lights don't come back on."

CHAPTER 49

August 23, 2016
Morgan Vacation Compound
Martha's Vineyard, Massachusetts

He was thankful for clear skies and a lack of turbulence. The short ride in the Sikorsky S-76 from Boston was devoid of the sudden sideways movements and occasional rapid changes in altitude typical of helicopter flights. The swooping motions that created a thrill for some presented difficulty for others. He requested the morning meeting to avoid a return trip at night, when the human eye struggled to find a reference point on the horizon. This could result in serious spatial disorientation and motion sickness—and his day did not need the added stress.

The newly designed Sikorsky was ideal for his trips to the Vineyard. Most people thought of the deafening *thump*, *thump*, *thump* sounds of the rotors, but inside the cabin, the redesigned Pratt & Whitney engines and noise-reduced tail rotor barely competed with his thoughts.

Flying over Buzzards Bay, he glanced out of the starboard-side windows, catching a glimpse of the Black Hawk helicopter that had shadowed them since they passed New Bedford. To his left, he observed the lines of cars, full of tourists and gawkers alike, waiting for the ferry trips departing Woods Hole—taking them to the island. Naturally, security was heightened due to the importance of the vacationers, but the appearance of Coast Guard coastal patrol boats throughout Vineyard Sound was a reminder of the state of world affairs.

As the pilot swooped across Menemsha Pond, he thought about

the words used in the past that drew so much criticism from pundits—you didn't build that. There was some truth to the statement. Nobody got rich on their own money. They leveraged their wealth on the backs of others. Similarly, power was achieved through the adept application of your strengths.

Machiavelli once wrote he who wishes to be obeyed must know how to command. A commander-in-chief might be anointed with power, but it did not necessarily provide him the ability to command. He needed guidance. Today, help arrived in the form of a message—one that must be delivered face to face.

The pilot gently set the Sikorsky down on the helipad built by the Corps of Engineers on his property just three weeks ago. Men and women in dark suits surrounded the landing zone, along with several golf carts. The welcoming committee was a little much—especially for his own home.

He loved the Chilmark House. Situated on the southwest part of Martha's Vineyard, the open floor plan and the floor-to-ceiling windows in each living space accentuated the panoramic views of the South Shore and the Atlantic Ocean.

After the obligatory security check, he was escorted inside as a guest in his own home. It was an odd feeling. He was not accustomed to meetings outside of the sanctity of his offices in Boston.

"Hello, sir," greeted David McDill, the White House Chief of Staff. McDill was not part of the inner circle. He filled a role as an intermediary, a conduit for the exchange of information. The President's real confidant, the person whom he trusted the most, was by his side—Valerie Jarrett.

"Good morning, David," he said. "It is nice to see you again."

McDill escorted him down the steps into the sunken living room, where the President finished a putt across the carpet to a makeshift cup. The President whispered something into the ear of Jarrett, who looked up at him and smiled. There was something between them—something more.

"Mr. President, your guest is here," announced McDill.

Jarrett hastily broke away from the President and smiled as she exited the room.

"Thank you, David, you can go now," said the President.

Silence filled the room as Jarrett and McDill exited, closing the doors behind them. Once the room was empty, the President smiled and spoke first.

"How are you, my friend, it has been too long."

The men shook hands and shared a brief embrace.

"We've come a long way in the twenty-five years since we met at Harvard," he said.

"I will always appreciate your assistance in landing the summer clerk's position at Hopkins and Sutter," said the President. "That summer changed my life." The summer Saul Alinsky changed your life.

"Well, Mr. President, do you have something against the nine-hole course I built on the grounds?" he asked. "We built it with you in mind—all doglegs turn left."

"Very funny!" said the President. "It's ironic. My swing produces a terrible slice, but it plays into a dogleg left perfectly because I'm left-handed. I absolutely love your place. It's difficult for me to find solace. Somehow, Chilmark gives me the opportunity to think and reflect."

He set the putter aside and motioned for the men to sit by the windows overlooking the pool.

"Your children seem to be enjoying themselves."

"Definitely. They start school soon and this gives them an opportunity to relax. It's not easy being the children of a president."

"How is your wife?"

"She hates me, to be blunt," said the President. "But you probably already know this. When I entered office, she envisioned an opportunity to effectuate a new direction for America in a dramatic way. Change isn't easy. I tried to explain to her there would be setbacks and false starts. She wanted me to crush my political detractors. She thought I was being weak, indecisive. In hindsight, I should have fast-tracked some of my initiatives while I had supermajorities in both houses. Frankly, I received bad advice from political advisors who were more concerned with an upcoming midterm election than my agenda. The party sustained heavy losses anyway."

"I suppose," came the reply. Let's get down to business. "Mr. President, the election is in ninety days. You know why I am here. A decision needs to be made."

"Here's the deal," started the President. "I still have a lot of work to do. When I came into office, I promised my constituents meaningful change. I told them we are greater together than we can ever be on our own. I am running out of time and I know it. I will not leave office without fulfilling my legacy."

"I understand, Mr. President."

He decided to allow the President a little more time to speak and reflect. He would encourage the leader of the free world to reach the necessary conclusion on his own. The President rose to his feet and stared out the window. He put his hands in his pockets and stood stoically for a moment.

"You've warned me for years of this possibility," said the President, breaking the silence. "I have watched as you expertly orchestrated events around the world to achieve certain mutual goals. For my part, I have purged the military. I have executed both executive orders and secret directives with a singular purpose in mind. Your associate, Mr. Holmes, has been useful in that regard."

"He's a good lawyer and appreciates the importance of our goals."

"I have spent the last eight years preparing for this eventuality," said the President. "In addition to advancing my agenda, I have taken measures to allow for a continuation of my work. In order to win the future, I need more time."

"What do you propose?" he said.

"There is only one way to circumvent the Constitution without a series of annoying courtroom spectacles," replied the President. "Martial law and the suspension of Posse Comitatus."

"I believe you are correct, Mr. President. I know you understand the ramifications of such a declaration."

"I do," said the President. "The groundwork has been laid. Over the last seven years or so, I have conditioned the American people to accept the presence of our military in their cities and towns."

"The law supports your approach, Mr. President. Never in the history of our country have we faced so many potentially destructive threats at the same time. Your leadership can guide the nation through a crisis, and if handled properly, a continuation of your presidency will be welcomed."

"Thank you for that," said the President. "Difficult times lie ahead and will require shared sacrifice by all. I know there will be pain inflicted upon average Americans. I can focus the government's vast network of assistance upon those who welcome our help and who agree with our vision for a new America."

"You will experience resistance from within the government, and beyond."

"Let me be clear," said the President with conviction. "This will be an opportunity for all Americans to choose a side. If they wish to be a part of an America that is open to fairness for all, then they will join me. Those who remain loyal to my vision will relish the opportunity to be placed in positions of power. I have no concerns about the American people who have grown accustomed to the benefits my government provides them. They will thrive with the full protection and care for their families."

"What about your most vehement opponents?"

"Oh, I have a plan for them," said the President. "Congress gave me fast-track authority for trade agreements last year. Under the TPA, I have the ability to issue domestic executive orders over virtually all goods and services produced in the United States. I can issue executive orders for weapons and ammunition confiscation, prohibitions on hoarding food and necessary supplies, gold confiscation and the required relocation to detention facilities for our citizens' safety. For those who choose to resist by clinging to their foolish notions of patriotism, guns and hypocritical religious beliefs, they will receive the full weight of my government upon them."

"Russia and China?" he asked, digging a little further.

"We'll toss them a bone," said the President. "And stop opposing them at every turn. What about your end? Do you have everything in order?"

"I do, Mr. President. With your assistance, I have planned a series of carefully orchestrated false-flag attacks this year. Everything is in order for the final collapse event."

"Perfect. I will be in Hawaii," said the President.

"And how will the Vice President react?"

"It doesn't matter," said the President. "He will be in an unfortunate location when it happens. Where will you be?"

"Initially in Boston with my daughter; then we will evacuate together to Prescott Peninsula."

"I am glad the acquisition worked out for you," said the President. "We can offer your daughter a position in the new government when things settle down. What about her patriot friends?"

"Their lineage dates back to the founding of America. They will see the big picture, as will my daughter. All of them realize this country needs a reset. They just don't know what that entails."

As for you, Mr. President, your entire career is based upon *planned obsolescence.*

CHAPTER 50

August 28, 2016
National Mall
Washington, D.C.

"In a desperate attempt to generate more excitement from her base, Mrs. Clinton made what has been characterized as a racially charged and divisive speech at the National Mall today on the anniversary of Martin Luther King's memorable speech—*I Have A Dream*. Let's take a listen to an excerpt," said Bret Baier, host of *Special Report* on the Fox News channel. The monitor changed to Hillary Clinton standing on a stage in front of the Lincoln Memorial.

"This nation was founded on the basis of freedom, but our Founding Fathers left one important task unresolved. They were slave owners and therefore were unwilling to address one of the original sins of this country—the inhumane ownership and mistreatment of African-Americans. While it is true the Constitution provided all Americans equal citizenship under the law, African-Americans were not considered people. They were property!" Clinton stood back from the podium and nodded her head as the crowd voiced their displeasure with the Founding Fathers' oversight. She continued.

"The Constitution did not deliver on its promise of freedom for all Americans and I am here to say our country has failed African-Americans for over two hundred and fifty years!" She paused for the applause to die down.

"This nation owes an apology to all African-Americans. This nation owes all African-Americans reparations for the sins of past slavery and the sins of current oppression. Elect me President, and I will see that all African-Americans receive their fair share of the pie that was stolen from their enslaved ancestors!" The monitor faded out and returned to the Fox panel.

"Charles, what do you make of this?" asked Baier. Dr. Charles Krauthammer, a board-certified psychiatrist, was best known for his political commentary, which earned him a Pulitzer Prize while at *The Washington Post*. Confined to a wheelchair following a freak surfing accident in college, Dr. Krauthammer stood tall, however, among inside-the-beltway conservative pundits.

"Bret, the Clintons have gone back to the basics and opened a playbook that was so effective for Bill in the 1990s—racial divisiveness," replied Dr. Krauthammer. "The difference is the extent of the rhetoric. Today's speech by Mrs. Clinton on this historic date was more than a speech to rouse the emotions of the democratic base. She fired heavy artillery at our Constitution and all American institutions. This will do more than gin up the base. This will whip them into a frenzy with potentially violent consequences—as this afternoon's riots show." The monitors switched to cars burning and rioters battling police in front of the Capitol. Another scene showed barriers being knocked down as the protestors attempted to climb the steps of the Supreme Court building. Tear gas was administered to disperse the crowd.

"To Charles's point, American cities have experienced a summer of discontent unparalleled in my lifetime," added Laura Ingraham, talk show host and frequent contributor to the FoxNews panel. "Racial disturbances have wracked Boston, Cleveland, Memphis, and Washington, D.C. Not only is the racial divide evident from these clashes, but the explanation is deeply divided as well." A poll was shown on the screen. The poll was labeled *Cause of Racial Tensions*.

"*The Wall Street Journal*, NBC poll seems to illustrate this," said Baier. "Seventy-four percent of African Americans blame longtime mistreatment and disrespect as the cause of the divide. Seventy-one percent of whites claimed African-Americans were simply seizing an excuse to loot. Charles?"

"This is not a racial divide, this is a chasm," replied Dr. Krauthammer. "It is a crevasse that is expanding and the political rhetoric we experienced today will not help bring the country together. Which brings me back to the Clinton playbook. She continues to fall in the polls and with ten weeks to go, she is looking for some traction. She needs the coalition of African-American voters to turn out in record numbers, as they did for the President in the last two elections, in order to overcome Senator Paul's momentum. This speech is just the first step in that direction."

"Let me add," said Baier. "There are protests organized throughout the upcoming Labor Day weekend by African-American activists and another core constituency of the democratic party—America's labor unions. They intend to make their voices heard in every major city across the country as the start of a fall push to get Hillary Clinton elected. The question is whether it is too late to turn the tide."

CHAPTER 51

August 31, 2016
Undisclosed Location
Boston, Massachusetts

"Is this kid ever gonna come out of his apartment?" barked Sharpie into the comms. "I went to Harvard and there was no way I could afford to live in Regatta Riverview."

Steven shifted his seat in the surveillance van as he watched through cameras identifying the entrance to the east tower parking garage. He hoped the overnight surveillance team didn't miss his departure.

"Stow it, Sharpie," replied Steven. "Bugs, sitrep."

"Oscar Mike," replied Bugs, who had picked up the young woman, Anna Fakhri, fifteen minutes ago.

"Roger."

Two days before, Steven was summoned to 73 Tremont to meet with John Morgan and Malcolm Lowe. Morgan instructed Lowe to create a state-of-the-art cyber facility in an old warehouse downtown. He asked Steven and Lowe to bring in the Zero Day Gamers—*quietly*—to finish their task in Morgan's facility. Morgan believed they were at risk of being arrested by the FBI.

The team arrived at the loft on Binney at *O Dark Stupid* and gathered up the tired-looking professor. He apparently slept on his couch a lot. The professor didn't protest excessively but seemed skeptical of Steven's explanation. As the Aegis team pulled hard drives out of the computers, the professor's look of concern turned to fear.

Steven was a good soldier and learned not to outwardly question his orders. But the abduction of the Zero Day Gamers *for their own good* was added to the growing list of questionable missions. If the FBI was hot on their trail, Katie would know. She hadn't mentioned it to him.

"Here we go," announced Sharpie. "Damn, there's a girl with him. Redhead. Copy?"

Steven thought for a moment. He was under strict instructions—no witnesses.

"I have them on the screen, stand by." Steven looked at his watch. The kid was nearly an hour past his normal routine. She must be a girlfriend. The Binney Street location would be less conspicuous at this hour.

"Ahh, how sweet," said Sharpie. "She gave him a kiss good-bye as he goes off to work. Fat boy is bangin' the Wendy's girl. He needs to lay off the cheeseburgers."

"Change of plans, Sharpie," said Steven. "We can't pick him up here because she'll notice the abandoned car. Follow him down to Binney Street. We'll grab him there, roger?"

"Roger that. Rollin' on," replied Sharpie.

Seven minutes later, the youngest member of the Zero Day Gamers was en route to join his associates in their new digs.

CHAPTER 52

August 31, 2016
Undisclosed Location
Boston, Massachusetts

Lowe and Steven emerged from the makeshift command and control post set up for the surveillance and abduction of the four hackers. Lowe was proud of his handiwork. In just a few days, he had transformed this dilapidated downtown car dealership into a brightly lit series of individual offices and cubicles. Other than the paint peeling off the walls and the asbestos-filled ceiling, this could pass as a state-of-the-art cyber center.

"Steven, have them all brought into the small conference room," said Lowe. "After that, my team will take it from here. You guys can wrap it up."

"Well, sure," replied Steven hesitantly. Mr. Morgan was explicit in his instructions—neither Steven nor his team was to be involved in the continuation of this project.

Steven waved to his men, who brought each of the Zero Day Gamers into the room. The looks of apprehension were obvious. He had to calm them down or they wouldn't be able to function. They sat down and Lowe joined them.

"Good morning, everybody."

"Was this necessary, Troutman?" asked Lau. He was brought into the facility the earliest and was now visibly suspicious of Troutman and his intentions.

"Professor, I truly apologize for the surreptitious methods we employed this morning to bring you all together," replied Lowe. "Unfortunately, our friends in Washington gave us credible information regarding interest in your past activities by law enforcement."

"What do you mean?" asked Lau.

Lowe noticed a tear run down the face of the young woman, Fakhri. Lowe learned long ago fear was the oldest and strongest emotion affecting man. The strongest fear of them all was the unknown. His approach would be to quell their fears of the immediate threat, but allow the unknown to lurk in their subconscious to keep them focused on their task.

"First, let me calm your anxiety for a moment while being aboveboard on the situation," replied Lowe. "Effective this morning, your location on Binney Street is closed—emptied out completely. We have removed every piece of equipment and our team has wiped every shred of latent evidence indicating your presence there. You are ghosts."

"Why?"

"Our contacts in Washington informed us the FBI has tied your Binney Street location to the security breach of Senator Abigail Morgan's personal computer," replied Lowe. "Apparently, the breach occurred several weeks ago and has been identified as cyber vandalism. Our sources tell us your intent was not to cause the senator any harm or retrieve information. It is being labeled as a possible campaign stunt." Lowe purposefully avoided eye contact with Walthaus. He hoped to keep the group together without animosity between them.

"That's ridiculous!" exclaimed Lau. "We have no interest in her computer. There is no benefit to us. Further, we are extremely careful, following all necessary protocols." Lau pushed his chair away from the table as if to leave.

"Please keep your seat, Professor," demanded Lowe.

"I don't like this at all," complained Lau. "The senator's problems have nothing to do with us!"

Walthaus slumped into his chair, hoping to disappear. "But—"

Lowe cut Walthaus off. "We believe you have been set up by Anonymous or a similar hacktivist group—perhaps out of jealousy or with the intent to eliminate you as a rival."

Walthaus showed signs of life as Lowe made direct eye contact. *Shut up, kid.*

"We're here to help you weather this storm. My employers are willing to continue working with you towards our goals but only under certain conditions."

"What conditions?" asked a still-agitated Lau as he settled back in his seat.

"The conditions of our original offer stand," replied Lowe. "Based upon our conversation the other day, you're prepared to initiate the grid-down scenario on Saturday night. Is that still the case?"

"Yes, we have a few details to iron out," replied Lau, who was calming down. "What are the other conditions?"

"Until we have more information on the intrusion into the senator's personal computer, we must take certain precautions. I hope you understand. I don't want to offend any of you, but we have to insure there is no mole in your group."

"Oh, come on," protested Malvalaha. "We know each other like brothers and sisters. None of us are working for the government and we would never expose each other to criminal prosecution."

Walthaus hid within himself again.

Lowe ignored the protest and turned his attention back to the professor. "We mean no disrespect to you or your associates, Professor, but the stakes are high for all concerned. The circumstances have changed and we all need to rely upon each other's protection."

"What are the other requirements?" asked Lau.

"You will each be assigned a dedicated workstation that will be connected via an enclosed intranet system. All activity will be continuously monitored by my team. Do not attempt to contact anyone via your computers, please. This is for your own safety."

"Okay."

"Once the task is completed, you will be paid in full together with an additional stipend for your stay."

"What does that mean?" asked Fakhri.

"You'll not be allowed to leave this facility until after the task is completed."

Lau exploded. "You can't hold us hostage. Are you crazy? Come on, let's go. I've had enough."

Lowe nodded his head, indicating for his security team to come in. The room was quickly filled with four Aegis operatives. "Please sit, Professor. It's not as bad as you make it out to be. There may be warrants for your arrest as we speak. Our people in Washington will take care of this for you in the next day or two if you can calm yourself, and let's move forward."

Walthaus spoke up. "Professor, here's the thing. The senator's laptop…" Walthaus trailed off. "The senator's laptop is irrelevant right now. These people have made us an offer that will allow us to disappear to some tiny island in god knows where. I don't mind hanging out here for a couple of days to focus on what may be the greatest hack of all time. Come on, guys, don't you agree?"

Again, Lau calmed himself and sat down. The Aegis security personnel left the room and Lowe was back in control.

"Fine, Mr. Troutman, or whatever your real name is," said Lau. "We'll move forward, but we want confirmation of half payment by the end of the day. We're not going anywhere and your *watchers* won't allow us to access it. We just need some assurances."

"Done. Now, it's a little hot in here, don't you think? Why don't we step out here and let me introduce you to my team. I'm anxious to hear the updated details of your plan."

Lowe led them out of the room, but he pulled Lau back in by the arm.

He whispered in his ear, "You and I will need to speak privately, Professor. My employer has an additional offer for you." *An offer you can and will accept.*

PART FIVE

CHAPTER 53

September 3, 2016
73 Tremont
Boston, Massachusetts

Morgan was uncharacteristically dressed in khakis and a polo shirt—
not because this was a rare day in the office—but because today
would be a rare day.

It was getting late, the sun having dropped below the western
horizon, leaving only a pale white remnant in his view. He left the
sofa and his dinner and looked at the museum case full of antiquities,
including a copy of *Poor Richard's Almanack* written by Benjamin
Franklin in 1739. He hadn't opened the glass door to the climate-
controlled piece in over fifteen years. He removed the book and
gently thumbed through the pages. He found the page he was
looking for, the one pointed out to him by his father when he was
very young. Morgan muttered the words aloud.

"By failing to prepare, you are preparing to fail."

The Morgan family built a financial dynasty on this premise. His
father, Henry Sturgis Morgan, the grandson of J. P. Morgan, took the
family investment banking business to the top of the global financial
world. Now, Morgan Global protégés held positions of power in
every European central bank, in the top fifty global lending
institutions and at all levels of the most powerful nation-states. *I have
prepared, Father.*

Morgan used his vast network of think tanks, corporate public
relation firms, and the corruption of government institutions from
the presidency to Congress to judges. This complex system was

created to insure profits and earnings would flow to the Boston Brahmin and any associated risks would fall on the shoulders of others.

He allured a delusional President, willingly, into a fool's paradise. Desperate to hold onto power, the present occupant of the office would sell his soul to remain there. He would be an excellent propagandist for the goals Morgan sought to achieve. The President, blinded by power, was easily manipulated to advance the geopolitical and financial strategies of the Boston Brahmin. But his term would also come to an end.

Now, decades of preparation were coming to fruition. With every shock to the system, governments were weakened and the wealthy oligarchs of the world became more powerful. As nation-states collapsed, the void was filled by the surviving power brokers. This nation had survived catastrophic economic collapses in its past. America, with his guidance, would emerge stronger, wealthier and more powerful—without the baggage that was dragging her down.

"Sir," said Lowe, bursting into the room without knocking.

"What is it, Malcolm?"

"I've received a text message from your daughter's chief of staff."

Morgan looked at his watch—9:10 p.m. "What does it say?"

"The campaign delayed her return in order to make an impromptu campaign stop."

"What? Where?"

"Tallahassee, Florida, sir."

CHAPTER 54

September 3, 2016
Triple Q Ranch, Prescott Peninsula
Quabbin Reservoir, Massachusetts

"The girls were exhausted," said Susan as she joined Donald, J.J. and Sabs on the front porch of the main building of the Prescott Peninsula complex—1PP. "All of that time swimming wore out our water babies, Daddy."

Donald took a sip of his Samuel Adams lager. The sound of a loon wailed across the Quabbin Reservoir as it tried to regain contact with its mate. This prompted a responsive night chorus of loon tremolos—a back and forth sound that sounded like a violinist playing the same note repeatedly.

"This is so serene, peaceful," said Donald. "If we didn't have to sleep on bunk beds, I could stay here forever. Tell me again why we live in the city?"

"It's not that bad at Brae Burn," replied Susan. "I think we would go stir-crazy with no activities for us or the children."

Donald stretched out in the chair in order to work out the stiffness setting in from today's *activities*. "I suppose. Besides, we can come out here whenever we want. We have security personnel rotating in and out per Brad's orders. The pantry is always stocked, needless to say. The Triple Q Ranch can become our home away from home any time."

"You two have performed a miracle here," said J.J. "I was amazed at 100 Beacon when you first took me on a tour. Sarge sits on top of a prepper fortress, and 1PP is equally outfitted, but can accommodate hundreds of people."

"And they did it in ninety days," added Sabs. J.J. reached out to rub her shoulder. Donald was happy for his friend and enjoyed watching their relationship grow. They were now inseparable and both of them contributed greatly to the development of the Triple Q Ranch. "What's the next step?"

"Nothing, really," replied Donald. "Any preparedness plan, regardless of the magnitude, is always evolving based upon everything from increased mouths to feed to the nature of the threats we face. Susan and I conducted extensive research considering our anticipated occupancy levels and the amount of time the Triple Q Ranch would be occupied during a collapse event."

Donald stood up to stretch his legs and continued. "The motto on the preparedness website I prefer most—FreedomPreppers.com—is very straightforward. *Because you never know when the day before is the day before. Prepare for tomorrow.*"

"There are certain threats we face—collapse events—that can occur without warning," added Susan. "Examples are an EMP attack, bioterror attacks, and certain natural disasters. Others, like solar flares, pandemic, near-earth objects, and economic collapse provide at least a modicum of warning."

"What is your biggest concern, Donald?" asked Sabs.

Donald thought for a moment, as there were so many reasons to prepare. He sat back down and looked into the dark woods as the loons continued to entertain each other with their crazy laugh. "Darkness. My biggest concern is any grid-down scenario, whether it was caused by a massive solar flare, a nuclear-delivered EMP, or due to a cyber attack. If all or part of the power grid goes down, we will quickly descend into economic and societal collapse."

Susan held his hand. They'd had this conversation many times before. "Our plan for the Triple Q Ranch assumed a long-term grid-down scenario," said Susan. "We consider it the worst-case scenario. Any collapse event which is less than the collapse of the power grid could then be dealt with unless…"

"Unless what?" asked J.J.

"Unless one or more of our enemies used our nation's bad

fortune to their advantage and piled on with an attack of their own. A fighter can take a punch and get off the mat. Several punches can result in a knockout."

Donald continued to stare out into the darkness. J.J. broke him out of the trance.

"Hey, buddy, how but another cold beer?" J.J. helped Sabs out of her Adirondack chair. "You stay put while we grab the burgers and potatoes for the grill." It was a new moon. *It was dark.*

"Deal. I could use another cold one."

CHAPTER 55

September 3, 2016
100 Beacon
Boston, Massachusetts

Sarge and Julia sat down at the dining table on the rooftop terrace at 100 Beacon. It was a cool evening indicating the end of summer and fall's arrival. Julia handed Sarge the corkscrew and watched as he expertly popped open a German Spätlese from the Mosel region of Germany near the Czech border. This was a very sweet wine, perfect for dessert and one of Julia's favorites. They were quiet for a moment as they both looked out across the Charles River and the Esplanade on Storrow Drive.

There was supposed to be a Boston Pops concert together with a fireworks show afterwards, but it was cancelled because Boston PD had insufficient manpower to provide security. Over the last several days, riots and unrest—typically confined to the South End—were now prevalent in all parts of the city. Boston was coming unraveled. Sarge saw evidence this was the beginning of the end.

Julia broke the silence. "I think the Quinns took their girls to Prescott Peninsula for the weekend. Susan said Donald wanted to admire his handiwork."

Sarge laughed. "As well he should. They worked miracles to bring that project together in a hundred days. Mr. Morgan was very pleased when I spoke with him the other day." Sarge poured them both a glass of wine and they toasted.

"Cheers."

"I think J.J. and Sabs went too," she said. "I guess they are officially *an item*."

"Donald told me J.J. was very happy and he referred to Sabs as being *good therapy*." Sarge laughed. "I wonder what he means by that."

"Oh, I know," replied Julia. "We had a girl talk the other day. Sabs is very much a soldier, but she is trying to retain her identity as a woman. They are getting serious and I'm very happy for them."

"Yeah, me too." Sarge slid a couple of chairs in front of them so they could prop up their feet. Julia kicked off her sandals and settled in. "Speaking of getting serious, my brother has gone through some changes this summer."

"I noticed that too. I never get an opportunity to talk to Katie much since she is in Washington. But I noticed Steven spends a lot of time with her."

Sarge took a sip of wine and paused as two police cars roared down Commonwealth—sirens blazing.

"Something happened to Steven when he was on assignment in Germany last May. Just a week before, he was his usual testosterone-driven whore dog. A week or so after he returned, he began to call Katie every night and visited her most weekends. He doesn't even talk about his usual man-child stuff."

"What happened to him? Is he okay?"

"Yeah, it's nothing like that. He is just serious now. He pays attention to the news. He stays with Katie every chance he gets. I don't know. Maybe he's growing up."

"No way."

"Way." That earned him a slug to the shoulder.

"Good for them. When I see Katie, I'll ask her how he's doin'. Girls know things."

"You do."

"Yep."

Sarge contemplated this for a moment. "I spoke to Brad. He allowed a substantial amount of the base to go on leave to visit their families. He has a trusted group that he keeps on base at all times—hard-core military and the nucleus of the Mechanics."

"How many does he have?"

"He told me last week he has around eighty to a hundred at

Devens, but thousands more nationwide under the command of friends."

"Wow, that's a great start."

"I thought so. These guys rotate in and out of the Triple Q Ranch, acting as maintenance and security. He and Donald have it very well organized." He refilled their glasses and they clinked them before taking another sip.

"Where is Abbie this weekend?"

"I thought she was supposed to be home, according to what her dad said the other day, but I caught a glimpse of her at a campaign stop in Tallahassee near Florida State University. They have her flying all over the country, putting out fires."

"Is Florida in play?"

"Must be. The ticket is slipping in the polls. Unless something changes, they will lose."

"After the conversation with Robby Mook, have they left you alone?"

"Yes. I brought it up to Mr. Morgan soon afterwards, and I'm sure he put the kibosh on it."

They remained quiet for a moment, enjoying their wine and the Boston skyline. There was very little traffic on the street. The downtown nightlife died over the summer as it became unsafe to be on the dark city streets. Following Sarge's encounter on Boston Common, people stopped visiting the park as often. The tension in the city had a chilling effect on all aspects of their lives.

"Is Steven's friend Drew still part of Abbie's security detail?"

"As far as I know."

"I've seen them interact together during raw news feeds. They seem to get along really well."

"I'm sure he is very professional." Julia's feet were starting to twitch. *She's on a mission.*

"Well, maybe they'll get together. She needs someone in her life."

Yeah, not me. "I agree."

"Do you think the Quinns will be the only set of friends with children?" *Twitch.*

"Oh, probably not. I mean, we're all still young, right?" *Julia's prying into my brain.* Her feet were twitching like an annoyed cat's tail. "What do you think?"

"Do you wanna have kids someday?" *Blindside!* Sarge finished off the rest of his glass of wine—which was nearly half full.

This was a long overdue conversation.

CHAPTER 56

September 3, 2016
9:11 p.m.
Undisclosed Location
Boston, Massachusetts

Lau sat in the dark staring at the computer terminal. The monitor was lifeless except for the faint glow illuminating his face like an X-ray. Its pulsating cursor, ever-patient, awaited an answer. His middle finger caressed the mouse. If his frayed nerves caused his index finger to twitch—an accidental press of the enter key—the decision would be made for him.

Am I going too far? There will be consequences.

Refusal was not an option—if he hoped to live.

I could try to run. I have money. I could easily disappear in Korea, China or Thailand. Live like a king.

Except these people would find me. You could not hide from these kinds of people.

He glanced over the top of the monitor to once again look in the eyes of his young graduate students, each in the prime of their lives, held at gunpoint.

Sweating profusely, Lau groaned aloud to the empty room. He made a decision.

The saga will continue in MARTIAL LAW

SIGN UP to Bobby Akart's Boston Brahmin mailing list:

eepurl.com/bYqq3L

and receive free advance reading copies, updates on new releases, special offers, and bonus content. You can contact Bobby directly by email (BobbyAkart@gmail.com) or through his website:

BobbyAkart.com

Stop by the Boston Brahmin website:

thebostonbrahmin.com

to dig deeper into the history, characters and real-life events that inspired the series.